Acid Rain

A selection of Short Stories by Vonnie Giles.

Following Vonnie's successful contributions to the short story anthology 'Picked and Mixed', Vonnie was invited to publish a selection of her unique and quirky short stories.

Acid Rain delves into her eclectic collection of dark and esoteric tales and promises to entertain and surprise.

Meet some of the darkest characters ever to send shivers into your dreams.

First published in Great Britain in 2016 by U P Publications Ltd
Eco Innovation Centre PetersCourt, City Road Peterborough UK

Cover © 2006 from the oil painting Acid Rain by Gaile Griffin Peers, reproduced in 2016 with permission

A CIP Catalogue record of this book is available from the British Library

Paperback ISBN 978-1-908135-06-3
eBook ISBN 978-1-908135-17-9

FIRST PAPERBACK EDITION

Published by U P Publications
Printed in England by The Lightning Source Group

www.uppublications.ltd.uk
www.vonniegiles.com

Acid Rain

Vonnie Giles

U P Publications
2016

Dedicated to
Dr Alex García Escrivá

Contents

A Little Odious Vermin

The man in the cloth cap and scarlet kerchief looked down upon her. "You're a little odious vermin, madam, and there's no mistaking that!" he shouted in his rough London voice. Catherine stared up at him in surprise...

Well, it was such an amazing remark to come from an obviously working-class man – a quotation from 'Gulliver's Travels', no less! For his temerity, the man was, of course, immediately hustled from his seat in the public gallery of Court No 1 of the Old Bailey and soon found himself outside on the pavement. The bronze statue of Lady Justice looked down upon him; for once depicted without her blindfold, her impartiality in no doubt.

Anyone who had acquired a certain level of notoriety, as Catherine had, was a target for all sorts of insults and gratuitous opinions and, she supposed, a charge of first degree murder could be said to fall well within that category... If you so wish, you can always read an account of her trial in the Proceedings of the Old Bailey for 1935.

She was, of course, acquitted – well, why wouldn't she be? Her defence, after all, had been in the hands of probably one of the best defence counsels in England. The fact that he was also her lover had, not unnaturally, been kept well and truly under wraps, for just imagine the furore if the press had caught wind of that snippet of information!

If she hadn't met him, of course, none of these awful events would ever have happened, but it was love at first sight, which is never a very good idea and any woman with a modicum of sense would know not to fall into its trap. Nevertheless, that's much easier to say than to do, is it not? The deed was done, all common sense swept aside when delivering a hatbox containing the wondrous, pink, frothy creation his mother was to wear at Ascot; she immediately fell under the spell of those amazing green eyes. Tall and elegant, with the sort of voice that always stirs the pit of one's stomach, he stepped aside to allow her to enter his mother's splendid Highgate house just as he was leaving, and thus it all began.

He was unmarried but, of course, would never marry her, especially now; well, no man of ambition would want to taint his reputation with someone with her unsavoury criminal record, innocent or otherwise, nor with someone of her class – well-educated, but the daughter of a millineress – a working girl of doubtful parentage, her father having simply disappeared into the mists of time on the night she was conceived.

However, she made very good mistress material; in fact, more than very good or so he had told her, and with this she had to be content. She was well rewarded for her services and he had, after all, given her so much happiness, brought so many advantages into her life.

Certainly, without him, she would not at that moment be sitting there wearing the most gorgeous, dark blue velvet gown in the world, one that even Wallis Simpson herself would have not scorned.

It was all such a pity though, because he was totally desirable: sexually, socially and spiritually. She was really the only stain on his conscience, but he simply could not do without her nor she without him, bound to each other by feelings that almost defied reason; lust, love, even hatred, she sometimes thought. She would just have to accompany her mother to church more regularly to confess her grievous sin but, of course, forgiveness was of no use to her whatsoever. For him she would commit the same error over and over again until kingdom come: her one and only love!"

She dreaded the day when he would tell her, as he surely would, that he was going to marry. It was after all his duty as the eldest son to provide an heir for the family; she understood that perfectly well. On the other hand, he would never let her go – there was no need to, for everyone knew that it was the accepted thing for men of his class to maintain a mistress. After all, you had only to look at the Prince of Wales!

Outside, curling around the tree-lined streets of Richmond, was a thick, yellow fog, but inside her beautiful, tastefully-furnished flat, (another of her perquisites as a kept woman!) she felt almost cocooned and protected by it. He sat opposite her, completely irresistible, dressed in an elegant, maroon, velvet smoking-jacket, a Sobranie Black Russian held in his long fingers, his hand resting on the arm of the chair, smiling at her with half-closed eyes. On a table by his side sat an empty brandy glass and at his feet a briefcase with all his legal papers and various notebooks spilling out onto the Persian carpet´

All at once the telephone in the hall rang, shattering the restful mood of the evening, and out he went to answer it, refilling his glass as he left the room. Obviously an important telephone call or he would not need another drink to fortify himself. Eventually, after fifteen minutes or so, his conversation was over and she heard the receiver being replaced. By that time, her heart was beating furiously as though it would burst within her body. She sat there desperately pinching her cheeks and biting her lips, trying to put some colour back into her ashen face.

She smiled wanly at him as, on his return, he kissed her on the neck, on the breast, then resumed his seat, taking a sip of his brandy; the glass still almost full. They continued to listen in silence to a concert on the wireless. Beethoven's Great Fugue was about to begin: her lover's favourite. Staring thoughtfully into his green eyes, she started to reminisce over the events that had brought her such doubtful fame.

The central figure of the drama had, of course, been her mother; in fact, not only had she been the central figure, but also the victim of the drama. Not an innocent one, just as Catherine had not been innocent of her murder. Sharp-tongued, sharp-featured, she had been a still dripping with his blood: her beautiful gown ruined.

The dramatic, insistent notes of cello, viola and violins continued to play unheedingly, as though completely detached from this scene of death that she had created. He should not have been so careless, so trusting as to think that she would not be tempted to look in his journal, lying so invitingly on the carpet among his papers.

There it all was – vivid descriptions, written in his own precise handwriting, detailing every nasty, perverted act he had committed with her mother, his dominatrix: the whips, the handcuffs, and far, far worse instruments of abuse with which he had satisfied his sexual deviation. There had obviously been a great deal more on his conscience than a mere peccadillo with her! Another little odious vermin to add to the working man's tally!

In the preparation leading up to her trial there had never been any hint that he had known her mother and, certainly, no regret over her death. He had, of course, loved neither of them; he'd used them both which, she supposed, was the way of men. It had all been smoke and mirrors – she could see that now. One day he would have grown tired of her, have sent her away and replaced her in the beautiful flat in Richmond with some other pretty, young woman. In this way, she had finally finished with the pair of them: mother and lover. In a few minutes' time she would call the police and supposed that her ultimate destination would once again be the Old Bailey.

As she sat there, her head still on his knee, she wondered what insults the members of the public gallery would think up for her this time; again, something literary, she hoped. She did like to think of her denigrators as being well read – Shakespeare, perhaps: "Thou unfit for any place but hell" – which, of course, was perfectly true. Once Mr Pierrepoint, the hangman, had finished with her, hell was assuredly where she was headed.

Let this be a salutary warning to those of you who are at this moment in the first throes of infatuation and think yourselves to be in love. Be careful who you allow into your heart and into your bed. Read about Catherine's trial in the newspapers and learn from her mistakes. Whatever opinion you form of the proceedings, one thing, however, is certain …the counsel for the defence will not be of the same calibre. Interpret that remark as you please!

A Lost Soul

Millions of stars twinkling and vibrating in the darkness of space: asteroids ambling past in their own good time: comets leaving their zooming, sparkling trails behind them: black holes: the effects of dark matter and all manner of gravitational conundrums! This was what he could see from his window. Interesting you might think, but not after the novelty had worn off, not if you'd been looking at them for the last forty years! Looking and looking and looking …condemned as he was to space imprisonment. The wickedest man on Planet Earth, they used to call him, with no hope whatsoever of remission for good behaviour. He had no choice but to keep looking.

So there he was enclosed within that aluminium space pod with windows on all sides, unable to communicate, to study or to write – but then, he had no hands, so writing materials or a keyboard wouldn't have been of any use there. He couldn't even talk into a speech sensitive computer or sing to himself for he had no tongue, no voice. It was all so excruciatingly, deadly, unbelievably boring!

He had experienced the odd bit of excitement, which had slightly relieved the monotony – a couple of exploding supernovae, and there had been that rather tense moment when he'd thought he was going to enter the event horizon of a black hole, from which no space traveller has ever returned to tell the tale!

In case you are wondering why he had no hands and no tongue, I perhaps should explain to you that, in fact, he had no anything – he was all dust and ashes, every part of him incinerated, except for his eyes which had been allowed to remain intact. Like this, you see, he didn't need to be fed, and what there was of him was kept together encased in his own personal transparent gravity bubble within the little space pod. Doesn't sound nice, does it? – but then, he had no ears with which hear sounds – no music, no crash, bang wallops, no nothing – sound-wise.

Really, he would prefer to have been frozen, but it had been deemed by the Department of Justice that a quick burn was always more satisfactory than a big freeze. It was allowed in exceptional circumstances, when, for example, the prisoner was of great intelligence and his brain might just have needed a quick thaw to be able to solve some tricky philosophical or scientific problem. This, you have probably realised by now, didn't apply to him, for he was as he was.

What did he do to deserve this, you may well be wondering – well, actually, not a lot – a couple of individual murders (richly deserved, he thought!) and even a massacre! (He was quite proud of that one). Not pretty, I have to admit, but it's not often that you suddenly come upon twenty or so people on their knees – sitting ducks as far as he was concerned, too good an opportunity to miss for somebody with his mind-set. They had been more or less asking to be shot, wouldn't you have said? So there they all were, kneeling in a church. You remember those? Strange buildings, strange ideas, but everyone to their own! At the time that his pod was launched into the ether, moon-worship was the up-and-coming religion, hoping that everyone's concentrated thoughts would prevent it from wobbling away into space and leaving us all up the creek without a paddle, as they say.

Hang on a minute though – something is happening there now. I'm telling you no lie, but his bubble is bubbling – and that was certainly not supposed to occur – and you won't believe this, but his dust and ashes appear to be coagulating! He was pretty sure that when the judge pronounced sentence he had mentioned nothing about this. Oops! – there came a brain – it had got to be his – and I have to say that it seems quite big as brains go. It's a good job that he had his eyes or he wouldn't have been able to see all this happening. It was certainly the most fascinating thing he had seen in the last forty years.

All the time there were more bits and pieces of him appearing – he just hoped that if this continued everything would eventually join up together – preferably, in the right places. It might look rather funny to have a hand on the top of one's head – handy, though – there's a coagulating space pun for you; not, however, a very original joke he somehow thought! Oh yes, he could see that it was all happening as it should have done. Why, he had even got his fingernails back and they were still bitten to the quick – you just wouldn't have imagined that that was possible, would you? Now his bubble was expanding – bigger and bigger and bigger …and it had just burst: exactly like a balloon! He heard it loud and clear, so his ears were still in working order, thank goodness!

However, something was wrong, something didn't feel quite right and he suddenly had a very funny feeling that he was not really there anymore; in fact, he had a strong suspicion that he'd just kicked the bucket, or, to put it more bluntly, that he was dead! That was a bit odd, a bit unexpected, wasn't it? Well, I wonder what's going to happen, he thought to himself.

Now this was really, really weird! Unlikely as it may seem, there was a light shining through the pod windows – an unbelievably bright light. How comforting, he thought, to see something that was not cold and dark after all this time. Suddenly it was as though he were moving: floating, floating slowly through the walls of the pod! That light was really amazing – so intense that it seemed to be filling the entire universe. The strange thing was that, although it was shining so brightly, it wasn't hurting his eyes, which was just as well as they hadn't thought to provide him with sunglasses for his journey through space.

He had always thought that floating among the stars would be rather like swimming and that you could go in any direction you wanted, but it wasn't like that at all; he had no choice but to follow the light. Not that he wanted to go anywhere else, because actually it was a very pleasant feeling, but he did feel a little unsure about it.

What's that? What are you saying! Am I sorry about the murders? No, I don't think so. Am I sorry about the massacre! Of course not, no.

He could hear this voice coming from the light and it had just more or less told him that he'd made a bit of a pig's ear of everything. Now, however, the light seemed to be moving away from him and it was growing dimmer – no longer did it seem to pervade everything that existed.

No, don't go, please don't. I've been so lonely all these years. So bored! I'll say anything you like, if you'll only stay with me. I just want someone to talk to. Surely death can't be this lonely!

As the light faded he could just about make out someone in the centre of it – must have had a very nasty accident, covered in blood… and what on earth was that? It looked as though somebody had placed a circle of spines or thorns on top of his head!

I can explain – you see, the people I killed were really very unimportant and of no use to the world… No please, don't do that! Don't your turn back on me! Nobody does that to me! Who do you think you are?

When he remembered the slight figure in the dimming light turning his back on him, his heart still skipped a beat and he felt a deep sense of what he could only describe as loss. He couldn't explain it in any other way

– loss was the only word for it! Goodness knows why; this strange apparition had rejected him, well and truly.

All this had taken place a week ago; he knew it was a week, because everybody where he now was seemed, for some reason, to be very conscious of how fast or how slowly time passed …as though it mattered, when they were all enjoying themselves so much!

Everything that happened after that had all been rather vague in his mind. He knew that he had again been found guilty, (surprise, surprise!) just as he had been in his earthly existence, and again condemned …this time to spend his sentence down here. He seemed to remember that it had been no big deal – his trial, that is – if you can call it that! No defence, no one to speak on his behalf, just this great, echoing voice rabbiting on and on. Nothing face to face, you understand – no big throne, no long, white beard, no choir of angels trilling away in the background. He thought he might have won a few plus points for not killing more people, which he could easily have done because, believe me, once you have the taste for it, it's hard to stop – such a feeling of power – but it wasn't to be. Still that was life for you – or perhaps that should be death for you – a bit of an in-joke where he was now living!

So it was in this manner that he'd descended to his new home – had come down in a great, creaking lift, together with a few others. What a great bunch of lads they were, and what a great time they'd all been having since then – not at all what he had expected – no fiery furnaces, no stoking the eternal flames, no pitchforks prodding him, no wailing and gnashing of teeth.

The boss was as ugly as sin, but he was an OK bloke when you got to know him – Big Luci they called him (of Italian extraction, maybe!) who always wore a rather natty, red suit, but what really made him stand out were his great charred wings that every so often sizzled and smoked. What great parties he gave – girls, booze, ciggies (and they had been out of fashion for a few centuries) and fab grub! Who said that sin didn't pay? He really did prefer it down there – it was much more of a laugh – and he really liked that little, forked tail that he'd grown – very cool!

The only blot on the landscape were a couple of nasty diseases that occasionally appeared – redemption and absolution they were called – and when you fell a victim to one of those you were herded once again into the lift and taken upstairs where, presumably, they had quarantine facilities. Could you imagine, he thought, being again with the Great Light (or G. L. as he was called down there for short.) – all those harps, those fluffy, white clouds, that interminable goodness – what a drag!

He was, at that moment, lying on a very comfortable blow-up cushion, gin and tonic in one hand, Havana cigar in the other, looking out at a wonderful, turquoise sea. However, ...oops ...he suddenly thought he must have had a bit too much sun or something, because all of a sudden his head was beginning to spin and everything was becoming rather blurred. Oh dear, he really did feel most peculiar. The air ...the air was now so stifling that he could hardly breathe and he thought that if his heart beat any faster he must surely die, except he was dead already, so that had been a rather silly thing to think! Oh no! This was awful, truly awful. He dared not open his eyes for fear of what he might see, for he could feel the flicker of flames beneath him and the pricking of needles in his skin and he knew that Big Luci was by his side! He could feel his hot breath on his face!

How stupid, how blind he had been! He just hadn't realised ...but it was him, Lucifer, the great, fallen angel himself, standing next to him, terrible in his anger, about to mete out his eternal punishment; something infinitely worse than anything he could have imagined; and here it came...

He really shouldn't have been so naïve, he should have known all along. In front of his eyes, deep inside his mind, was a vision that would never, ever cease, which would continue until the end of time. Quite clearly now, he could see the broken bodies, the bloody corpses, and hear the cries of anguish of his victims and the wretchedness of those who mourned for them. The vision progressed remorselessly, letting him enter the hearts and minds of those he had destroyed... *Just take it away...please, please, let it stop!* Now he saw everything! Now he understood everything!

This truly was Hell, and even to be allowed to travel once again as dust and ashes among the stars in his little space pod would have seemed to be Heaven itself compared to what was now happening to him. Something, from somewhere, told him that his only hope was that the figure in the dimming light would one day take pity on him and let him share in the Redemption and Absolution of which he had spoken so scornfully, and which was still perhaps possible for those who lived in that barren, inhospitable place called Hell!

A Woman in Transit

Flavia and her little boat were as one, inseparable, never to be parted: the boat unable to travel without her and she unable to move an inch without it. In some magical way, they had truly merged, both metaphorically and physically, which meant that Flavia, that most solitary and self-contained of women, was never alone. They were forever on the move, never still, always on a quest, always looking for their own holy grail that changed almost daily.

It was a darling little boat that anyone would have loved – so cute – not unlike a pudding basin and, of course, it was only big enough to carry one person. Flavia and her boat looked so good together: colour co-ordinated, a vision in muted orange and fawn; she in her trench coat, set off by a smart, black, bowler hat that mysteriously melted into the high back of the boat, against which she leaned, so that they were truly as one.

To assist with its propulsion through the waters the boat boasted a rather elegant, pleated rudder that might have been mistaken for an exotic fish tail. The finishing touch to the whole ensemble were small, pale pink, angel-like wings that protruded from the back of the bowler hat and were attached by a series of string pulleys to the boat and to the trench coat, so that Flavia was able to steer easily through the water and even to fly over it. Certainly, it was a sight for sore eyes, for a more eccentric form of transport could not be imagined: a perfect blending of the mechanical with the human.

They had travelled all over the world together and even into different dimensions, for Flavia was a marvel when it came to all things scientific and this dedication was reflected in the serious face that she always wore when they were exploring. It was the voyage of discovery, rather than having a good time, that interested her more.

The murky water of that most famous of all rivers the Umbalala was swirling about as the fish-tail rudder churned it up and brought all sorts of objects to the surface, animate and inanimate. Flavia, that intrepid traveller, now in full research mode, reached over and took from the boat's breast pocket, which mirrored that of her trench coat, a small exercise book and, with her faithful, stubby, HB pencil, scribbled down all that she saw.

Today's aim was to find the Umbalala's source, but as there was a dense haze, through which it was difficult even to make out her hand in front of her face, it wasn't as easy as she had predicted. A dark canopy of ancient, gnarled trees didn't help matters either and she could hear the rather irritating call of a persistent bird, a sinister sound that made her unable to concentrate fully.

Imagine, therefore, how surprised she was when the boat nearly collided with a tree trunk, carved into the front of which was a tall, hollowed-out arch. Even more amazing for her was seeing, within the arch, a small, round, three-legged side table, rather like the one in her mother's sitting room. On top of it was a very peculiar and very special crystal wine glass. Streams of water tumbled out over its rim, even though the glass was only three-quarters full – some magical quality must be giving the water the impetus to propel itself of its own accord onto the floor and, from there, down into the river. This, surely, must be the source of the Umbalala River; so another aim had been accomplished, another holy grail discovered.

Flavia, brows furrowed, licked her pencil and crossed this off her list of things to do. Losing no time, she then disconnected the rudder and, lo and behold, in two shakes of an alligator's tail, the little pink angel wings on her bowler hat were flapping nineteen to the dozen like a humming bird. In no time, she and the boat were air borne, bursting through the tree cover and into the blue sky, ready for more exploration.

This was a tricky moment for Flavia because she was conscious of a feeling of redundancy emanating from the boat; after all it was a denizen of seas and lakes and watery places. There was, too, a sense of humiliation vibrating through its hull at being controlled by a distinctly feminine pair of pink wings. However, she was in a hurry and so it would have to like it or lump it!

On and on they flew coming eye to eye with all sorts

of strange, mechanical, flying machines, some of them cranking and creaking as though they were about to fall apart, some as eerily silent as a bird on the wing.

Gradually the weather had become unsettled and beneath them the sea was roiling. The blue skies were replaced by menacing, dark clouds tinged with orange, perhaps bringing sand from some faraway desert.

As Flavia searched the sea for somewhere to shelter in case the weather became worse, she spied what looked like a spiral island winding round and round a canal of green water. The island itself consisted of curved, raised, stone terraces interspersed with tall, pointed, black-tipped towers and trees. She knew that many of the buildings must be boat houses, for she could see the slipways leading down to the water. It was a sight that, for some reason, made her tremble with joy: the warm orange and yellow colour of the brickwork seemed to welcome her, the coiled shape of the island drew her in. She could feel that the boat too, within its pudding basin body, was excited and eager to explore, for it was making her bowler hat and the string pulleys shiver. She reconnected the rudder and, immediately, it began to wag happily like a dog's tail.

Until the moment they entered the canal at the beginning of the spiral, Flavia and her boat had always considered themselves to be the cat's whiskers of the boating fraternity: immaculately turned out and completely in tandem; in other words, perfect in every way. So, imagine her surprise when a flotilla of small boats appeared, coming towards them, one behind the other. Several were shaped like bananas inside which nestled the owner, a small sail ballooning out from the top of each tall stern. Another boat was like a miniature paddle steamer with a tall, thin woman, perched on the seat peddling away for all she was worth. There were others resembling water-borne bath chairs. In fact, the plethora of imaginative designs set out before Flavia's eyes all shared what Flavia had considered her unique characteristic, for each boat and owner melded and merged together as though the owner were wearing the boat.

As she passed the flotilla no greetings were exchanged. Everyone was too intent on avoiding accidents to bother with social niceties, for the canal was really too narrow for more than two boats to pass at a time. In fact, just to change direction required a very skilful three or four-point turn or, at times, even a twenty-point turn, although some didn't succeed at all and merely drifted out into the wide sea never to be heard of again. Nonetheless, there didn't seem to be much sense of purpose to all this movement and Flavia suspected that there was not a true explorer among them. They weren't going anywhere – just idling about on the water, showing off to all and sundry.

Apart from being slightly miffed that she and her boat weren't quite as special as she had always supposed, Flavia thought this spiral island to be the most cutesy, adorable place that she had ever seen. There were, for example, woolly detergent-white sheep nibbling away on a patch of grass by the side of the canal and, as if this wasn't delightful enough, well, she completely fell in love with a pair of cats that were sharpening their claws on a tree trunk; their huge yellow eyes with green iris centres looked her fully in the face and she was smitten. Even so, what she really loved about them was that they were made of ferns – what sweeties they were! Whoever would have believed such a thing? She just wanted to pop them into the side of the boat and take them along with her.

Then it all went wrong, the gilt most definitely going off the ginger bread – well, death has a habit of doing that to a person. It was such a shame because at that precise moment Flavia was actually starting to think that, perhaps, it might be rather pleasant to stay on the spiral island, make it her home – at least until, once again, she was overtaken by wanderlust because she always thought of herself as very much a woman in transit. A little holiday – that's what it would be!

Flavia found a boat house that was empty and, as the darkness of night descended, she sat watching the brilliance of the stars and moon above the enchanted island. Soon she and the boat fell into a deep sleep – it had been such a long, long day and they had both travelled over such a long, long distance, all the way from the source of the Umbalala River to the spiral island. No wonder they were both exhausted; so much so that when they awoke the next morning, they were not as alert as they should have been, which is when the trouble started.

Down the slipway and backwards into the water they went, but Flavia, still yawning and half-asleep, did everything too quickly, and simply failed to see that another boat, one of the bath-chair models, was passing behind them. Before she knew what was happening the two small vessels had collided, sending such a wave of fear and panic through the hull of her mortally wounded little pudding basin boat that it lost all control and, in very few moments, had sunk to the bottom of the canal.

Being a woman with great presence of mind and an instinct for self-preservation, as soon as the collision took place, Flavia automatically removed her bowler hat and quickly untied the string pulleys. So that, by the time the boat had died, she found herself swimming freely among the aquatic reeds and weeds, among the carp and the pike.

As she surfaced, helping hands pulled her out of the canal, took her into the boathouse, dried her off and soon had her wet clothes replaced by a long, black mourning gown, her head and face draped in a black veil so that her tears could fall unseen. They all knew what it felt like to suffer such a loss and they left her there alone for a whole week to grieve at the site of her boat's final resting place.

Dragonflies and butterflies were her only companions until, on the last day, she sensed that she was no longer alone and turning round saw the green fern cats playing together on the grass.

"Come and sit by Mummy," she suddenly said. Speaking was something that Flavia hardly ever did for she had never spoken to the boat because their relationship had been such that words were unnecessary, nor was she in the habit of talking to herself. So she hardly recognised the sound of her own voice when she finally did speak.

She was amazed when the cats reacted and did, indeed, come and sit by her. She stroked their ferny backs, while they purred and meowed with pleasure at her touch. They were such little sweeties, such little darlings that the empty space in her heart gradually began to fill once again. Like a bolt from the blue, she realised that she had always been alone, but now everything was going to be different. Despite the fact that she and her boat had been as one for so many years, she was no longer solitary, no longer held in thrall by an inanimate object,

She recalled the great satisfaction she had felt when she had discovered the source of the Umbalala, but the magical, crystal goblet, beautiful as it had been, would never have reacted to the sound of her voice. She needed living things, so off came the black veil, off came the mourning gown, soon to be replaced by all the colours of the rainbow; no more bowler hats, no more trench coats, just creations that would have looked simply marvellous on Ladies' Day at the races!

Right in the centre of the spiral island was an empty tower, the highest one there, and it was this that she decided to make her home. No one else wanted it, for they were all much too occupied with their boats. It had the most gorgeous views over the island and the surrounding seas. Encircling it, at the very top, was a gallery where she and the fern cats could stand and admire the rising and the setting of the sun.

Now, finally, she was happy to leave her past at the bottom of the canal: no longer was she alone, no longer was she a woman in transit.

Beautiful Losers

The smell of cigarette smoke: Galoise: the scent of perfume, Chanel No 5, and the sound of music, Tommy Dorsey's "I'll Never Smile Again" ...all these sensations engaged Jake as he sat sipping his bourbon. His head was resting against the back of the upright wooden chair. He listened intently to everything that was going on in the room: to the rustle of Rose's dress as the zip was lowered and to Freddie's breathing coming in short, excited bursts.

He contemplated the shadows in front of him as the pungency of the cheap alcohol set his teeth on edge; a harsh, unequivocal taste that he always enjoyed. He could feel Rose's long evening dress touch his knees as she began to sway in time to the enticing notes from the gramophone. "I'm so in love with you" crooned Frank Sinatra and that was exactly how Jake felt about Rose: an all-enveloping, all-consuming emotion. All he wanted at that moment was to run his fingers through her long, silky hair, feel the smoothness of her skin, let his face nestle in her neck and kiss her breasts. There would never ever be anyone else who could replace her, but tonight she was Freddie's and he would have to like it or lump it. That was an unpleasant fact of life.

Freddie, the perfect American man, or so it would

seem: young, handsome, well educated – Princeton, no less and, of course, rich. Yes, he had to be rich, for Rose had very expensive tastes. Her beautiful dresses, her jewellery, her perfumes, well, after all, they didn't come cheaply did they? Freddie and Rose, such beautiful people!

However, nemesis awaited Freddie, and his come-uppance would not be long in arriving – perhaps today, perhaps tomorrow – whenever those who decided these things had made up their minds. Make no mistake about it, come, it surely would! Jake smiled to himself and thought of the revenge that would shortly be meted out to Rose's lover. One of the harsh lessons to be learned was never, ever to take from Jake something that was his, for he was totally ruthless.

Unexpectedly, Jake put down his drink, and banged hard on the table with his fist in an uncontained moment of frustration, making the glass jump off like a jack-in-the-box, spilling its contents all over the carpet. Rose and Freddie, surprised, stopped what they were doing and watched the drops of bourbon that still clung onto the edge of the table slowly following the main downpour. It was rather like the remaining drops of rain that were dripping from the guttering outside. Tears might have been a more appropriate simile, for Jake wanted to cry, desperately, with a great longing to release his feelings but, of course, circumstances wouldn't allow that to happen. Rose lifted her eyes to heaven in mock exasperation at what Jake had just done. She then smiled at Freddie and placed her hand on his neck, kissing him, not bothering to pick up the fallen glass or to replenish it.

Rose was tall, blonde and slim, but not intellectually first-rate! She had probably never read a book from cover to cover in her entire life and as for the war in Europe, well, that would be a complete unknown to her – most of the time that is! She was too easily distracted by material considerations. Outward show, physical comforts, the little luxuries of life, these were what mattered most to her, but there was a sweetness in her that was irresistible and Jake dreaded what life would be like without her.

On the surface not too bright, Rose possessed, however, an almost unique, very valuable, talent: an eidetic memory. It was not just a photographic memory, but one that could remember sounds and words almost unerringly, repeating them parrot fashion: a completely unexpected accomplishment that Jake had not fully realised when he first took up with her. He might say, "Did you enjoy the movie, Rose? Do tell me all about it. I would so much have liked to have seen it!" ...or, "Did you ask Freddie about Princeton, Rose? Did he tell you about all the interesting people he met there? Do tell me! You always get so much more out of him than I do!" ...or yet again, "Tell me, Rose, what did Freddie say about what is happening in Europe? What was that about Hitler? Now tell me again – it's so fascinating!" ...Then, off she would go, describing every detail and regurgitating the dialogue almost word for word. Such a useful talent, if she had but known it!

By this time the evening shadows were beginning to gather in the moist air outside and the street lights were throwing an eerie glow into the room. Freddie took his arm from around Rose's waist, while she continued clinging to him. He was just about to bend down to turn on the table lamp when there was a loud banging from the corridor outside and voices could be heard yelling. The suddenness of the commotion immediately caused Freddie to loosen Rose's arms from around his neck and, by the time the door burst open revealing three fully-armed members of the FBI, there he stood with a revolver in his hand.

The standoff was easily resolved, however. Although Freddie was the first to use his gun, two minutes later, it was also he, firmly handcuffed, who was being led outside into the evening drizzle while Rose, desperately hanging onto his sleeve, wept and sobbed, calling out his name as she watched him go.

The door closed and so did Rose's life.

"Going to miss Freddie, are you, Rose? Well, in that case, let me put an end to your grief! I would hate to see you suffer!" The tone of Jake's voice frightened her as, choked with tears, she looked into his sightless eyes, not understanding the words he spoke with such anger and bitterness.

"But, Jake, you made me do it. It was what you wanted, wasn't it?" she whimpered.

"Not with such relish, Rose, not with such passion."

Jake stood up holding behind his back the knife that he'd been saving for just this purpose. Unfortunately for Rose, he didn't need to see her to know exactly where she was: her perfume, the movement of her silk dress, the warmth of her body, her very act of breathing …all were obvious to his heightened senses. He suddenly clasped her round the waist as she gave a little cry of fright, drew her close to him and, allowing her a quick glimpse of the knife that would kill her, stabbed her so deeply in the chest that anyone seeing them would have thought them fused together, melded into one body.

Listening, as her final breath vanished into the air, he removed his arm from her waist and let go of the knife, so that she slowly slid down the length of his body until she crumpled at his feet. He could feel the wetness of her blood on his hands, could imagine the scarlet staining of her white, soft skin and knew that he would soon have that awful, unmistakable metallic smell in his nostrils.

She had been bait in a game of espionage, a willing victim, but it was for her willingness, her too obvious enjoyment, that she'd had to pay the ultimate price. Under orders or not, nobody betrayed Jake and got away with it, even in a good cause. It was a shame to do this to her, but that was the way of the world, wasn't it?

It had not been difficult to fathom Freddie out for he wasn't the best of spies. He really should have been less loose-tongued and better informed about the facts of his sham life as an American. That accent really had not been up to the mark. Just one or two little German inflections too many for his own good! When you were blind, as Jake was, you noticed these things. It was part of his success as a counterintelligence agent. As for Freddie's true identity – well, so entangled was the web woven, that no one ever quite managed to work that out. It was enough to know that the day of his retribution had finally arrived and he would become just another feather in old Edgar J's cap, another traitor condemned to the electric chair …and how Jake would smile at that!

He nudged Rose's body with his foot, almost to convince himself that she was still there. By tomorrow morning she would be far away, lying somewhere under the Interstate Highway, her beauty vanishing as the liquid-cement hardened around her. An easily accomplished task when one had dubious friends!

Later that evening, Jake, sitting alone, smoking his Gauloise and drinking his bourbon, pondered upon Rose and upon Freddie, such beautiful people, such beautiful losers! Why on earth had they done what they did? They'd both had everything going for them and above all they had been able to see the world and all its wonders, a luxury denied to him for five, long years.

All he could do was look forward to the darkness of night when, in his dreams, he would be able to see Rose again, be able to watch her in her black dress, her blonde hair shining, standing before him, swaying to the music – just for him and for nobody else.

I'll never smile again, Until I smile at you.
I'll never laugh again, What good would it do?

Bloody Roger

Maureen wiped the blood off the knife and smiled at Fred, showing her ageing, yellowing teeth. She thought it was a job well done and perhaps, now, there would be enough money for some cosmetic dental treatment! They should have done it a long time ago, but you know how these things are; little matters like murder need a bit of planning, a bit of time to work up the courage to do the dirty deed.

"He was a nasty little sod, wasn't he, Fred?

"Quite right, Maureen, quite right! He certainly was a nasty little sod! Bloody Roger!"

"But he was tall, dark and handsome – in his younger days, anyway – he got away with a lot because of that."

She thought of the times when the three of them used to walk down the road or around the park and all the girls' eyes would be focused on Roger, but he would just ignore them and put his nose in the air as though there were a bad smell around. Even when Trina, with her beautiful, golden hair, came to stay with them and used to come on strong to him he would just leave the room, doing his Greta Garbo act; they really had serious doubts about his sexual orientation. Fred reckoned he was definitely gay and that the older he got the more apparent it had become. So, here was poor Roger lying dead as a doormat at their feet – they reckoned that he must be at least seventy because they'd first got to know him years and years ago.

"You know, Fred, I honestly think he was a few sandwiches short of a picnic! You remember how affected he was when poor Curtis died – well, that wasn't natural, was it? What a drama queen! We all loved Curtis – he was such a good cat, but Roger took it really hard and stayed in bed for days on end, moping and sighing – refusing to eat a thing. Silly sod! I really hate mopers – you've just got to get on with life, haven't you? Anyway, he finally came round, but I don't think he ever fully recovered from the tragedy."

No, Curtis's death, from falling from a great height, had definitely been the turning point in Roger's development. He became permanently bad-tempered, morose and moody in a matter of only a few days and indeed, as the years passed, grew worse. Fred had wanted to kick him out at one point. He even offered to pay his board and lodging if only he would find somewhere else to go, but no one seemed to want to take up the offer; well, you couldn't really blame them; he did whiff a bit and was embarrassingly incontinent. On the other hand, Maureen and Fred certainly didn't fancy the idea of his becoming a vagabond, wandering the streets where a crowd of yobbos might have ganged up against him. Also, how embarrassing it would have been to be taking your evening walk and to have bumped into Roger sheltering in a cardboard box, hidden by newspapers. What would people have thought, what would they have said?

"Look, Roger, it's up to you," Fred used to say to him, slapping his rolled up newspaper on the table, "Either mind your manners or you're out." Usually, the only reaction was a disdainful, dirty look; there was no need for words, for he always got the message.

Maureen looked down at Roger, still with the knife in her hand. What were they going to do with the body? They couldn't very well stick it in the large wheelie bin at the end of the road under the darkness of night – he was far too big for that; so much for the diet he was supposed to have been on. Anyway, he might have given anyone, discovering him, a heart attack! They would just have to fetch the wheelbarrow and bury him in the garden, perhaps even put a little cross over the grave as a small token of respect, although his religious beliefs had been completely unknown to them.

They knew that he would enjoy being in the earth for, when they used to go down to Weston-super-Mare together, there was nothing that Roger liked more than burying himself up to his neck in the warm sand and lifting his head towards the sun. Unfortunately, his behaviour had become so bad of late and the relationship between them so strained that, on their last visit, Fred had been sorely tempted to finish it there and then, by placing his foot on Roger's head and pushing him firmly and more deeply into the sand so that he would suffocate and die with no more ado. It would have certainly saved them today's palaver.

The final straw had been yesterday evening's little episode when Roger, sitting hip to hip with Maureen on the sofa, had suddenly fallen asleep, his head coming to rest on her shoulder, but then, all at once, he'd put his nose against her neck and nipped it – a love bite, no less. She supposed that he must have been having an erotic dream! What on earth would everyone think, seeing it – a woman of her age apparently indulging in such lewd behaviour? If it were to be discovered that it was Roger who had caused this embarrassment – can you imagine it? Fred was beside himself with anger and Maureen absolutely mortified – after all they'd done for him, all the money that had been at his disposal – no expense spared. She supposed that she'd now have to pop into Marks and Sparks to buy a new scarf to hide the offending stigma.

Maureen and Fred then spent the next quarter of an hour standing looking out of the window at the garden, waiting for the evening gloom to descend. They certainly didn't fancy drawing the attention of the neighbours to what they were about to do, so they had time to reflect on some more positive sides to Roger's character: trying not to speak ill of the dead! Needless to say, the list was inevitably somewhat short.

"I must admit, Maureen, he did give me a bit of a laugh when he used to watch the tennis on the telly – backwards and forwards, up and down went his head – then during the intervals he'd rush out like greased lightning into the kitchen to get himself a drink so he wouldn't miss anything. Wouldn't have anything to do with any other sport, only tennis."

"Yep, funny old so-and-so was Roger; now he's gone, we'll be able to save a bit of money at last and, perhaps, I can have my teeth done!"

In the meantime, a strong wind had begun to blow outside, whipping the trees and bushes from side to side and whistling noisily down the chimney. They watched as the dustbin lid flew into the air, hurling itself against Erica and Ernie, the garden gnomes; they gazed as the plant pots chased each other across the small lawn; they listened to the sound of a police siren somewhere nearby, which was a bit worrying in the circumstances. Indeed, there was a veritable cacophony of sound going on all around them. So much so that they almost, but not quite, failed to register that something was happening behind them.

When they turned around, there was Roger, now lying on his back, his dark eyes wide open, looking at them accusingly, his two black front paws waving about in the air. A familiar, pitiful moan escaped from his throat, the one that he used when he did his Lady of the Camellias act.

"God, Maureen, what happened there then? Didn't make a very good job of that, did you?"

"I can't believe it, Fred! Oh dear, oh dear …what on earth made me do it; as though I don't know! Greed, sheer greed – that's what! Oh you poor, poor love, poor Roger, our darling big, black, curly boy! What has Mummy done to you?"

"For goodness sake, Maureen, put a sock in it! Look

at his chest, you've hardly touched it. Where's all this blood coming from then, Roger? Bloody, little bleeder aren't you?"

"Listen to Mummy, Roger, you've just got understand. Vet's bills, visits to the poodle parlour for all those fancy cuts you like, special food for your sensitive tummy, an hour's walk a day, a dog psychologist for your neuroses, it's all very, very wearing and costs a lot of time and money. We thought I'd do it to spare the cost of yet another visit to the vet and that it would be kinder here at home with just the two of us and you are getting on a bit, aren't you, sweetie?"

At that remark, Roger gave them both a dirty look and, licking his wound, wobbled over to the sofa where he snuggled into his usual corner, with his head resting comfortably against his own personal cushion. "And now," said Fred, "I suppose it'll be more expense to put a stitch in that silly, little stab wound!"

So, Maureen's dream of a mouthful of blindingly white, perfect, Hollywood-style teeth was over until Roger, that darkly elegant, debonair figure of a poodle, went in his own good time to the great doghouse in the sky.

Blue Eyes

Gideon had always been a sucker for girls with blue eyes, especially those with dark lashes like spiders' legs; her skin was porcelain pale and her cheeks had the delicate, pink bloom of youth, of the naturally healthy. She shut her eyelids for him, then opened them, looking directly at him. He was totally smitten. Love at first sight!

She lay there, her legs modestly covered by an ankle-length, black dress, but he could see that they were invitingly open, which immediately made him think of his wife, Jessica. This blue-eyed beauty was obviously a naughty girl – anyone could see that – and there was a lot of interest in her. He wanted to buy her, but suspected that she would cost much more than he could afford. Even the reserve price was £80 and he recognised several dealers who specialised in dolls, so he knew he didn't really stand much chance.

A woman, standing next to him, physically backed away from the object of his desire and shivered, for those piercing, emotionless, blue eyes followed you wherever you went and she felt totally spooked by them.

The doll herself could still feel on her aging body the flesh of the hands that had shaped her a hundred years ago in Germany. He had been a young apprentice called Fritz and how she had loved him for breathing life into her, for creating her personality, for talking to her, for calling her 'mein liebling', for singing sweet songs to her as he worked away. However, as things turned out, she had spent most of her life wrapped in paper and left at the back of a cupboard – no child had ever played with her. She had never been cuddled and loved, which is what should happen to all dolls, which is what they all need to be happy.

She had been left alone to vegetate, to grow embittered. She remained untouched, her beautiful china face still perfect, her dress as pristine as the day when Fritz's mother had put it on her; always living in the shadows had ensured that she remained forever unchanged. The only little girl to whom she had been given had screamed at the sight of her, crying out, "Take her away, Mummy, take her away! Why is she looking at me like that?" There was obviously something about her that kept affection at a distance.

The auctioneer seemed, that day, to be off form and wasn't working the room in his usual enthusiastic way, so the prospective buyers reacted likewise and Gideon, within a few minutes, had won his bid.

"What the hell's this then, Gideon? I thought you were supposed to be bidding for a solid-silver tray!" Jessica's dark, brown eyes looked at him with disgust and amazement. "So what are you going to do with this damned doll? No way is it going anywhere on show in this house! It's totally ghastly – and it smells! £80 down the drain. Take it to the sale in Overbury next week and just get rid of it and I don't care what you sell for it. In fact, a car boot sale might be the best place for it. Better still, stick it in the dustbin!"

"What's the matter with you? Just look at those blue eyes – enough to make any man's heart break… *You're a beautiful girl, aren't you, liebling?"*

"Liebling – just listen to yourself!" she said and, picking up Gideon's darling, she flung her hard against the brass fender in front of the blazing fire. The pretty fender had been a good buy – how it shone as the light from the flames made it glitter and gleam. However, the doll was never again going to reach a reserve of anything like £80, for her nose now lay as a little pile of broken, white china and chalky dust upon the carpet.

"You stupid bitch!" screamed Gideon. "How could you have done that?

Gideon had her nose restored, of course, but she was never quite as beautiful as she'd looked when he first saw her in the sale room. From then on there was something different about her; well, would you ever feel the same if you'd been flung around and your nose ruined? So where did she end up? Why …on a shelf in Gideon's little computer room, under a mountain of files and folders, in a box tied up with green ribbon! For Jessica it had been hate at first sight and for Gideon the magic had now gone, but obstinacy made him determined not to get rid of her.

The doll pondered upon her situation. It looked as

though it would be another hundred years of sheer boredom with nothing to look at and she was simply not going to allow that to happen. Her lovely Fritz had been a strange boy, had possessed strange powers and she reasoned that some of these must have passed into her during her creation. The bitch Jessica who had spoiled her lovely face would be her ultimate aim, but until then she would spread mayhem wherever and whenever she could, not so much from malice, but simply to relieve the boredom. Nevertheless, she wasn't sure that she could do anything, so it was in the nature of experiment.

It took Gideon and Jessica some time to realise that they had a problem – starting with the beautiful brass fender. It gradually became tarnished and, however much they polished it, it never regained its beauty. In fact, after a few weeks it had become so stained and ugly that only its pretty shape was a reminder of how it had once looked. Eventually they threw it out. This, however, was only the beginning and Gideon and Jessica had no idea what was in store for them. As you can see, something of Fritz's gifts had, indeed, been passed on to the doll.

Gideon, as he lay asleep in bed, drowsily heard Jessica getting up to make her way downstairs. The kitchen door opened so he knew she'd gone to fetch a chocolate yogurt from the fridge – it is strange the cravings that pregnant women suddenly acquire, isn't it?

Two minutes later the delicious, chocolate yogurt was spread all over her face and the kitchen was like a war zone – plates smashed into pieces, rather like the doll's nose had been and the flames on the hob burning at full pressure. The contents of cupboards and drawers were heaped on the floor; jam, rice, cornflakes, everything edible and non-edible, was out of its allotted place.

As Gideon opened the door the first sight to greet his eyes was Jessica, a living work of art, her back as though it had been super glued near to the top of the kitchen wall, her arms, legs and head flailing helplessly in the air, her screams deafening; at least there were no near neighbours to hear her!

"What's the matter with me, Gideon? For God's sake, just help me! This has got to be a nightmare – tell me it's not happening". Her large, brown eyes were full of terror and tears. Then suddenly it was as though someone had released her and she just crumpled onto the floor, cutting her arm deeply on a knife as she landed so that everything looked even more of a mess. Her flowing blood added to the scene of destruction.

Once Jessica's arm had been cleaned and bandaged, the sheer mystery and fear of what had happened was too terrifying an experience to ignore and, as no rational explanation could be found, a priest with a goodly supply of holy water, and later a medium with all the powers at her disposal, came to exorcise whatever spirit of evil had caused this horrific event. Both priest and medium were well-rewarded financially for their work and eventually the memory, except in the world of dreams and nightmares, disappeared.

The doll, meanwhile, her blue eyes seeing nothing, lay in her box, as though in a coffin, and smiled to herself.

Sylvia clambered onto the chair in Gideon's little office and looked at him appealingly with her large, brown eyes focused on him as he leaned against the wall drinking his coffee. "Please, Daddy, let me click the mouse!" The screen was black, the computer hibernating.

Normally she was never allowed into the office – he didn't want her touching any of the electronic devices or moving papers around, for it was from here that he ran his business, made his money.

"Just this once – but promise me faithfully, on Tabby-Cat's life, that you'll never do it again."

"I promise!"

"On Tabby-Cat's life!"

"On Tabby-Cat's life!"

So she clicked the mouse, but the monitor remained dark, until suddenly a word appeared in the middle of the blackness; one word and one word only, written in red gothic script – "Liebling" it read.

Gideon's stomach turned a somersault and his heart leapt. "Get out of here, Sylvia – now!" he said, dropping his almost-full coffee cup onto the carpet as he grabbed her by the arm and pushed her out through the door. The little girl began to sob, not understanding Gideon's shock and dismay.

"What did I do, Daddy? I'm sorry!" she wailed.

Gideon, without any further ado, simply yanked the plug out of wall so that the computer died on him – anything just to remove the word as quickly as possible from the screen.

The poison had been laid, however, and all Sylvia wanted from that moment was to be able to creep back into the forbidden room, to play with the mouse, to explore the computer, to discover why it had seemed to hold such power over her father. Small as she was she understood that something strange had happened when she had clicked the mouse.

A couple of days later Jessica was in the kitchen baking cakes and Gideon had gone outside to mow the lawn, unaccountably leaving the office door unlocked. So, of course, Sylvia, curiosity burning away, crept quietly along the corridor to Daddy's office, silently opened the door and entered. The computer, much to her disappointment, was locked and so there was no entertainment to be had there. However, dragging the chair away from the desk she set it under the shelves and unsteadily climbed onto it, rummaging through all the bits and pieces that she found.

Paper, paper clips, pencils, rulers, all soon found their way onto the carpet and Sylvia knew that she would be seriously told off for what she had done. Suddenly she found a little, white, cardboard box tied up with a pretty green ribbon. It was like her birthday all over again so all thoughts of having done something wrong disappeared completely from her mind. Perhaps it was even an early Christmas present that had been hidden away from her.

Sylvia carefully climbed down off the chair and sat on the small sofa that stood against the wall. She always loved to undo presents slowly, not like some children who desperately tear and spoil their parcels. The anticipation was always such a large part of the fun. So, taking her time, she undid the ribbon and tidily wound it into a ball. Then off came the lid and there staring at her was a doll whose threatening blue eyes were so full of hate that Sylvia stood up letting it fall to the floor.

The little girl screamed and yelled as if she'd seen the devil; perhaps, in a sense, she had. "Take her away! Take her away! I don't want her. I don't like her! Give her to somebody else!" Jessica rushed into the room, looked down at the doll with horror and at that moment, thankfully, Gideon walked in and saw the terror in their faces.

"It's all right, Sylvia," he said, "we'll get rid of her, I promise you. In fact, you can come with us and see her go. We'll put her in the wheelie bin at the end of the road – so there is nothing more to frighten you! Go and find Tabby-Cat and then he can come too." So off went little Sylvia to find her cat.

"What is it about that doll, Gideon? God only knows why you had to buy the damn thing. Liebling you called her – nothing very darling about her, is there?"

"No, not the wheelie-bin! We'll burn her, Jessica, that's the best thing to do. We'll get rid of her completely and of whatever it is that she does. Have a ritual burning! And we'll do it now, without further delay. And you're right, of course. I should never have bought her in the first place!"

"It was she, wasn't it, who attacked me in the kitchen? I've always felt that it had something to do with her. But how could a doll possibly have caused so much damage? She's not even a particularly big doll, is she? She's only an inanimate object, after all! Such a foolish idea, but I've never quite been able to get it out of my head! And those blue eyes – they're so weird, as though they're looking into your very soul"

So down to the bottom of the garden they all went, including Tabby-Cat. The doll was put into an old paint tin and a match was set to her. No scream came from the paint tin while the fire consumed her – though deep in their hearts they had almost expected it, ridiculous as this may sound.

"But her ashes are still here, Gideon!" said Jessica. "Let's put them back in the box and take them to the small bridge in Overbury and drop them into the river. Then they'll be right away from us and we'll be able to forget that she was ever here."

Gideon, Jessica and Sylvia stood beneath the afternoon sun and looked down into the river. They could see their reflections glinting in the water, but if they'd looked more closely they might have seen that there was a faint, almost invisible, fourth figure standing at their side.

Jessica held the white box, again tied up with the same green ribbon. Inside, reposed the doll's ashes.

Meanwhile, Gideon and Sylvia retreated to lean with their backs against the opposite side of the bridge so that Jessica could alone perform the ritual of consigning the ashes to their watery grave. She untied the ribbon, opened the box and let the charred remains fall into the water. If she had known a spell suitable for the occasion she would have said it aloud. The box and the ribbon then followed the ashes into the current.

For several seconds she stood with her hands held over the water as though in benediction and then turned very slowly round to face her husband and her daughter, so slowly it was as though time had stood still.

Her stunningly blue eyes pierced their souls as she looked at them.

She smiled at Gideon as she said, "Mein Liebling."

She smiled at Sylvia as she said, "Mein Liebling."

Acid Rain

That was the summer when the Acid Rain began to fall – a summer that was to change the world, a summer that would be forever unforgettable. It was, of course, completely self-induced – the rain, that is – not the summer! Completely self-induced by… well, let's see, shall we?

Contador, tall, scrawny and past his best, was the controller of the Great Weather Machine, with Malden close at his heels, waiting to step into a dead man's shoes. Poor Contador, not terribly accurate in his forecasts, nor in his attempts to bring the weather under control – not daring enough in Malden's opinion, but when had meteorology ever been an exact science? Certainly not in the year of Our Great Omnipotent One 3001!

All that anyone knew was that each summer had become rainier and hotter. In fact, it was like a dripping furnace and, before long, the polar bears, the penguins and the seals, after a long, hard struggle, finally lost their fragile homes for ever. That year, however, the humidity, the thunder, the lightning, the rain and the unnatural deep orange of the sun had increased a hundredfold and no one knew why – or, at least, almost no one.

It was only as they walked down the great flight of steps towards the lake and through the huge, dark arches leading from the GWOC – the Great Weather Operational Centre – that Malden suddenly realised that he had just made a catastrophic mistake and could clearly foresee the awfulness of what was about to happen. Indeed, already drops of rain were beginning to fall upon his bare shoulders from the grey, lowering sky; immediately, his skin started to burn and blisters to appear on his arms and upon his hands; birds were falling from the air; animals were crying and dying among the trees that surrounded the lake and leaves were falling from their branches as though autumn had arrived prematurely.

Contador, his eyes smarting and streaming, looked Malden in the face and snarled at him. "You did this, didn't you? It's your fault, all this suffering. When you see the pain, the cancers, will you feel any guilt? Of course, you won't – guilt's not your thing, is it? You never take the blame for anything. You always step back, with your wide-eyed innocence. 'It's not my fault. How could it possibly be?' you'll say."

Malden had to stand there and take the accusations, unable to say a word, his mouth too full of the sulphurous, acrid taste of the rain to offer anything in his own defence. What Contador had said was completely unjust though, possibly, just possibly, might there be the merest smidgen of truth in it? No, the one to blame was Malden's woman. Lilith! After all she was the Supreme Leader, the ultimate point of reference for everyone, but what a psychological mess she was: ambitious beyond belief, frighteningly unpredictable, completely ruthless. Two brothers and an uncle had all made an untimely exit from this world for blocking her way to the top. So, you see, you wouldn't have liked her one bit – his woman – hard-faced, hard-hearted, but powerful and influential, which he admired very much indeed.

Why Lilith picked him out as her lover had always worried him a little – certainly nothing to do with love or affection, for she was incapable of either. Truth to tell, like everyone else, Malden was scared to death of her. When the great acid invasion got under way she was alone but for a single servant plus, of course, a gaggle of Martians – but more of that later! She sat high up in her tower in the middle of the lake, watching the fish and the last pod of dolphins on Earth struggling and fighting for breath, watching the water turning a reddish brown. No ugly, ulcerous sores appeared on her skin as the great machines that sucked out any impurities from her environment did their work. Nevertheless, if she were to leave her sanctuary, she, too, would fall prey to the great disaster.

Stepping over the scattered, spoiled bodies of the furry, feathery creatures that had been their neighbours, Contador and Malden hurried to the lakeside and signalled for the boatman who plied that stretch of water, in the service of the GWOC, to approach. Soon they were able to breathe more easily in the hermetically sealed craft, but the full horror of the situation only hit them fully once they had the leisure to look through the windows at the scene in front of them. To say it resembled Hell was an understatement. It was as if some artist had had a field day while mixing the colours on his palette. The dull, grey, yellowy skies of the morning had changed to horizontal stripes of vivid colour; reds, pinks, blues and greens filled the horizon while the huge sun, now hung colourless: a white snowball whose reflection on the lake resembled moonlight. The rain looked only semi-liquid, like chewing-gum stretched between fingers, seeming to solidify as it descended,

The sleek, streamlined, black craft soon approached the tall tower that stood completely isolated in the lake. Made of bronze, the massive edifice normally shone and shimmered, by sunlight, by moonlight, even under an overcast sky. Today, however, it looked as if some giant hooligan had attacked it, its usually perfect surface was spoiled by the thick, congealing rain that ran down it from top to bottom.

Lilith's servant ushered them inside through the great bronze doors. Up the spiral, metal stairway they went, until a door automatically opened before them. There was Lilith, Malden's woman, that red-haired demon in human guise, standing to greet them, if it could be called a greeting. It was certainly not a greeting of welcome. No words of kindness came from her lips, but then when did they ever?

Malden clenched his fists and tried to ignore the

cramps in his stomach. "Ye gods!" he thought, "what have I done, why did I do it? Damned weather machine! If only I'd resisted the temptation to fiddle and kept my hands off it, this would not be happening."

The wispy, wraith-like inhabitants from the depths of Mars – that dried-up, barren, red planet – floated at Lilith's side. "You were warned!" they whispered to Malden, smiling evilly. "It was forbidden, but you would have your own way, wouldn't you?"

Lilith glared at Malden "You've ruined the world, Malden. I can never leave this tower because of you. I shall starve and I shall die because of you!" The alien chimera smiled again, but no-one saw this, because in an instant they could disappear as though into nothingness, so it was not surprising that for nearly a thousand years no one had realised that the red planet was inhabited …blink too quickly and you missed them. However, ten years ago these nebulous, diaphanous creatures, suddenly and finally, lost patience with the unwelcome interest shown in their home by strange earthlings. Why would they want machines from Earth continually trundling over their rocky hills and plains, snooping and spying? What happened on the surface of their planet and, especially below ground, was no one's business but their own. That they were wrestling with the great problem of how to conquer the Earth was also their own business. You would have thought, after a thousand years of trying, that men from Earth would have arrived on Mars in person, but somehow things just hadn't worked out as expected. Not one single imprint of a human shoe had ever made its mark on the red planet's surface. Far easier to send machines and fool themselves into thinking that great scientific advances were being made!

The trouble was that the vast majority of people had spent far too much of their time in virtual worlds, living second-hand lives, interacting with holograms. Their brains had atrophied, their bodies almost unnecessary – except for sex, and even that was not as exciting as it was in their artificial existence. Even the greatest physicists and astronomers in the world had rather given up on their quest for solutions to the great scientific conundrums of the universe. It was all too much effort and, like everyone else, they'd just about given up bothering about the wellbeing of the Earth, let alone what was happening on another planet

So let pollution contaminate the atmosphere; who cared as long as they could continue to live in their wonderful dream-world? No, it was only people like Contador and Malden and Malden's woman, Lilith, who could really be said to be alive and this was one of the reasons why Lilith had ended up as Supreme Leader. Really there was hardly any need for people at all and, of course, the world was populated mainly by robots …and no, there was no chance at all that they would ever take over the world. Not with a programmer like Lilith in command!

"You've been interfering again, haven't you,

Malden? I really should have kept a firmer eye on you.
I should have realised what was happening. My big, big
mistake, but you'll pay for it, Malden – you just see if
you don't! And what about you, Contador, you're
supposed to be the one in charge – couldn't you see
what he was doing? The prime rule has always, always,
been never to interfere with the Great Weather
Machine. Isn't that right, Malden?

"It wasn't my fault, none of it," Malden said, but
with a very large, niggling doubt somewhere in the
recesses of his extremely brilliant mind. However, on
and on and on she went until finally he could stand no
more of her. All he wanted was for the sound of her
voice to cease and so he killed her, there and then –
strangling her, squeezing the breath of life out of her
body, so quickly, so decisively that neither Contador
nor the servant, nor, indeed, the boatman who had
followed them in, could prevent it …an absolutely
unpremeditated, spur of the moment impulse that he
would never have imagined doing! What had brought
that on, where had he found the courage? The shadowy
wraiths smiled slyly.

As a matter of fact, the strange, floaty beings from
Mars were awfully grateful to Malden on several fronts.
They had been intending for the last thousand years or
so to take over the Earth, but being only half there and
half not, being so very insubstantial and hazy, had made
things difficult for them. On the other hand, Malden, by
meddling, by thinking that he knew best had, through
the years, solved their problem. Forever clicking the

keys of the weather computers when he had no business to be doing so, he'd finally pressed one finger too many on the Great Weather Machine's sensitive numerical keypad that morning, thus ruining everything from the earthlings' perspective.

The only thing those shadowy, indistinct aliens really wanted was water and the wonderful, gooey acid rain was right up their street. Now they could all leave dried-up old Mars and drift down at their leisure to Earth. All the people, all the animals, all the birds in their new home would just gradually disappear, with no effort at all on their part, whilst they would thrive and multiply.

As a matter of principle, the Supreme Leader's passing had to be avenged, which is why later that day Contador, the boatman and the servant watched Malden as he lay on the floor of the tower, manacled and gagged. While, from the shadows, the chimera silently laughed, for aliens they may have been, but they did possess a sense of humour, of a sort! Suddenly, they saw Contador open the window and cough as the contaminated air entered the room. They wafted around just below the ceiling like puffs of pale smoke, giggling hysterically, as the boatman and the servant threw Malden, manacles and gag still in place, into the fetid air and down into the lake. There his body bubbled and burned in the simmering heat of the water. As he hurtled downwards he must have heard Contador's last words to him. "Always remember, Malden, obey your betters, keep your hands to yourself and never touch the

Great Weather Machine!"

The chimera simply adored this entertainment and decided that they would do the same. So, after a considerable amount of difficult manoeuvring, out of the window went poor old Contador, the boatman and the servant. Down through the wonderful acid rain to join Malden and the dead dolphins in the wonderful acid lake!

So that is how The Acid Rain Fiasco, as it became known, enabled the Martians to become rulers of the Earth and how its whole evolutionary development, thereby, took a completely different turn, simply because one silly man, by the name of Malden, could not keep his hands off the Great Weather Machine!

Yes, indeed, what an unforgettable summer that was!

Conway Street

Daisy and Harold, Bertha and Marvin and so many others, plus, of course, all the cats and dogs, budgies and gerbils, even pigeons in their lofts, all lived in Conway Street. Alongside were four pubs, two baker's shops, one refined ladies' clothiers, one barber's, Miss Sweet's Sweetie shop that always smelled wonderfully of the tobacco that she also sold and, of course, Fretwell's, a general store. It was small, but stocked with everything under the sun, a real jumble of a place, which was run by two ladies whose sexual preferences were probably recognised, but not talked about – suffice to say that one of them had extremely short hair and always wore brown corduroy trousers and bulky suede shoes.

I mustn't forget, of course, the Baptist Church, the Congregational Church and the Sally Army just round the corner. Also, at the top of the street, was the Methodist Church, which faced the war memorial that, in the form of a cross, was the central focus of the town.

At the other end of the street stood the Cottage Hospital where Daisy's mother had had her appendix out – that had been in the days before anyone had ever heard of the national health service and she'd had to borrow five pounds from her sister in Scotland to help pay for the operation. It was also the place to which Daisy was always dragged by her mother whenever one of her habitual whitlows needed to be lanced.

Daisy could still, all these years later, remember having a terrible tantrum in the baker's, lying on the floor screaming and making no end of a fuss, until her mother had had to remove her from the premises. In fact, it was her first real memory, probably because she'd been the centre of everyone's attention, which every child liked to be. Those were the days when her mother used to push her under the kitchen table whenever the enemy planes passed overhead. Not that that would have done much good against the military might of Germany! Those were the days too when, if there was a problem with the wireless, you just gave it a good slap to set it on its way again.

Daisy had first met Harold at Conway Street Junior School where she regularly used to cross rather daringly over to the boys' side of the playground so that she could talk to him – she'd fancied him even then. She could still remember how when they were in the top class they had laughed themselves silly together watching the headmaster's false teeth almost making an embarrassing exit from his mouth and, of course, all the kids used to have a good giggle whenever his underpants could be seen peeping over the top of his trousers. They used to laugh at such daft things, but those are the sort of memories that made up their childhood.

Every Sunday afternoon, without fail, both Daisy

and Harold were sent off to the Sunday school at the Baptist Church because it was the nearest to where they lived. It was there, at some point during their first year, that they decided to become real Baptists, God's little helpers. Well, they had suddenly realised that the platform where they used to stand helping out the choir on special occasions, could be transformed in the twinkle of an eye into a swimming pool. That was what they thought it was, until they saw people dressed in white robes being pulled backwards by the scruff of the neck and submerged below the water.

'What fun' was that they thought and, from then, on they spent hours at a time walking up and down Conway Street their hands together in front of them, repeating the Lord's Prayer.

Perhaps if their holiness shone brightly enough and they were seen by the minister to be showing sufficient devotion to their religion they too might be chosen to descend the steps into the pool.

This phase didn't last long, however, for Harold, in a particularly prayerful moment, had closed his eyes and walked straight into a lamppost. So off to the Cottage Hospital he was sent to have a couple of stitches put in his forehead.

Harold's dad worked on the railway and they used to live behind Conway Street in what, nowadays, would be termed a bijoux residence with a river view. In other words, a small, humble house which, when it rained heavily, was in grave danger of being invaded by flood water.

Harold's mother was famous for the birthday party that she unfailingly gave for Harold each year. Daisy always remembered the lovely, iced fairy-cakes that she made, but above all the wonderful box of assorted chocolate bars that she gave each little guest at the end of the party: all this, despite the fact that money was tight. What lovely people his mum and dad had been, but unfortunately they never got to make it to Daisy and Harold's wedding.

Such a pity, but she'd never forgotten their kindness to her and to everybody. Harold, completely without ambition, had gone on to the Secondary Modern School and then progressed to the local flour mill where he still worked happily. It was a very picturesque spot and, during his lunch of cold, bacon sandwiches with plenty of margarine, he used to stand on the bridge outside the mill watching the anglers on the river bank and the boats passing through the locks.

Well, that's Daisy and Harold done and dusted – pleasant, ordinary people – nothing more really to be said about them …and you've also got the general idea of Conway Street… Goodness, I almost forgot to mention Conrad, their son!

Well, most people forgot about poor Conrad.

Not too well endowed in the brains department, he was a bland, quiet, simple soul, the highlight of whose life was the annual visit each October of the Mop Fair. How he loved the bright lights, the loud music and wandering amongst all the rides and the stalls. As this all took place in Conway Street itself he was absolutely in his element.

He would even follow the Mop Fair by bus to its next destination, so loathe was he to see the last of it. I suppose I should also mention the family cat upon whom they all totally doted, but I can't possibly tell you what he was called because he was black and his name began with a capital N. So it would be politically incorrect to say it, though in those days nobody gave it a second thought. Big, fierce with a huge appetite he ruled the house and absolutely adored watching the small black and white television set that was everyone's pride and joy. So, yes, there you have it – Daisy, Harold, Conrad and their anonymous cat all dealt with – for the moment.

Now we come to Bertha and Marvin. A completely different kettle of fish! What a pair they were!

"Marvin, you can't possibly wear that tie – it's got a stain on it. What on earth would people say if they saw their barber with a dirty tie? And do remember that unlike most people in the street we own our building."

No, there was certainly none of your rented rubbish for Bertha and Marvin and, therefore, standards had to be particularly high. Poor, henpecked Marvin virtually paled into insignificance against Bertha who, if she had but known it, was rather a source of amusement for the rest of the street. There she was with her blonde hair piled up high on her head, her long, brilliantly-coloured earrings almost touching her shoulders looking, everyone thought, rather like a barmaid. A considerable dent would certainly have been put in her airs and graces if she'd only realised this.

Bertha, naturally, did not work.

Although, on days when business was particularly good, she would nip into the shop from their private premises at the back just to make sure that the floor was clear of hair and that things were shipshape and Bristol fashion.

Apart from that she did very little: just spent her days flicking the occasional feather duster delicately over the furniture and perhaps giving the floor a bit of a sweep.

As for cooking and buying food, why bother when it was so obviously more Marvin's forte than hers?

Most of her time she was to be found in one of the coffee shops gossiping and giggling with her friends …and my goodness, how she bitched! Not a good word to say about anyone! Poor Daisy and Harold were especially focussed upon and, of course, Conrad.

Surely, she said, they could have found him something better than a job sweeping the streets!

Bertha had no children of her own and, therefore, felt free to offer her opinion on parenthood in general.

In fact, Bertha was a true expert on everything. In other words, she was a smug, self-opinionated, old windbag.

So the years passed and it was already coming up to the first anniversary of the horrendous Mop Fair that people would talk about for ever and a day.

Harold, his clothes not unnaturally dusty with flour, was standing in his favourite place on the bridge eating his bacon sandwiches, while the tears ran down his face.

Poor Daisy, what a cross she had to bear and poor, poor Conrad! Who would ever have imagined such a thing happening to him.

In all the years of following the fair Conrad had never quite had the courage to go on any of the rides. The eternal spectator, that was Conrad, until one evening he had suddenly, for some unknown reason, become mesmerised by the flashing lights and the up and over, up and over motion of the Big Wheel. So he'd gone on, up and up right to the top, the seat swinging as the wheel turned.

Suddenly, filled with fear, he had found himself stranded at the pinnacle of the ride as the wheel slowed down to allow people to get off at street level.

He completely panicked at this point, feeling so isolated and vulnerable as though he were going to be fixed for ever at the top of the world.

He shouted out for help, but no one took him seriously. After all, it was just silly Conrad getting a bit excited, though they were rather surprised to see him up there.

He then grabbed the safety bar trying to open it, but it wouldn't budge.

So onto the seat he climbed and stood there swaying with his arms outstretched until the wheel started going round again, giving a little jolt to the seat as it did so …and out into the autumn air sailed Conrad as the spectators shouted in horror.

He would probably have died, perhaps a better

outcome, but for the fact that the Big Wheel had been erected outside the cottage hospital as it was every year, so that help was immediately at hand.

It was that same evening at the fair that Daisy had won Alfie, a fine-looking, brown teddy bear with a bright red bow around his neck. She was so pleased with it that she was going to put it in the cat's basket so he'd have a friend. Silly idea, really, but that's just the sort of thing that we animal lovers do, isn't it?

That didn't happen, of course, for destiny had had different plans for Alfie! Everyone in the town now knew Alfie, for he sat always, without fail, on Conrad's lap as his wheelchair was pushed along the pavement, always firmly clasped in his hand.

Why, they even shared a bed together.

Conrad sadly, as you might expect, didn't really recognise anyone who didn't live in his house except, of course, Bertha, that surprising trump card in the pack.

What a friend, what a help! They couldn't have survived without her.

Even the not-to-be-named cat had taken to her!

Bertha, heaven only knew why, had cast just one look at Conrad sitting in his wheelchair with Alfie, one look at Daisy's strained, sad face, one look at Harold's despair and she knew as sure as night follows day that she had to help.

Now coffee mornings were a thing of the past and gone were her afternoons spent reading silly novels –

she now had a mission, a purpose to her life – she was needed!

As for Marvin – well, it's an ill wind, as they say – for while she was looking after the house down the street it meant that he could lead a nice, quiet life without her continual squawking.

What a relief that was!

In fact, he thought that poor Conrad had probably saved Bertha's life, for many was the time he'd looked at the razors in the shop and wondered if he might use one for a rather different purpose!

Well, such was life in Conway Street!

Dysfunction

"Daddy doesn't love me," said William.

"Don't worry about that, William. Daddy doesn't love anyone."

"Does he love you, Mummy?"

"No, William, he doesn't – in fact, he especially doesn't love me."

"Why not, Mummy? Why doesn't he love you?"

"I'm not too sure to be quite honest. Probably, I think, because I'm stupid".

"You're not stupid, Mummy."

"Oh yes, I am, William. I'm stupid all right. I'm very, very stupid."

"Why are you very, very stupid, Mummy?"

"Because I married Daddy, William, that's why!"

Well, this little conversation went on, in a similar vein, for quite some time, by the end of which both William and Mummy had decided that as they didn't love Daddy anyway, it didn't really matter much whether he loved them or not. However, as he was the one bringing in the dosh, they must always remember to be nice to him if they wanted to continue living in their beautiful, big house with all its beautiful furniture and to go twice a year on lovely, lovely holidays to the Caribbean. The most important thing, of course, was that William and Mummy loved each other.

"If you promise to be polite to Daddy this evening and not call him a silly old fart, I'll let you have a sip of my gin and tonic. I'll even let you have a puff of my nice, sweet-smelling ciggie if you swear not to carve your name again on the door of Daddy's new car with your penknife."

So there they sat in the garden as the sun went down, drinking and smoking. In fact, within a very short time, William was feeling quite squiffy and rather light-headed and Mummy was completely plastered. Then the sound of Daddy's car was heard on the drive and, before they knew it, there he was, standing in front of them, home from his office where he was a very important person indeed, who shouted a lot and threw his weight around all over the place.

"What is that hanging out of your mouth, William?"

"It's a spliff, Daddy."

"I've told you before not to smoke pot, haven't I?"

"Yes, you have, Daddy," said William, putting on one of his innocent, angelic faces before giving Daddy a punch in the stomach that looked playful enough, but which, in actual fact, hurt like hell, so much so that Daddy seriously thought about giving William a good slap, but he knew that if he did William would be on to Child Line or Social Services as quick as greased lightning.

William, if only Daddy had but recognised the fact, was a real chip off the old block, for Daddy was a mobster, a gangster, a high-up member of the English branch of the Cosa Nostra and there was nothing in life that William wanted more than to follow in his footsteps. You can see for yourself that, even at his young age, he was already showing considerable potential for the job: drugs, booze and even murder, for who had just been expelled from school for putting poison pellets in the gerbil's cage? Daddy had been really, really angry with William for doing that.

"Why did you poison the gerbil, William?"

"I don't know, Daddy."

"Where did you get the pellets from?"

"I can't remember, Daddy."

"Don't be silly, you must remember. Tell me!"

"No comment, Daddy!"

At this reply Daddy had to hold his hands behind his back, clenching them until the palms almost bled, to stop them from giving William a good clip round the ear.

As the weeks passed by, William began to notice that Mummy seemed to be spending an awful lot of time in the potting shed with Mr Dobson the gardener.

"Talking about the birds and the bees," said Mummy to William with a wink, but he thought this was very odd, for surely they should be talking about trees and flowers and things like that. He sometimes tried listening at the potting shed door, but heard nothing except loud, grunting sounds – Mr Dobson must be working very hard indeed to get so out of breath and Mummy had always been a bit of a giggler. However, as the door was never left unlocked and the window was too high to look through, William was unable to discover more and usually wandered off with his catapult to see if he could down a bird or two.

At the breakfast table one morning Daddy seemed to be having a real go at Mummy about Mr Dobson and was talking about sacking him. Poor Mr Dobson, thought William, he'll just have to work even harder! That very same evening at about ten o'clock William, unusually for him, was snuggled up in his nice, warm bed with Reginald the Robber, his fluffy rabbit, lying on the pillow next to him – he was feeling very tired having had an exceptionally busy time trying to pull out the saplings that Mr Dobson had planted the day before.

Suddenly, there was great deal of noise coming from downstairs: screaming and shouting, scraping and dragging, pushing and pulling, comings and goings, until William, yawning and grumbling, got up to see what was happening. Peeping out of the window, he was just in time to see a long, wooden box, with brass handles that shone in the moonlight, being loaded into a white van – and as Mummy didn't appear at breakfast the next morning or, in fact, at breakfast ever again, he could only come to one conclusion.

He didn't really mind too much, however, because soon there was a new lady to look after him, one who always allowed him what he knew was called a full English breakfast, instead of the cornflakes and fruit that Mummy had made him eat. The first time he met her was a few days after the box had been carried from the house. She seemed a nice person and, in answer to William's very first, anxious question to her, was able to reassure him immediately that, yes, he would still be able to go on his lovely, lovely holidays to the Caribbean twice a year – so that was all right, wasn't it?

"Did you ever meet Mummy, Felicity?"

"Of course I met her, William."

"And did you like Mummy?"

"Yes, of course I liked her, William."

"And where is Mummy now, Felicity? Is she still in the long wooden box I saw that night from my window?"

"I rather think she is, William, but a good boy would say nothing about that to anyone. Let's just pretend that you didn't see anything, shall we? Promise?"

"Yes, Felicity, I promise."

"Good boy, William!"

William was rather shocked later that same week when he saw Mr Dobson, moaning and groaning loudly, hanging around by the potting shed. Now he knew perfectly well what the word `violence´ meant, from all the very unsuitable programmes that he liked to watch on television, but he'd never actually met it in person before – only the odd scuffle in the school playground – but nothing on this level. Why ...poor Mr Dobson looked as if his face had been run over by a bus and he didn't look as if he had any fingernails left.

However, thought William, it'll save him the trouble of having to clean them, for by the end of the day, what with all that digging and delving around in the earth, they were usually pretty dirty.

William was just about to speak to him when Mr Dobson turned on his heels and stumbled away as quickly as it was possible for someone in his parlous condition to do. A few moments later, to William's great surprise, who should then come out of the potting shed but Daddy and one of the men who worked for him. Daddy smiled broadly at William and William only just managed, by the skin of his teeth, to stop a very rude word escaping from his lips.

"Who loves his Daddy, William?"

"I do, Daddy"

"And who loves William?"

"You do, Daddy."

"You didn't ever meet Mr Dobson, did you, William?"

"Mr Dobson? No, Daddy, I don't know anyone called Mr Dobson."

"The gardener, William?"

"I didn't even know we had a gardener."

"Good boy, William!"

William with his little repository of secrets, and the others that he was to gather as time passed, was, of course, as you can imagine, a very powerful little boy, but as he grew a bit older he promised himself that he would never forget the wooden casket or poor Mr Dobson. On the other hand, he was sensible enough not to flaunt what he knew in front of Daddy – keep it for when it would really matter, he thought.

Sometimes, he would catch Daddy looking at him wonderingly, but William would simply smile back at him with a reassuring glance and the look that had hovered on the edge of fear would disappear. Meanwhile, Felicity grew increasingly frail and sickly – well, so would anyone with a regular diet of poison pellets in her food – a diet suitable for a little rodent who slept in Mummy's place in Daddy's bed! The name of the game, of course, was payback and a ruthless young boy was more dangerous than dynamite when crossed.

The only ambition that William had in this life was to become the big boss of the Cosa Nostra in England and now the position was vacant, but Daddy was the main contender and Daddy couldn't even speak Italian, whereas he, William, had an Italian tutor who came to the house once a week – the only time when he'd ever applied himself to learn anything.

In time, of course, William had lots of dangerous information, which he could share with the police, with the public and the press. In the end, poor Daddy, so tantalisingly close to realising his dream of true power – within a millimetre of achieving greatness – was pipped at the post and William became the youngest boss in the history of the brotherhood.

William had once said that Daddy didn't love him, but Daddy did: too much for his own good. He'd seen the signs, had known all along how William's mind was working, but had done nothing to stop him.

William, of course, had never forgiven nor forgotten what Daddy did to Mummy and to poor Mr Dobson's fingers. So one dark night on Hampstead Heath, with two henchmen by his side, he watched as Daddy died.

"Do you love me, Daddy?" William asked.

"Unfortunately, William," Daddy replied with his last breath, "I do."

Footsteps

My brother, that bastard, that bitch's spawn, where is he tonight, do you think? Well, he's exactly where he deserves to be, in prison awaiting tomorrow, awaiting the arrival of the infamous Mr Pierrepoint, chief hangman for England. While I, poor Tweeny, mad as a hatter, where am tonight? Can you guess…? Well done! Right first time! I too am just where I deserve to be …in a lunatic asylum, awaiting my doses of camphor, of veronal, of metrazol.

My brother, you see, trained me too well for his own good. "This is how you do it, Tweeny, this is how you kill a chicken. Just put your hands very tightly round its neck and you'll be able to feel its head come away. Good girl, Tweeny, that's the way! Now you can go out and buy thruppence-worth of sweeties."

Buy sweeties for killing a chicken! That was on a good day, of course, (well, as good as they were ever going to get) before my little world became really dark and hateful.

I was even allowed, at that point, to listen to the wireless: to the kindly voice of Uncle Mac; to the exciting, innocent world of Jennings at School; to Toy Town, with the lovely baaing of Larry the Lamb.

I used to imagine other little girls listening to these

same programmes, but wearing big bows in their carefully brushed hair, wearing clean, neat dresses and being looked after by loving mothers and fathers. They were my refuge from a world that was gradually becoming increasingly hard to understand.

I wonder if you know how it feels to follow in the footsteps of someone, with such rage and loathing in your heart that they're barely controllable. My brother's footsteps were bloody, carmine-red, scarlet-stained, mud-spattered – the footsteps of a psychopath without one jot of human kindness, without one smidgen of sympathy towards another living creature.

There were lovely animals on our farm, but they were the most unfortunate of creatures, whom I many times, for their own sake, wished dead: a donkey purposely maimed for pleasure or a cat cruelly blinded and so on and so forth. "But they're here for my enjoyment, Tweeny, just as you are. There's no difference between you and them. Consider yourself fortunate, Tweeny. Just think about what I could do to you."

Well, that's me accounted for, my brother accounted for, but where's my mother tonight? Well, she's deep in the earth, removed from the sight of decent people, rotting in some hellish world, far from the presence of God.

I wanted to ask her something, wanted my mother to explain what was happening to me, but I couldn't because she would have slapped me, hit me, kicked me for my insolence, but I wanted to know! Why was he starting to touch me in that way? Why was he beginning to make me do such unspeakable things to him? Why did my mother watch and do nothing? "Be nice to your brother, he is such a clever, handsome, young man. And you, Tweeny, what are you, but a stunted, ugly, little piece of humanity?"

I cannot even now say his name, so filthy did he make me feel and you may wonder why I bear such a strange name; not the one, I hasten to add, to be found on my birth certificate, though it might as well have been. It was just another nasty, cruel joke between my brother and my mother at my expense. For a tweeny, as I learned later, was the name once given to maids in rich households and that is what I had become in the farmhouse where we lived. I was a servant, a slave, constantly fetching and carrying for my mother and for my brother.

Ecstatic, my heart fills with joy, as I picture my brother's bewilderment all these years later when he faced the judge, saw him don the black cap, heard him utter the dread words that were to send him to the gallows. Finally, he had become the victim. So, tomorrow I wish him all the pains of Hell and pray that when he arrives there, as he surely must, he will be made to suffer as he made others suffer.

The justice system is still unaware of the mysterious disappearances through the years of occasional seasonal workers who used to help us at harvest-time; still unaware, I am sure, of the full extent of his cruelty and depravity and certainly unaware of why I, his sister, am as I am.

So what was his crime?

Why has he an appointment with Mr Pierrepoint tomorrow morning?

Why?

Matricide: that was his crime.

Or was it?

The old bitch had finally turned against him, needless to say, not on my behalf. Only because she had caught him trying to steal from the cache of money and jewels, which she had so lovingly hidden in the loft of one of our barns.

From that day onwards, their relationship was never the same, both obsessed with keeping a close watch on the other, suspicion and mistrust constant presences.

Hardly ever was she allowed so much as to step out of the house, but he would slip out quietly after her, to see if he could discover the new hiding place of her treasure and one fateful evening he did.

It had been a successful market day for my mother and she returned with a purse full of money, which she kept close by her until after supper time, when, believing my brother to be dozing by the fire, she quietly opened the kitchen door and disappeared into the rainy darkness.

As the latch clicked, I watched my brother open his eyes and put out his hand to pick up the heavy, iron poker that rested against the fender.

He slowly rose from his chair, his face blotchy from the heat of the fire and from the tankards of home-brewed beer that he had downed during supper. He took his time, deliberately waiting until he thought our mother would be close to the new hiding place where she now so carefully secreted her treasures.

After he had closed the door behind him, I watched him from the window, then slipped out into the night to follow him.

There was just about enough moonlight to be able to see the mud the rain had caused. In the sodden earth I could see his footsteps, together with those of our mother and I followed those footsteps resolutely, some instinct telling me that the end was in sight.

As I approached the barn, I could hear their raised voices, but my mother's ceased abruptly and I saw my brother running out into the moonlight, towards where his little car was parked. So, away he drove, the stars shining down innocently upon this rustic scene of evil.

It was the last time I was ever to see him, except in my nightmares.

I crept into the barn and, by moonshine, saw my mother lying on the hay, blood streaming from a terrible head wound. A gurgling sound came from her throat and she looked at me beseechingly, begging me with her eyes to help her. She may or may not have survived, but how was I to know?

I couldn't let that happen though, I couldn't take that chance, could I? "Tweeny is sending you to Hell! Mother!" I shouted at her. "Where you belong!" Then, remembering my brother's lesson on how to kill a chicken, I put my hands tightly around her neck, twisted hard and so she died.

Hours later, at dawn, I was found wandering in the village, unable to speak and gibbering like the mad girl everyone now believes me to be.

Neighbours who, up until then, had barely known of my existence, took care of me until I was removed to this asylum, my home for the last five years.

The police searched the farm, finding that my brother had long gone.

Soon the hue and cry was out for him, but it was only a year ago that they found him and he was imprisoned and tried for his crime.

I suppose you may find it hard to believe, but I actually choose my moments of madness, for my symptoms immediately worsen if I ever hear anyone suggest that I am recovering and that one day it might be possible for me to be released!

How could I ever allow that to happen?

Why on earth should I ever want to leave this safe, comfortable refuge to go out again into the harsh, wide world?

So I scream and I scream, I tear my hair out from the roots as though all the demons of hell are after me, I scratch my arms until they bleed.

Then, thankfully, out comes the straight-jacket and, when I see that happen, I know that I'm safe and sound for the foreseeable future within this cloistered world of the mad, where I've always been treated with kindness and respect.

Whenever I emerge from my cosy, woolly, drug-induced dream-world, the other inmates spare me no detail of my brother's trial so that is why, tomorrow, I will hide the pills and potions I am given.

My dearest wish, you see, is to be as alert as possible so that, in spirit at least, I can be fully present at the scaffold to see, in my mind's eye, the noose tight around his neck, his body swinging over the open trapdoor.

By the way, Mr Pierrepoint, I should just like to say to you that if, by any chance, you fail to make a quick, clean job of it tomorrow, please, please don't feel aggrieved, for I would go down on my knees and thank God most sincerely for your incompetence.

Godrum's Tale

The huge, stone monolith felt cold against his back, the dampness of the night entering his old bones as he sat on the grass watching the scene in front of him. Godrum the Magician, a man of mystery who put the fear of the Devil into nearly everyone he met!

Of course, there were inevitably those who resented, rather than feared, his great powers and would like to have seen him taken down a peg or two …or even three!

No one, of course, knew of the fear that he himself felt: that of being in an alien place, not really knowing how to act, relying solely on instinct.

The flames of the torches fluttered and spluttered as the priests made their way up the processional path towards the great stone circle in the middle of which stood the sacred altar.

Tonight there was to be no human sacrifice for the gods were obviously sufficiently satisfied making this unnecessary.

The wonderful harvest, the perfect weather were proof of this although of course, within the next few nights, blood would be shed.

One couldn't, after all, be too confident, too sure of the minds and intentions of the gods.

At the end of the proceedings the tall figure of Ælfric

the high priest came and stood in front of Godrum.

Gazing at the mysterious light that shone from the small box resting on Godrum's lap and looking at the shapes that moved across its centre, he swallowed nervously.

"Put your box of magic tricks away, Godrum, and come to eat with us. The villagers will dance and sing. You know you will enjoy it."

"I have somewhere else to go, Ælfric, and other things to do. Forgive me, but I cannot stay." After all, he was merely a visitor to this place, a stranger. He lived in a different dimension of space, in a parallel world; his home was just a breath away from this bleak ring of huge stones, less than the merest fraction of a millimetre from the straw and mud huts in which the inhabitants of this ancient world dwelled. He had to leave, for there was business that required his attention.

"You know I'm only here sometimes, so please allow me some privacy and let me go in peace!"

So the High Priest turned his back and walked away wondering about him and about the meaning of his words, while Godrum Ashdown returned again to the real world, or perhaps it was to the dream world. Who could possibly tell which was which?

He slipped silently, effortlessly, through the thin veil that separated the two, carrying his laptop under his arm, and found himself once more seated at his desk in rural Barton-under-Marsh.

He was still able in his mind, however, to hear the drum beats, to smell the burning flesh of meat as the villagers prepared the feast that always ended the nightly ceremony in honour of the gods.

Why was he able to do this, he wondered yet again?

Why could he always understand what was being said and in turn be understood. He had no facility for languages whatsoever, but wherever he went there was no problem. As for his clothes, well, that was almost just as extraordinary, for he always arrived suitably attired so that he never stood out from the crowd.

It was only two years ago or so that this strange wandering through time had begun; it had coincided with the start of his illness, but whether the two were in any way connected he just didn't know.

Tonight it had been this pagan world of gods and blood sacrifices, but he was never able to decide for himself where he would go.

Someone else or something else obviously made the choice for him, but, for some unaccountable reason, he could almost always return home of his own volition.

A quick whisky and soda to steady his stomach and he would attend to the pressing business that still urgently awaited him: the proof of his latest book to be checked, a lecture to be prepared that would, next month, be delivered at Thrisham College. He was, after all, at the cutting edge of the world of quantum physics, but this had in no way helped him to explain satisfactorily what he was experiencing.

Why his encounters in other worlds were usually so violent and bloodthirsty he had no idea: nothing to do with his subconscious, he hoped!

Was there perhaps a hidden side to him that impelled him into these situations or was it simply that there was just so much violence in the universe in general that it was hard to miss it?

The mud-filled trenches of the First World War and brutal happenings that had not even taken place as yet, so much he had experienced.

One minute he would be standing knee-deep in bodies in some long-past conflict. Then the next moment he would find himself standing at his lectern in front of his students, with seemingly not a pause between words to indicate the wealth of experience through which he'd just passed. In a very short time, of course, he would not be able to stand at all and supposed that he would have to give his lectures from a wheelchair.

At times he was astounded at what he found on his travels. For example, he'd visited a Berlin where a very unpleasant and irascible octogenarian named Adolph Hitler was the Emperor of Europe. So quantum physics had obviously got it right when it stipulated a choice of possibilities and probabilities; nothing was fixed, nothing was assured.

The place, however, to which he truly wanted to go, was Jerusalem on the weekend of the Crucifixion, to discover if it could really all true! It was something so alien and unbelievable when compared to what logic and his scientific training had taught him: a truly incomprehensible dichotomy of beliefs. Could it possibly have really happened? The genuine stuff of martyrs! A meek and mild man who could save our souls and send us to Heaven! The promise of a life to come! Could it all really offer him some sort of hope for when his illness finally overcame him?

Yes, his illness would worsen and eventually death would claim him but he had made certain arrangements to ensure that this would happen at a time, and in a manner, of his own choosing.

He heard a key turning. It was Angela, back from the university library where she was Acquisition Manager. A good sort, a woman who, he knew, would miss him terribly! There had been no great passion in their marriage, but they had existed agreeably enough for the past twenty-eight years and he had no regrets.

She popped her head round the door of his study. "How are you feeling, Godrum? Did you remember to take your pills…? You've been travelling again, haven't you? You really should write it all down, it would be such a shame to let all this go unrecorded."

"I shall one day, my dear, but not quite yet. There's too much to do. I must first finish my book, perhaps my only chance for a bit of posthumous fame!" he said, giving her a wry smile.

Godrum, indeed, always told her about his travels while they sat at night in the sitting room with a nightcap of whisky and soda.

All that is, except for one journey, which he would find too difficult to put into words, his feelings too deep to express, almost he thought, the ravings of a madman.

For there were times when he felt an undefined something, formless and without gender, calling to him from the other side of the universe.

It was as if he were half of a whole, a soul separated from its twin although the two halves, without any shadow of doubt whatsoever, belonged intractably together.

There would be an emotional spark, an inward flash, an indescribable magnetism. Then, for there was no other way to describe the sensation, it was as though his soul were travelling, unswervingly and at an unbelievable speed, towards its destination, until there was a merging of their two parts ...or spirits ...or personalities, so that they made a single entity. He didn't know what to call this feeling, this fusing, but when it occurred there was no adventure, nothing to see, merely a completeness such as he'd never experienced before. Each time this happened the less he wanted to return to his normal life, or, indeed to the other worlds that seemed to claim him more and more.

This was the one journey where there was no friction – only total peace and fulfilment: just as a particle in physics calls miraculously to its twin, light years away, and is answered.

However, Angela knew Godrum so well that she had an intuition that she hadn't heard the whole story, that something very important had been omitted, but she wouldn't ever intrude, wouldn't ever question him about it.

Everyone, she thought, was entitled to a secret place

that was his alone.

A week later, Cladworth, both town and gown, was shocked and abuzz at the news in the evening edition of the Echo that the badly mutilated body of Godrum Ashdown, Thrisham Professor of Physics, had been discovered lying on the prehistoric altar at the centre of the ancient ring of stones comprising Hilbury Henge. His laptop, so the report went on to say, had been found nearby. So his book was abandoned, his tales of travel through time left unwritten …while Angela wept, knowing that she would now never know him completely, his secret gone with him to the grave.

The gods of that ancient world, after all, had had to be placated and a human sacrifice offered up to them.

The gods of growing things needed the earth to be fed by human blood and Ælfric, deep in his heart, was glad that it was the magician who had become the chosen victim. Primitive hands, unable to endure the mystery of his magic, had prised open Godrum's laptop and removed the strange object that they found inside, which is why, of course, the hard drive was never recovered. Then they had taken their revenge for the fear that he had caused them.

The two policemen who first arrived at the crime scene were totally unnerved and absolutely discredited by their colleagues when they described having momentarily glimpsed a very tall man in a druid's costume hovering, like a ghost, above the dead professor's body.

None of this, however, was of any interest whatsoever to Godrum, for his spirit, by now far, far away from Hilbury Henge, had winged its way across the universe, never to return.

Complete harmony had been achieved, a perfect symmetry formed, as his spirit blissfully merged with its partner. Godrum's travelling days were over, his tale finally told.

Jeremiah

There he stood – John Croft – self-designated Witch Finder General.

"It's no good!" Hannah thought. "I can't do this!" She scrunched her eyes up trying to avoid seeing what was in front of her, trying not to weep with pity, longing to be able to place her hands over her ears. She wanted to shut out the screaming, the roaring, the shouting, but such a gesture would have been noted and suspicion aroused. The saintly women of Salem were always on the alert for any sign that indicated sympathy towards the Devil's minions.

The poor, poor girls! They were either mad or they had truly been taken over by Satan himself. They were lying on the floor of the courtroom: all four of them shrieking; limbs flailing; saliva and foam running from their mouths. So young, one of them only nine-years-old! It was just not possible that they had made a pact with the Devil …so who amongst the gathering had drawn them into his power? Who amongst them were witches?

The tension that Hannah could feel in the courtroom was almost unbearable. She glanced at the soberly-dressed townsfolk seated near her. They were breathing heavily, fists tightly clenched, some lips so nervously bitten that blood had actually trickled annoyingly down onto to their pristine, white collars. Cleanliness, after all, was next to Godliness and the folk here were nothing if not clean – in body if not in mind!

"What a shocking exhibition of licentiousness!" remarked Mistress Foley seated next to Hannah, as she looked at the girls. "They should be removed from the sight of decent people," she added, looking anxiously at her husband, whose eyes were gleaming with religious zeal and also, she strongly suspected, with common-or-garden prurience. Sanctimonious and hypocritical, Silas Foley was enjoying the spectacle of those young girls uncontrollably writhing around in front of him. "Disgusting! Truly disgusting!" he murmured to himself as he fidgeted uncomfortably on his chair.

The crops had failed badly that year, sickness of one sort or another was rife and mishaps had seemed to follow so quickly that, surely, there was something not quite natural about it all. God would not allow such misfortunes; only Satan would do that. So who here was at his beck and call?

Then the girls, to everyone's horror, started to bark like dogs and to meow like cats, faces taking on animal-like features, which almost frightened to death some of the more sensitive souls who were watching…

Now …here she came, the most eagerly-awaited of the accused; poor Goody Bright, chilled to the bone from her two freezing nights in the town jail. She was the most charitable of souls, the kindest of women, loved by all the children of the town, and yet accused of being a witch. According, that is, to John Croft, a man with no mercy and no love for his fellow human beings. He stood tall and straight, his arms firmly folded, staring at Goody with eyes so dark that they seemed to resemble those of the Devil himself.

Only Judge Crater, seated on the great, wooden, carved chair of the courtroom, had perhaps more power and influence than the so-called Witch Finder. No, Witch Finder General, for we must give him his correct title – that was of paramount importance to the bombastic, puffed-up Mr Croft. No witch could escape his beady eye, especially this simple, little woman in her threadbare dress, her stomach empty... Nobody would dream of giving sustenance to a servant of the Devil.

The crowd gasped as they watched Goody enter, for she was not alone. Jeremiah had come with her. Indeed, he had spent the past two nights waiting in the bitter cold for her outside the jail, so why should he abandon her now? His black fur was silky and sleek, his yellow eyes took in every detail and he gave a loud meow of disapproval at what he saw, his long, dark whiskers seeming to brush the air in anger.

Goody, tears coming into her eyes, looked over at the afflicted girls and, desperately wanting to help them, went and placed her hands upon them, thereby, it would seem miraculously causing their hysteria to cease. An immediate furore erupted from the crowd – she had just condemned herself to death – there was now no need for a trial, for it was a well-established fact that only a witch could stop these fits ...and this she had done.

"Death to the witch! Death to the witch!" screamed the good folk of Salem, their faces ugly with malevolent fury. "The gallows! The gallows!" they demanded mercilessly, their harsh, screeching voices growing more and more insistent. The quiet, reverend tones they used in church were quite forgotten! So immediately, without any further ado, her face as white as a ghost, her whole body trembling, poor Goody was bundled outside.

At least she would be spared another night in the numbing cold of the jail, for later in the day she would be carried on a cart to a tree and a rope placed around her neck, then the cart, moving onwards, would leave her dangling from a branch. So, either the fire of Hell or the kindly warmth of Heaven was going to spare her more chilling discomfort.

John Croft smiled; it was another victory for him, but Judge Crater seemed less pleased with the result. He liked to give the court a good, well-considered verdict, which this little show had certainly prevented – too short, not enough argument, no time for preaching and a bit of sermonising, he complained ill-temperedly to himself. However, last night's stewed mutton did not seem to have agreed with him entirely, so perhaps a short break in the proceedings would not go amiss at this point in time.

Mistress Crater, sitting amid the crowd in her best,

brown dress and knowing of his little problem, looked at him anxiously, for even at the best of times he was not the most equable of men, but today there was an added element of tetchiness, which did not bode well for those unfortunates who were still to be brought before him.

All at once, everyone could hear rain beginning to fall and the court room darkened, so that candles had to be lit. In the distance, thunder grumbled and growled and bounced around the skies of Salem, and lightning illuminated the eager faces of those awaiting the next part of the proceedings.

Then, as if by magic, the brilliance seemed to focus exclusively upon the small figure of Jeremiah as he stood bereft and lost, wondering at Goody's absence.

Everyone's eyes were upon him as he slowly turned, looking at all those present.

Suddenly he stood absolutely still, for he had found what he was seeking and made his way towards her. It was Hannah whom he had found. The witch's cat had chosen his next mistress! He leaped upon her lap and sat gazing at her, their eyes glued upon each other.

John Croft uttered such a roar of anger that Judge Crater dropped the Bible he was holding. The Witch Finder then stepped forward into the centre of the room, raised his arm and pointed firmly at Hannah, his meaning quite clear to everyone there.

For all that, not a word, escaped his lips for there was no need for speech. Hannah, clasping the cat in her arms, stood up, whilst those around backed away from her in fear.

Mistress Foley almost fell off her chair – a witch was someone to be avoided.

Judge Crater's face darkened as another rumble of thunder rolled and raged right over the courthouse. It seemed as though the cat's choice obviously pleased Satan. This too, apparently, was going to be a short trial, with but one end: the gallows.

Mistress Crater sat watching the terrible scenes unfolding in front of her and felt sick at heart. Goody and Hannah, both virtually condemned without being tried.

Traitorously the thought entered her mind that the Judge might as well have stayed at home to nurse his ailing stomach for he'd certainly made very little contribution to the proceedings so far.

It was all such a nightmare, she thought – who to trust, who to doubt, what was fake, what was real. Who was really in charge, God or the Devil?

Anyhow, Mistress Crater's main concern was for Goody's little family, soon to be motherless. Who would look after her three young children in their humble, little home from which their father had disappeared many years ago?

The virtuous, Christian townsfolk of Salem would look upon them as the Devil's spawn, so no charity could be expected from that quarter!

The fascinating spectacle continued as Hannah stared at John Croft and gently placed Jeremiah at his feet, causing the Witch Hunter to kick him viciously out of the way. The cat then slipped out through the door unnoticed

"Are you really not going to say one single word to me?" she said to John Croft. "Is this all that ten years of marriage means to you? It seems to me that swinging from a branch with a rope round my neck is perhaps preferable to what you have to offer me."

In the meantime, circumstances had changed, things were now different, for a choice had been made, Jeremiah's and thus the Devil's choice!

It was as though there had been an anointing and Hannah could not remain the same.

Her sweet, pure heart was slowly being transformed into something completely unrecognisable. The people in the courtroom could sense it, Judge Crater could sense it… and John Croft, under his stern exterior, was filled with dread.

There was never to be any utterance from Hannah to reveal whether she was a witch or not, but she was spared the gallows because John Croft and the Judge had decided between them that a different death was to be her destiny. There would be no swinging from a tree for her, with eyes bulging, tongue swollen.

The rain swept and lashed around the men of Salem that dark evening as they pushed and pulled her up the incline that led from the courtroom until they found a flat piece of land. There she was laid upon the ground and, for more than twenty-four hours, those valiant, pious churchgoers placed more and more heavy rocks and stones upon her, waiting for a confession, which never came.

Some distance away, hidden among the drenched, autumnal leaves of a tree, sat Jeremiah, enduring the heavy rain falling upon him.

His big, yellow eyes missed nothing. As for Hannah, all she did was silently to offer up prayers to her master, whoever he might have been, that her tormenters, would receive just punishment for her suffering, for crushing her to death so cruelly …and, indeed, they did, for the next year there was virtually no harvest, the cattle sickened and died and a terrible fever decimated much of the town.

Most strange of all, of course, was the dark fate of John Croft, destined within a very short time for the mad house where, in his befuddled mind, he was accompanied always by a black cat with yellow eyes.

He kicked it!

He threw stones at it!

He tried to kill it!

In the Devil's name he shouted at it to leave him in peace!

All to no avail!

Only he could see the cat, until, that is, the dawning of the day of John Croft's death, when once more Jeremiah became visible to all, just as he had been on the day when Goody and Hannah breathed their last.

The final words that the Witch Finder General uttered on this earth were witnessed by Judge Crater who was seated by his bedside as he died.

Mr Croft, looking straight into the face of Jeremiah,

who was sitting on his chest, was clearly heard to say, "Hannah, I don't hate you, but I don't ever want to see you again." In response Jeremiah just winked a yellow eye at him.

After Mr Croft's unfortunate demise Jeremiah, his presence fully noted and remarked upon by the sharp-eyed townsfolk, followed the Judge back to his home where Mistress Crater was inordinately pleased to see him and he her. In fact, it was like the meeting of two kindred spirits, for no sooner did she set eyes upon him than a comfortable cushion, a saucer of warm milk, a plate of last night's left-over supper were quickly found for him.

Jeremiah's yellow eyes followed intently every move that she made. Naturally enough, none of this remained a secret, for her neighbours were eagerly gathered outside, peeping through the windows and listening at the door. Thus, they were all able to bear witness to Mistress Crater's soft tones and to Jeremiah's contented purring. What transpired then is not hard to imagine.

Madame Proust

Madame Proust, spare-framed, was vicious hearted: Madame Proust, rabble-rouser, cheer-leader of the unwashed masses, citizen of the New France! Let her draw you into her unforgiving, barbaric, violent world. Heed her words well and pray that you will never see what she sees, never enjoy what she enjoys.

"I love knitting, always have done, always will... One plain, one purl, drop one, two plain, two purl, drop one – a bit like a poem, isn't it! And I knit all sorts of things: gloves, socks, scarves. You name it, I'll knit it! In fact, I'm addicted to knitting! Such a nice, cosy, comfortable little hobby I always think."

Madame Proust, inciter of rebellion, fiend in woman's guise, is also addicted to death and the bloodier the death is, the better. She feeds on hatred and on pain, and of those there is always an abundance. Therefore, in that sense, she never has to go hungry.

"Well, believe me when I say that there's nothing in this world quite as enjoyable as a morning spent sitting at the foot of the guillotine. What a lot of knitting I manage to get done there! See, it's all so interesting because no two beheadings are ever the quite same."

However, even Madame Proust has her reservations!

"I have to say, though, that I'm not too keen on those

where the victim keeps a stiff upper lip and goes proudly to his doom! No, what I like is a bit of emotion, a bit of drama, a bit of weeping and wailing. Otherwise, it all gets a bit boring, especially as the beheading itself is usually all over in the winking of an eye and you hardly have time to see the head plopping into the basket."

However, in Madame Proust's line of work – and it is work, because, believe it or not, she and her fellow tricoteuses, actually receive a small pittance for witnessing such events – there are enjoyable little highlights that prevent the monotony from setting in. She will explain.

"Sometimes, of course, things don't always go according to plan and the head completely misses the basket, rolls down the steps and almost ends up in your lap …and what a laugh that is, especially if the eyes are still blinking!"

As you might imagine, Madame Proust has so many fond memories, but the one nearest to her foul, little heart is the day when Madame Guillotine met Citizen Capet, formerly Louis VI, King of France. Expect no milk of human kindness in the telling of her tale, for she has none.

"What a day that was! I remember it all so clearly: cold and drizzly, with a pale, watery sun hanging in the sky. There were thousands upon thousands of us crammed into the square, with not an inch to spare between! Most of the citizenry were carrying pikes and guns, so that if Madame Guillotine failed us, we would

be able to take matters into our own hands, find our own solution. We knitters had all assembled at dawn so that we would have no trouble claiming our normal places, for we wished fervently to be able to look directly into the eyes of the deposed king, and even to spit on him, given half a chance. Anyway, finally, after what seemed like an eternity, he arrived: not in a tumbrel trundling noisily along the streets, as did normal villains! O no, in a fine carriage comes he, finely dressed, with a priest, no less, by his side. Too late for God to help him now, I would have thought! There were over a thousand, red-coated soldiers accompanying his royal person, and what a fat, royal person he was; it was plain for all to see, that he hadn't spent much time wondering where his next meal was coming from, (nor, I suppose, that fat, foreign bitch he was married to) – not like us poor sods – grubbing around for the smallest crumb!"

So up went Citizen Capet to the scaffold and what a disappointment he was at that moment to Madame Proust and her fellow knitters. No histrionics, no railing against fate; just a firm refusal to have his hands bound and his coat removed. Then came his fine, brave, noble words, because, in truth, he was a fine, brave, noble man, but really all that could be heard was the rolling of distant thunder, the beating of the drums, the insidious clicking of knitting needles and, of course, the frenzied, hysterical shouts of the good citizens of Paris. All this was more or less normal fare for Madame Proust: nothing here out of the ordinary, nothing to dream about on her cold pallet of straw during the bleak winter nights. However, she was soon to have her recompense! Listen to what she has to say, if you can bear to …and be amazed at her enjoyment!

"The drums were beating loudly as we tapped our feet in time to the rhythm, as Citizen Capet made his way towards the arms of lovely Madame Guillotine, our dear friend, who once again didn't disappoint us. For, when the blade fell with a mighty swish, it failed to disconnect his head completely from his body and a great cry of agony and anguish issued forth from his lips. What a moment of triumph that was, but, unfortunately, a bit of quick manoeuvring on the part of the executioners soon stopped his voice forever …shame, that. Well, it would have been nice to have heard a bit more screaming from him, wouldn't it? A sudden silence from the crowd then followed, which I didn't like at all, so I quickly climbed up a couple of the guillotine steps and exhorted the citizens to give voice to our victory. 'What's the matter with you all?' I shouted. 'Why so silent?' So, gradually, a great cry of 'Long live the Republic' began to echo around the square. One of the executioners then plunged his hand into the basket where the head had finally landed and held it up in the air, so that all might see that Citizen Capet had been well and truly dispatched. Blanched like an almond he was, with blood oozing from where his body should have been. I can't tell you how much I enjoyed that…a sight for sore eyes he was!"

You will not, by this time, be surprised to learn that

Madame Proust was, of course, one of those who swarmed round the place of execution in order to dip their handkerchiefs in the blood of the fallen king.

"Well, it had been such a memorable day, I just had to have a little souvenir, didn't I? In fact, I've kept it underneath my pillow for the last few months, but I think that, now it's getting warmer, the flies are starting to take a bit of a liking to it".

After the execution, as Madame Proust and her fellow knitters, cold and shivering from the drizzle that had rained down upon them for most of the day, made their way home through the shabby, rat-infested, back streets of Paris, the broken body of the unfortunate king was being buried, in the cemetery of the Church of the Madeleine: in quicklime so that no trace of him should remain. By this time, the rain had stopped and above his final resting place appeared a rainbow.

As to what enjoyable little thoughts were going through Madame Proust's mind while she was eating her meagre supper that evening – well, believe me, you just would not want to know!

Pillow Talk

Do you remember that time when you gave me twenty pounds? For my mother, you said! Though we both knew that that wasn't true, didn't we? ...but it sounded so much better – so much more casual, so much less business-like. As for that Flaminaire cigarette lighter – well, it was so prettily packaged and, oh, what fun I had trying to persuade you to hand it over! You remember...? And what fun you had for that matter, which, of course, was what it was really all about, wasn't it? In fact, I've got the lighter with me here in my handbag – it's so gorgeous!

I know I really shouldn't be here at all, but I just couldn't resist it. I wanted to see for myself what the place is really like and not just read about it in the newspapers. Most especially, of course, I wanted to see you, here where you really belong, so well-groomed, so much in control. Believe me, you haven't disappointed me one bit, that lovely voice, those elegant hands. Without any shadow of doubt, power really is the aphrodisiac they say it is! Nevertheless, you silly, silly boy, why on earth did you send me that letter ending it all? You know you didn't mean it. Why else would you have called me "darling" if you did? I can see the look in your eyes now, as you glance up at me. You just have to keep looking, don't you? I'm irresistible to you, aren't I? You know I am! However, I won't cause you any problems because you know that your little secrets are all quite safe with me, but if you keep staring up at me like that your colleagues are going to begin to notice and that won't do either of us any good, will it?

I don't think anyone saw me creeping in here …well, not looking like this, in a headscarf and no make-up, which all goes to prove, I think, that I can be as discreet as the next person when I want to be. However, I know there are some people who consider me nothing more than a silly goodtime-girl with a loose tongue.

If someone did see me, though, that would really put the cat among the pigeons, wouldn't it?

Just one press photo of me anywhere near here and then the wolves really would begin to bay.

People are so priggish, so hypocritical in this country. Don't you think so?

Look at all the to-do a couple of years ago over Lady Chatterley's Lover. You would think that the British had never heard of sex, despite the fact that in some miraculous way, most people seem to have been able to produce children. They obviously don't mind doing it, but don't want to read about it!

I suppose, that in one way, I'm really your own private version of Lady Chatterley, aren't I? In reverse, of course, because you're no gardener and I'm certainly no lady! OH look, the Prime Minister has just come in. He's just like a droopy-eyed, shaggy teddy bear, isn't he?

You could be sitting in his place one day, Jack, I know you could. People have such very short memories that they'll soon forget all about this! After all, you haven't done anything that they themselves wouldn't secretly like to have done, have you? Of course, they don't know that you've been – well, telling them lies, do they? In this hallowed ground of all places, you naughty boy!

They might suspect that the rumours are true, but that's all they can do. They can't know for sure! Anyway, it's only me and Mandy and Stephen and Bill Astor who know what you've really been doing and, of course, our good friend from the Russian Embassy; mustn't forget him, must we? Well, really, more my friend of course, but he's so charming, so good looking and that lovely accent of his! So you see you're really quite safe!

You would love to be Prime Minster, wouldn't you, Jack?

I know that I'd absolutely love to live at No 10 Downing Street, but I don't somehow think that Valerie would allow that to happen because, even if you were to confess the truth about your little peccadilloes, I have a strong feeling that she would stand by you.

There would be no divorce. A very beautiful and, I would think, very upright lady, your wife! Anyway, I don't imagine that a party-girl brought up in a converted railway carriage in some backwater of Berkshire would make a very acceptable hostess at No 10, do you? Neither can I honestly see myself attending receptions at Buckingham Palace, though I have to say that I'd probably know quite a few people there, if you see what I mean!

I'm sure that all this is gradually going to die a natural death! You just see if it doesn't! I mean what can people say about me, other than I'm someone who earns her living making ageing British aristocrats happy and the odd Russian spy or two, of course, but we'll keep quiet about that won't we?

How you all love us girls with our working-class backgrounds and our common ways: very common sometimes!

I think I'll go now, Jack.

The Public Gallery of the House of Commons isn't the most comfortable place to sit, and all this pent-up testosterone here is making me think that perhaps I could spend the rest of the morning in a more financially profitable way! So, Jack, you probably won't hear from me again but if you should ever be curious about me, I'm sure that you would only have to ask Bill Astor and he would be able to tell you...and I do faithfully promise that I'll never, ever breathe a word of what went on between us.

Well, it only remains for me to say goodbye or, as the Russians would say, dosvedanya, Minister, dosvedanya!

Shopping Around

"Look, Mave! Isn't it pretty? You'd look nice in this!"

"Don't think so, Coral! It'd be miles too small for me."

"Course it wouldn't! You've lost weight, haven't you? Must have done – with all that dieting. Not had any sugar or carbs for weeks now, have you?"

"I know, but just the same, I don't think mum would like it!"

"What you mean you don't think mum would like it! Look, Mave, your mother's been dead for fifteen years and I very much doubt that she's hovering over you waiting to see if you buy a jacket or not!"

"I know, but all the same…"

Then, suddenly, what Mave has since described as a dark-brown voice, piped up from behind us. "Well, ladies, need any help? If it's this smart jacket you're interested in, we also have it in a very attractive orange …only the one left, so it looks to me as if it could very well have been waiting just for you!"

That was our introduction to Mr Fender – doing his 'departmental manager' bit in his dark suit and his Ariel-white shirt: shoes shining enough to give you sun-blindness. Bit heavy on the Old Spice I have to say, but then, anything is better than BO no5, isn't it?

So, before we knew where we were, Mave had become the proud owner of an orange jacket. It was a bit snug under the arms and, not wishing to be unkind, I have to say it does makes her look rather like a Belisha beacon. If she perseveres with the diet it might eventually, I daresay (in some parallel universe) become the perfect fit! Anyhow, once she'd got the idea that she must have it – well, there was no stopping her, was there!

I always enjoy going round Swithin's Department Store and I especially like going with Mave. She's quite a bit older than me, but somehow I always feel comfortable with her – it's a bit like having a big, lolloping, untidy dog at my side. Nevertheless, she is what I can only describe as rather morose, to say the least: even worse since she's started the menopause. She never has a great deal to say for herself at the best of times but, as we made our way back to the car park, she seemed even more downcast than usual. What's wrong with her, I thought? Probably worrying about wanting to spend a penny! She always leaves it until the last moment! However, as soon as I started up the car, up started Mave as well!

"I've got to have him, Coral, I've got to have him!"

"What was that, Mave – got to have who?"

"Why, Mr Fender, of course!"

"Who's Mr Fender when he's at home?"

"The man in the store, Coral, who else! His name was on his lapel!"

Now this was as lively as I'd ever known Mave to

be, so you'll get the general idea of how scintillating she usually is! "He's lovely, Coral, really, really lovely."

"But you don't know anything about him, Mave – he's probably married with a dozen kids… For goodness sake, let go my arm, will you, or we'll be on the kerb in a minute!"

"We couldn't go back to the store tomorrow, could we, Coral? There was another jacket – a lime green one that I quite fancied. *(Subtlety is not Mave's strong point!)* I think I'd like to go back and try it on, if you wouldn't mind. If you don't want to go with me, I could always take the bus."

"Yes, all right, Mave, I'll take you, but just don't get your hopes up too high!" I agreed to take her because the fact is that Mave and the public transport system don't always hit it off together terribly well. She hardly ever has the right change and if she does, pound to a penny, she'll drop it. Unfortunately, while grubbing around on the floor trying to find it, she has been known to root about in other people's baskets which, as you can imagine, doesn't go down too well. "Well," she had protested, "it's not my fault that I'm all fingers and thumbs, is it, Coral?"

I'm very fond of Mave in spite of her peculiarities. Believe me I need to be, particularly at this present moment in time, because it transpires that Mr Fender is not married! Hence the almost daily trips to the department store during the last few days and the mounting collection of brightly-coloured jackets hanging in her wardrobe!

You've never been in Mave's flat have you? Well, you certainly haven't missed much, I'm afraid. I usually go there and sit with her on Monday afternoons while she gnaws away at her biro, filling in the little crosses on her Vernon's coupon. I go then because, while her mind is on the football pools, I don't have to listen to her sobbing over the more tragic details of Sunday's EastEnders Omnibus.

As I look round I can't help thinking what a shame it is that Mr Fender doesn't manage the furniture department because the contents of her living room really do look a bit like a job-lot from the charity shop! I'm sure that with the amount of money she's spent on jackets, she could well have bought herself a really nice new sofa. However, I'm afraid that when Mave's on a mission you just have to go along with her…!

"A comedian… at the end of Brighton Pier! No, he can't have been!" This was to my friend Monica who works in the personnel department of Swithin's Department Store. "Are you sure, Monica? But there's nothing very comical about Mr Fender. How on earth did he earn a living making people laugh …and how on earth did he go from that, to being a departmental manager? I just can't imagine him in a clown costume, or in a straw hat and striped jacket, telling saucy seaside jokes!"

Having said that, though, I just so wish that he could put a smile on Mave's lips! I'd give anything to see her face light up and to hear her having a really good laugh! I'm sure I could count on two hands the number of times I've seen her smile, let alone laugh. The light seemed to go out of her when her mother died and I don't think even Mr Fender could manage to rekindle it ...not completely!

"That cat needs to see the vet," said Mr Fender yesterday evening. "Just look at him. Poor thing's in a depression!"

"No, Alfie's all right, really he is," I said.

"He does mope a lot though, doesn't he, Coral?" said Mave – this coming from someone who could well mope for England! By which fascinating conversation you will have gleaned that definite progress has been made in the love stakes.

Personally I don't think Alfie's problem has got anything to do with depression. More likely to be fleas, the amount of time he spends scratching! I mean, what on earth has he got to be depressed about? His every wish is catered for: nice food, a lovely fluffy igloo to sleep in and his own personalised little blanket with his name embroidered in the corner. Even the cat-flap has been oiled – by Mr Fender – to make it as easy as possible for him to go in and out. Having said that, however, I suppose with Mave being the cheerful little soul she is, perhaps some of it is rubbing off on Alfie and he's finding life somewhat of a trial ...So we're off to the vet tomorrow!

In the meantime, Mave and Mr Fender are going to

spend an exciting evening together, sitting on the sofa, cosseting the ailing Alfie. There'll be no champagne and caviar, no hearts and flowers, no Frank Sinatra and certainly no laughter, that's for sure. I think it's more likely to be a bit of Beethoven on the record player and a cup of cocoa with a nice digestive biscuit; that's more Mr Fender's idea of an exciting time. As for Mave, well, as long as she's got her man, I don't think she really cares. Although I think she might well find herself missing quite a few episodes of EastEnders! Anyway, whatever makes her happy!

It's been a funny sort of day today – showers and a watery sun – not the sort of day when you want to go traipsing through the streets carrying a resentful Alfie in his cat-carrier but, as he gets car sick, bus sick, train sick and, I dare say, air sick, there's no other way that Mave will take him to the vet other than shank's pony!

Well, here we are in the waiting room, Mave sniffling and snuffling, her big, white moon-face streaked with tears! Bit of a black soul is Mave as you've already gathered – always fearing the worst in life. Whenever she sees all the budgies and cats and dogs gathered here together, her mournful little mind always thinks that they're for the big drop – simple vaccinations and infestations just don't enter into the equation for her. As far as she's concerned each one of them is at death's door. Mr Fender is sitting with us, a glazed expression on his face, trying not to show his embarrassment, which is not a good sign, this being his first appearance in public with Mave.

"Oh, Coral, poor innocent things. It's just not right, is it? At any minute their little lives are going to be snuffed out just like a candle!"

"Don't be silly, Mave! There's Mrs Sargeant with George, he's obviously got a few years to go, hasn't he?"

"You don't know that for sure though, do you, Coral?" Well, at this point Mr Fender looks as though he's seriously thinking about throwing in the towel.

"And just look at Benny Budgie, Mave, he looks like he's in for the long haul, doesn't he? Nothing much wrong with him! Why don't you say hello to Benny, Mave? See, he's all right, isn't he?"

"I suppose so! If you say so, Coral!"

The reason that there are the three of us sitting here, me and Mave together with our prize-catch Mr Fender is that – well, I've been a little bit devious in my dealings with him. You'll probably think I've been a very naughty girl, but I just feel so sorry for poor Mave. I mean, it's years since any man has looked at her twice and I thought well, where's the harm! So, a couple of days ago, I had a quiet little word with Mr Fender, just letting it drop, en passant as they say, that Mave had had a very nice little windfall on the pools a couple of months back that she's keeping quiet about.

Well, as soon as I told him that, I could just see the look of greed on his face. He tried very hard not to show it, but there was a definite glint of anticipation in those beady, little eyes of his! Actually, she did have a win, so I wasn't telling him any lies – just under ten thousand pounds, it was – not to be sniffed at I know, but not the vast fortune that's giving Mr Fender such a nice, warm feeling.

He'll take it all away from her, of course, in one way or another – there's no doubt about that – but what should I have done? It is her last chance, isn't it? And when it's over I will be here helping her to pick up the pieces, won't I?

I expect you're thinking I've done the wrong thing and I probably have! I'm just hoping and praying that he won't learn the truth for at least a few months and will stick around even after that, for as long as he can stand her that is. After all, better to have loved and lost than never to have loved at all! Poor Mave!

Singer for Money

The beginning, of course, foretells the end.

She's lost, completely lost, without hope, without dreams, without him. He didn't want her, he didn't need her. He recognised that she's not worthy to be loved, or, indeed to be in this world at all. So she lies here, under the pulsating light of the stars, contemplating her death, she lies here in the darkness of the wood, the damp grass beneath her, the chill air around her, the gun in her hand.

She has murdered and, therefore she's an outcast, unfit to remain here. She is unloved, unwanted, superfluous to the world and, worst of all, alone. Therefore, extinction beckons to her.

So she will do it!

Her hand fondly strokes the shiny surface of the gun and she lifts it to her head, her finger poised on the trigger. Love sleeps and soon she will sleep.

So she will do it!

The reverberation of the bullet fills her everything and now death is upon her and she's spiralling, whirling inevitably down the dark tunnel, but here there is no promised light at the end.

Only bleakness and the eternal darkness of night.

No sweet welcome, no familiar arms to encompass

her, no love in which to drown. No lovely sounds, no singing of angels. Only his voice murmuring hazily to her from afar, but he doesn't want her, doesn't need her. So she did do it.

The beginning, of course, foretells the end…

You could see that they were bad girls, Cleo and Birdy. The way they stood, hips thrust forward, heads thrown back. Well, that was in itself an open invitation to the sort of men who frequented that particular club in one of the most seedy, downtrodden areas of Los Angeles.

The fact that there were two of them together, arm in arm for moral support, was just too much of a temptation for those smoothies in their fedoras and cheap off-the-peg suits, looking around for what was on offer.

What Cleo and Birdy had to offer was only too obvious – the smoke from their cigarettes making its swirling, sinuous patterns in the air, the wine glasses held aloft while their fingers suggestively stroked the stems, their scarlet nails, their too-thickly-applied makeup.

All this made its own statement.

You can imagine the type, can't you?

The men would come up and whisper discreetly to them, making suggestions that perhaps on other evenings might have interested them – but not tonight, for tonight they had other fish to fry, as the saying goes!

"Are you sure he'll be here, Birdy? It's not exactly the Ritz, is it?"

"Oh, he'll be here all right. Don't you worry your little head about that. He may be a Hollywood star, but Sam Albinoni likes a bit of rough now and then.

Then suddenly everything seemed to intensify, from the volume in conversation to the amount of sweat and cheap perfume hitting their nostrils. Excitement was at fever pitch for he was just entering the room. He was surrounded by his bodyguards and everyone there had to stand on tiptoe to get a glimpse of him.

No, no, that wasn't him, there must be some mistake…!

Oh, what a disappointment he was!

Where was the tall, handsome cowboy that the girls so adored to watch at the movies, the lips that they would have loved to kiss, the body that they caressed in their dreams?

This was someone else completely!

To reach Rita Heyworth's lips he would have needed to stand on a box!

However, he was, at least, smart and tuxedoed unlike most of the other clientele – and famous and rich!

Meanwhile down the wrought-iron stairs in the depths of the club, in her dressing room, Gracie prepared herself for the show. Gracie was another fast one – well, you had to be, to get to where she had got – which wasn't, truth to tell, all that far. Particularly when you weren't actually all that talented! A larger crowd than usual was expected that evening.

Word was out that it was Sam Albinoni's birthday

when he would slum it with lesser mortals. So it was important for her to make a good impression. Let Sam hear how good a singer she really was! Her stomach was churning, her heart racing at the prospect.

This evening there were so many dreams that could become a reality.

No one in the world, of course, could have described where she was as a dressing room. It was merely a makeshift space at the bottom of the stairs among cartons of wine bottles that couldn't be stored elsewhere, but it was space enough in which to make herself beautiful.

Her slinky, black dress, her black, darkly-seamed stockings, her wondrously sexy, black, patent, high-heeled shoes – this was the business!

Sam would love it.

After all, she knew just what he liked.

Ten years ago they had meant everything to each other, or, so it had seemed, until luck had catapulted him to fame and he had begun to see her as second rate. He could do so much better for himself, he'd thought. Inevitably it had all crumbled apart, as easily as a sandcastle when the tide comes in.

There she stood, a slim, beautifully-shaped leg poised seductively on a wooden chest while she held a cigarette in one hand and, with the other, applied her lipstick. Her bottles of creams and powders lay around her, and she knew that she had made herself look lovely in spite of the dim light, in spite of the speckled mirror.

Perched on a shelf behind her was a gramophone

playing her favourite – "As Time Goes By"…and go by it certainly had, at an unbelievably fast pace.

She knew that she still looked good, but her loveliness was fading, the age on her birth certificate frighteningly distant!

Barbiturates, alcohol, so many late nights, and so many demanding men – all these had taken their toll during the last ten years. It could all have been so different if his love had only been as strong as hers.

"And when two lovers woo
They still say, "I love you"
On that you can rely
No matter what the future brings
As time goes by."

Completely untrue, of course, for love had seriously betrayed her, let her down big time; it was nothing to be relied upon! There had never been anyone in all those intervening years like Sam, but here perhaps, tonight, in this shabby club she might unexpectedly have another chance with him.

In the meantime, upstairs, Birdy and Cleo, their lips pouting, breasts suggestively pushed forward, had soon made their move and, almost before he'd had time to take a breath, there was no doubt as to who were to be Sam's companions for the evening and, if things went well for them, for the whole night. His bodyguards had had a losing battle with two such insistently strong-willed girls!

Now came Gracie's big moment!

Overwhelmingly nervous, she'd dealt with that in

her normal way, though perhaps this time she'd overdone it a bit. She certainly felt much more relaxed and confident.

So up the wrought-iron stairs she clattered to join the jazz trio who were already entertaining the audience with popular numbers from the hit parade.

Ten minutes later, as she stepped on to the little stage, she was immediately conscious of the brilliance of the spotlight, which seemed, for some reason, overwhelmingly bright that evening.

Then, coming from some distant place, she suddenly heard her introductory music start up ... but why did she feel so totally disconnected from it and why, when she began to sing, did the notes that came out of her mouth seem so at odds with those being played by the trio? "I really know this song! I know I do, so why can't I hit the notes?" Gracie knew she was badly out of tune and, for some reason, she was having the greatest difficulty remembering the lyrics too, but there was absolutely nothing she could do about it – the gin for Dutch courage and the downers to calm her nerves that she taken before coming up stairs had beaten her to a pulp.

Absolute, total panic had now overtaken her. She just wanted to escape, to be a million miles away.

Then from the table right at the front came the worst sound in the world, that of Sam's laughter, but who could blame him?

When she glanced at him she saw his look of scornful amusement. He was sitting between two young women, each one with her glittering, gaudy, low-cut dress leaving nothing to the imagination. From her private hell Gracie watched them, Birdy and Cleo, pointing at her, giggling and whispering into Sam's ear.

Birdy sniggered nastily. "She should have been put out to grass a long time ago. She must be forty if she's a day!"

"Nothing but a lush!" added Cleo helpfully.

Then suddenly Sam's heart missed a beat and he stopped laughing. Gracie Frost! Who would have believed it after so many years?

Gracie was beside herself with all sorts of emotions as she staggered off the little stage, when the seemingly endless nightmare had mercifully ended. She made her way unsteadily down the stairs, her face by now wet with tears of humiliation. The whole audience had by this time caught the humour of the situation and she could hear them jeering and whistling.

Biting her lips and conscious of the ringing in her ears, she went to her makeup case and, with trembling hands, removed from it a beautiful, blue, silk scarf which she carefully unwrapped, revealing a small, chic Smith and Wesson handgun. Nobody was going to laugh at her!

This little gun had for years been her protection in the violent world that Los Angeles sometimes was but, in truth, she'd never ever needed it until tonight. Now, however, it would come into its own!

She could feel the anger burning away inside her as she made sure that it was well and truly primed.

She'd show them all, especially that bastard Sam

Albinoni!

Above her she could hear the trio playing her favourite song: *"Hearts full of passion Jealousy and hate..."* and the words cut into her more deeply than ever before. Again she made her way up the wrought-iron stairs, but this time her confusion was accompanied by the most awful, overpowering rage.

How dare they mock her and how could Sam, who had once loved her, be so cruel?

The unsuspecting audience was about to have a performance as good as anything they'd ever seen at the movies and Sam, about to have his heart really broken, remembered.

He had truly loved her, but circumstances and his new, unbelievably glamorous life had overtaken him completely.

Who was he after all, he now suddenly thought?

Really no better than thousands of other hopefuls who'd come to Hollywood, but he'd just struck lucky.

Suddenly there she was again on stage, the spotlight upon her, but this time there was to be no singing.

"You'll all pay for this! And," she cried, as she pointed the gun in Sam's direction, "especially you, you bastard!"

The trio dropped their instruments and fled back stage, while the audience, opened-mouthed and overcome with fear, yelled out in panic and hid themselves as best they could behind tables and chairs, but watch they had to, because what was happening was, somehow, strangely fascinating!

Gracie, however, had never really learned how to use a gun properly, so she completely missed her target. Instead it was poor Birdy who screamed out in pain and collapsed to the floor, blood streaming from her wound, while Cleo looked on in horror.

Gracie, shocked and appalled at what she'd done, turned on her heels and raced off again, down the stairs and out through the back entrance of her meagre dressing room into the chilly, Californian night.

She ran as fast as she could and luck was with her, for only one block away from the club, she found a cab, which carried her to a wooded area…

She can hear his voice, its sweetness filling the air, she can smell the freshness of his skin, she can feel the warmth of his body, she feels that he is by her side …but that is impossible because she is dead, killed by her own hand, heading for the fires of hell to pay for all the sins that she's committed – mostly, of course, for the darkest sin of all: murder! Nevertheless, she doesn't feel dead; she should at least be able to feel the damp grass on which she is lying, to smell the trees and the earth, to hear the rustling sounds of small animals as they explore the world by night.

However, none of those things is here.

So where is she?

What has happened to her…?

I'm not dead.

I've failed utterly.

Gracie was very much alive and had simply woken up in hospital with Sam sitting by her side, talking to her, holding her hand and watching as she was injected with painkiller for a minor shoulder wound.

She really was indeed a very poor shot!

Birdy, too, had lived to tell the tale and acquired, thereby, a sort of dubious fame. It was just such a pity that her very pretty face was, thereafter, marred by such an unsightly scar.

Of course, when you attempt to murder someone in full view of a hundred people or so there is a price to be paid. Well, that's only right, isn't it?

Gracie was sentenced to four years in prison for the attempted murder of poor Birdy Halston. Only she herself, of course, knew who her intended victim had really been, but about that she kept her mouth firmly shut, just as she firmly tried to blot out the feelings of guilt from her mind.

Poor Gracie, for her there would be no more singing for money and trying to make the big time.

However, perhaps performing in front of her fellow prisoners was much more suited to her talents.

One week after her release, Sam Albinoni, Hollywood idol, married Gracie Frost, former Californian prison inmate…

What headlines that made on the front page of the Los Angeles Times.

There was even talk of a film!

So some stories do have a happy ending: of a sort!

Spider's Web

The black spider sat comfortably ensconced in her web in the corner of the sitting room, watching and waiting, her eyes on their little stalks missing nothing of the action, aware of all the subtle nuances vibrating around her. Physically present, but with no emotional involvement, she was enjoying every single moment of the entertainment. She laughed inwardly at what was for her the greatest joke in the world.

There they all sat looking at the black widow in her deepest mourning, her eyes dry, her heart unaffected by her loss. How could she possibly grieve for Lennie, the little shit? Nevertheless, that's what they were all waiting for – some sign that, perhaps after all, she had finally felt something for him. If only they knew what a wicked, old spider she really was; for they had absolutely no idea of how deeply buried within her the venom lay. They had not an inkling that they could all lie dying at her feet and she would not raise so much as a finger to help any single one of them.

Lennie had been disposed of, face downwards, in the marshlands of the Thames estuary, among the wetland plants and the burgeoning wild life: butterflies and dragonflies fluttering and soaring happily over his bloated, putrefying body, no flowers or blossoms capable of alleviating the unforgettable stench of human decomposition. A gangland killing the police had said, but no further progress had as yet been made than that!

Now, four pairs of brown eyes were suspiciously fixed upon Liliana as the gloom of the evening seeped into the room. The lights had been switched on, but were dimmed; the atmosphere had to be totally conducive to what they were all about to do …bring Lennie back from the dead.

Liliana, still beautiful and naturally blonde at sixty, looked a million dollars in her slim-fitting, black widow's-dress, a gold collar gleaming around her smooth neck, as she rose from her corner seat to fetch the home-made Ouija-set from the sideboard cupboard. There was no proper board, no planchette, merely cards – on each of which she'd scribbled a letter of the alphabet – and a tumbler on which they would each place a finger, hoping it might move to reveal a message, and all the while she smiled to herself!

Liliana didn't in the least like the Ouija idea, for you never knew what spirits of evil might be roused from their long slumber, wanting to meddle maliciously in the world of the living. However, her step-daughters desperately wanted to have serious words with Lennie; they needed to ask him what he'd done with all the money. The will had been read, but there had been nothing left!

As a precaution, not really knowing what else she could do, she had brought in garlic from the kitchen and had placed it on the table, together with a wooden crucifix and a rosary – relics from Rosalind's fleeting flirtation with Rome – well, you could never be too careful, could you? Rosalind was any step-mother's worst nightmare: mouthy, lazy, scrounging all the benefits the state would allow, hooked on food and horse racing: every afternoon spent in front of the television, filling her mouth with junk food and watching the gee-gees. Neither must we forget all the bets that she placed via her mobile and her forays down to the Turf Accountants, as she so grandly liked to call them. Liliana, however, had failed to place the most important object on the table – something made of silver, which would assuredly have kept malicious spirits away – but she had not known that this is what you were supposed to do.

It was at this point, while trying to contact poor murdered Lennie, that everything got out of hand. For there they all were, fingers lightly touching the very expensive glass tumbler that Lennie had used for his evening bevies of whisky and water, the cards spread round the table in a circle, eagerly waiting for something to occur but nothing happened; the glass stayed obstinately where it was, absolutely refusing to budge, as if glued to the table. Liliana even tried to give it a surreptitious push, but to no avail. What silly girls they were to waste their time like this, but it was such fun, Liliana thought, her poker face giving nothing away. How she loved seeing the look of hope and greed on their faces. It would have been far better for them –

though not for her, of course – to have invited a medium to the house, someone who really knew what she was doing – so much more entertainment value, Liliana thought – in fact, rather like their own private performance of 'Blithe Spirit'.

However, that was exactly what they were going to get, for the lights dimmed even more and began to flicker eerily. Perhaps a little problem with the electricity mains, they wondered? So there they were, seated in a disappointed circle, barely able to see each other in the gloom when, suddenly, there was a flash of light, and a little puff of smoke arose from the centre of the table, drifting up towards the ceiling. The cards all rose in a flurry and whirled around in the air, while the tumbler threw itself against the wall and, despite being heavy lead crystal, smashed into smithereens.

The circle was unbroken; the five of them were so shocked at the sight that they were all by now gripping each other by the hand, just hoping that it was a nasty dream and would be over soon. Unfortunately, more followed and real fear set in when a familiar voice suddenly addressed them from the great beyond.

"You witch!" said Lennie, in the typically spectral tone that you might expect from someone who was no longer alive. Well, there was no mistaking to whom he was speaking, was there? "Spinning your lies and deceit! Trying to cheat my babies... And, of course, all the other things that you've done!"

The so-called babies were totally gob-smacked – things like this just did not happen in the real world –

only in films or in books! The dead simply did not return from wherever they had gone. They absolutely did not leave messages for the living.

It seemed that that was all they were going to get from Lennie at the moment, for the smoke simply floated away and the voice disappeared into the void. Why had he not said more, instead of leaving tantalising hints, wondered Rosalind, the fattest of his babies and what was that about Liliana cheating them? They had never liked her from the moment she first walked into the house, did not trust her farther than they could throw her and they had even hired a private detective to see if he could track down the missing money. There seemed, unluckily for them, to be no hidden bank accounts, no evidence of money going where it had no business to go.

Liliana breathed a sigh of relief that his visit had been so very, very short, but what did Lennie know, what had he seen from his pole position behind the veil, what had he observed from Abraham's bosom, from the Elysian fields or, more likely in his case, from the Stygian shore? Liliana just hoped that, from wherever it was, he would keep his other-worldly mouth shut and not visit them again. Knowing what she knew, it was all rather a giggle but not, however, as much of a giggle as she thought it was, for they had not bid the spirit a polite goodbye. A fundamental mistake that meant it was probably going to hang about for a considerable time, maybe even forever!

Liliana was sitting on the dining room table, her legs around Roger's waist, fingers in his mouth feeling his tongue licking them, his hands stroking her neck, which she so adored that she could have raped him on the spot. She was a tough lady, but Roger was a definite little weakness of hers: a long way, of course, behind her love of money, but a definite attraction. It had been so easy to ensnare him: "Will you walk into my parlour?" as the Spider had said to the Fly! After all, men were such gullible creatures, easily enchanted by flashing eyes, a few empty compliments and suggestions of what might happen if they were good boys. It had all, of course, been going on for quite a while, certainly long before Lennie's totally tragic demise!

Part of Roger's appeal for Liliana was that he was a banker, but very much on the shady side, who knew all about moving money around, who knew very well what commodities to buy with it. We do not, therefore, have to ponder too deeply about what happened to the wicked step-daughters' inheritance.

By now the valuable rosewood table was in grave danger of being rather badly scratched by Liliana's scarlet toenails enthusiastically digging into its fine surface. Her lust was at full tilt, her libido in overdrive at the thought that tomorrow they were off to Miami: simmering sex under the hot Floridian sun, reckless abandon under the breeze-swept palm trees, cuddling and caressing while hidden in the warm waters of the Atlantic: the rampant spider and her mate!

Sounds wonderful, doesn't it? Except, of course, that it didn't quite turn out that way! Liliana first realised that something was not quite right when, sitting in her roomy seat in Business Class, she felt a definite third-presence accompanying them. Little puffs of smoke began to pop in and out of sight in front of her eyes. Then things took a more serious turn when she suddenly noticed, out of the corner of her eye, a nebulous, vaguely man-shaped apparition taking possession of the empty seat on the other side of the aisle. By this time the cabin crew was in a frenzy trying to hunt down the forbidden smoker among the passengers.

Roger, who didn't in the least like flying, was asleep during this little drama, having had a tad too much alcohol in the airport bar to steady his fragile nerves. This, together with the valium, had proved just too much for him. Yet he was soon roused out of the land of nod when safety instruction cards and in-flight magazines began to whiz through the air in his direction. This was Lennie in poltergeist mode, out to make the most mischief that he possibly could. The spooky voice from beyond the grave had been replaced by this more playful mood.

"Are we here? Have we landed?" poor Roger mumbled almost incoherently.

"No, we aren't here, Roger, but Lennie is!" Liliana whispered discreetly, with her hand in front of her mouth; Lennie's bionic hearing had been almost legendary.

So the potentially erotic fortnight of sun, sea and sex went very wrong indeed and Roger was completely unable to rise to the occasion, which is hardly surprising when you know that you are being watched and your manhood judged by a third party. The only occasion when Lennie was of any help at all was at the carousel on arrival, when some rather travel-worn passengers thought that they must be dreaming as they watched two pieces of wheelie luggage moving of their own accord through the airport concourse.

Yet all was not lost. Well, let's face it if you can conjure up one departed soul from the deep abyss, surely you can produce a second. As long as you are discriminating as to whom you choose! Which is why, four days into their celibate holiday, Liliana and Roger sat staring at the infinity pool and sipping their piña coladas while giving considerable thought to possible candidates.

"Fred – that's who we need!" said Liliana suddenly. "He used to scare the living daylights out of Lennie until someone put a bullet through the back of his skull. A bit of victimisation is what Lennie needs to take his mind off us. It'd give him something else to think about."

"Come on, Lil, you can't just conjure up dead people at the drop of a hat. For all you know Fred might have repented of his evil ways. Perhaps that's what happens wherever he's gone to! Or perhaps he's on a different astral plane to Lennie!"

Liliana, nonetheless, had made up her mind. So, that evening, there they were, in their hotel room sitting face to face at a small table, knees touching, this time with a proper Ouija board and a piece of silver between them. They had closed the curtains and lighted a pair of candles to create a more spiritual atmosphere. Then they waited, all the while concentrating hard and murmuring Fred's name. The planchette seemed to shudder slightly, but apart from that there was again no reaction whatsoever, until the board suddenly rose, which it wasn't supposed to do, and hurled itself time and time again against the top of the table – a sign of temper if there ever was one!

Alarmed and surprised, with their eyes glued upon this display of anger, they suddenly became aware that they were not alone. When they looked towards the other side of the room a puff of red smoke had manifested itself. In the middle, they could just make out a wispy Fred-like figure.

"What the flipping heck do you two think you're playing at? I've got more things to do with my time than bother with whatever's troubling you," said Fred's familiar, gruff voice. "And, by the way, yes, I do know that Lennie has arrived here and, no, I do not want to carry on the feud with him. So count me out of this one."

"Please, Fred, please, just keep him occupied if only for a little while."

"You're a sneaking, conniving madam, Liliana, weaving your little plots, and I feel sorry for Lennie, the poor sod, having had to put up with you!"

Off Fred floated, but not back into the great unknown, for no one had said a nice goodbye to him and, therefore, he didn't feel disposed to go. So the situation remained unresolved as Liliana and Roger continued their frustrating American idyll, now with both Lennie and Fred keeping tabs on them.

As this was to be the last holiday that Roger was ever to have, it was a bit of shame for him that things hadn't worked out better. Poor Roger was destined to return home deep in the hold of the plane, resting in a wooden box with the words 'human remains' marked clinically on the outside. A heart attack was the given cause of death, but it could possibly, probably, indeed unequivocally, have had something to do with the fact that they had again both failed to say a courteous farewell to Fred which, as you already know, was asking for trouble! Never forget your social graces where ghosts are concerned or you'll soon find out that a sulky astral entity like Fred is seriously someone to be reckoned with …so Roger was found face down in the pool after one of his little midnight swims.

Liliana, however, was not as disappointed at this dreadfully tragic outcome as you might have imagined. After all, Lennie was the one who had stolen the money, who had laundered it, who had washed it until it was squeaky clean. Why, therefore, should his widow not have the full benefit from all his efforts? Roger had merely been the conduit for making the most of these assets, so really it was better for her that he was out of the way. A dead man tells no tales and, more importantly, doesn't need his share of the filthy lucre! Her flight to Heathrow was, therefore, quite a journey of unexpected celebration. Having been upgraded to first class, she arrived back in England feeling cosseted and definitely hung-over from all the complimentary tip-top champagne that had been on offer.

Liliana was, however, just about to become tangled up in her own web, for as she dragged her luggage up the path to the house she could see a light shining from the sitting-room window. This was rather strange because no one was supposed to be in; Lennie's babies had been scheduled to go off on a girlie weekend to the Cotswolds, hoping to meet the landed gentry and take a step up in the world. Rather belatedly, it has to be said, but better late than never! So she quietly slipped her key in the lock, hoping not to meet a burglar for her trouble, and went into the hall without closing the door so as to make the least sound possible. The sitting-room door was slightly ajar. As she pushed it open she heard an unwelcome voice addressing her.

"You can come in, Liliana. Don't be frightened. It's only me! Fat Rosalind, the slob who does nothing, but I can think, Liliana! I'm not stupid!"

Liliana was appalled to see her step-daughter sitting on the spider's chair, now moved out from its usual place in the corner, a floorboard lying on top of the carpet, the hiding place exposed for all the world to see. Rosalind looked like some Indian queen: a magnificent tiara on her head; her arms decorated with at least two dozen gold bracelets; a splendid, but rather gaudy, necklace of emeralds and rubies hanging at her throat. At her feet lay sixty or so gold bars each about the size of a mobile phone. In other words, the little nest egg that she and Roger had accumulated at Lennie's expense!

"Daddy came back to me yesterday, Liliana. He's apparently been keeping a very close watch over you, ever since his departing spirit saw Roger pushing his body down into the mud of the estuary, with you standing by egging him on! So what have you got to say for yourself, stepmother dear?"

Surrogates

Where the train had come from and where it was going is completely immaterial, for it will not make any difference whatsoever to the tale and, therefore, is not worth the telling. Suffice to say, that it was very crowded and Cynthia found it overwhelmingly tiring to be surrounded by so much bustle and noise.

As she sat in her aisle seat she could feel her arm constantly being nudged and knocked by her fellow passengers as they squeezed by each other whenever the train stopped and started – not always very politely – the f-word and the sh-word turning the air a dark shade of blue, which she really didn't care to hear.

She then directed her eyes once more towards the old man sitting in the seat opposite her as the train swayed and rocked its way towards its destination. She should have got off at the previous stop for she was heading for her mother's house, but he was so unpleasantly fascinating and his presence so totally unexpected that she had to go with him right to the end of the line.

She had not been able to believe what she was seeing as she had sat down and glanced towards him. Of all the people in the whole world, that it should have been him. It was for a purpose, of course, because they always say that there is no such thing as a coincidence. Six degrees of separation and here they were, after so many years, actually face to face. How she hated him!

On the table between them he had placed three books: his attention, however, focused not on reading but on watching the passing scene. This was just how he was supposed to look, how she'd always imagined him: an exact older version of the grainy photo she had found tucked into a book of poetry in her mother's bedside table. He didn't know, of course, that she was his daughter, but why should he? He had only seen her once – on the day of her birth, forty years ago, after which he had disappeared into the sunset.

She studied him minutely, hoping that he wasn't conscious of her searching gaze, hoping that no one was inspecting her as closely as she was him. It was for this reason that she tried to keep her arm tight against the side of her body, her hand firmly between her knees so that the uncontrollable twitching would go unseen. She could feel her lips trembling too, but there was not much that she could do about that, thinking that it must always look to other people as though she were on the point of bursting into tears. She knew that one day soon she would end up in a wheelchair, completely dependent on other people, but until that day came she would just soldier on.

She'd misunderstood the situation completely, however, for this thin, old man with his toothless mouth and his grey hair combed straight back from his forehead was certainly not her father and why the confused idea had come into her head was just one of the peculiarities of her illness. She sat there contemplating how she could avenge the terrible wrong he had committed, for he had left her mother, abandoned her, when Cynthia had been only a few hours old. So she'd always lived her life as a poor, fatherless child. The knowledge that her father had died in a road accident on the night of her birth and had been a good and loving husband had completely gone from her mind. It was yet another sign of how much her grasp on reality was becoming day by day more nebulous.

"Do you know what it feels like not to have a father?" she suddenly asked him softly, leaning towards him so that he could not ignore her. His pale, grey eyes turned away from the beautiful country views outside the window and stared at her wonderingly, sadly.

"I don't know, but I can imagine. When did you lose him? Is it a recent bereavement?"

"He's not dead. He just left us to our own devices, to fend for ourselves. What do you think of that?"

He did not want to think of it at all. Truth to tell, it was the last thing in the whole world he wanted on his mind – too painful for words, which is why he read such a lot. Always three books on the go at once – a thriller, a biography, a travel book, only ever this combination!

"What's your first name?" she suddenly asked him. A trick question! She supposed that he would lie and he did! The old man was surprised by her question and felt slightly patronised as though he were too stupid, or too old or not worthy enough of respect to be called Mr

Burberry. "Charlie," he answered. Yes, obviously a habitual liar, she thought!

"I shall call you Thomas." However, this brought no sign of recognition to his face, merely bemusement, so perhaps he was not only a good liar, but also a good dissembler.

"Do you know what love is, Thomas? In the whole of your life have you ever selflessly loved anyone? Have you ever had a wife? Have you ever had a child – a daughter perhaps? What is your honest opinion of men who desert their families? Don't you think that they should be punished for what they've done?"

Her words sounded like the voice of a wrathful God! The voice of his own conscience!

"I don't want to go on with this conversation – my life and my feelings are nothing to do with you."

"But I have to know, Thomas. I want to hear you speak loud and clear to me. I want your answers so that there can be no mistake."

A strange stillness had by this time descended upon the passengers seated nearby who were absorbed and rather amazed by this strange exchange. It was like being in a theatre listening to the opening words of a play at the point when you don't know where the plot is going. Charlie and Cynthia were, however, both oblivious of their audience and there was certainly no irritating coughing or the rustle of sweet papers to spoil their concentration while they spoke their lines.

"I have nothing to say and I really don't understand what you're talking about."

"You're a lying little weasel, Thomas, and should go to hell for abandoning us".

"I'm already there. I've been there for years."

The train was on the point of arriving at the next station and everyone around was just so pleased that they were not about to get off and miss the next part of this fascinating little drama.

Cynthia's voice suddenly, however, began to trail away and she looked at Charlie aghast. "I'm so sorry! Forgive me! Sometimes I just don't know what I'm saying." In fact, not only did she not know what she was saying, neither could she remember what the argument of two seconds ago had been about – only that she had been extremely insulting to this poor, old man.

By this time the tears were stinging Charlie's eyes. Who had put these words into her mouth? Was it God punishing him, making him feel even more remorseful than he already felt?

The atmosphere among the audience, meanwhile, had relaxed, as the tension on the stage lessened, but they were still none the wiser as to what had been going on between the characters; the script remained a complete mystery. Cynthia looked around at them all, overcome with embarrassment and smiled weakly as though apologising for making such an exhibition of herself. She was a formal woman who would never have wished to cause a scene in public or to have presumed to call any man by his first name unless she knew him well.

"I'm so sorry, Mr…!" "Burberry!"

"I don't know what you must think of my strange behaviour, Mr Burberry. Please just forget that I ever spoke to you. And I really am very, very sorry!"

Charlie, too overcome to say a word, opened his thriller and tried to concentrate, but the words were meaningless and swam before his eyes, his mind now on the very subject from which he so desperately wanted to escape. This strange woman had done that to him: opened up the great wound that was, in reality, never ever completely closed. For Charlie Burberry had been a wastrel, a drunk, a gambler, someone for whom the grass on the other side was always greener. So he had left his wife and child for a little flippertigibbet who seemed to offer the excitement he craved, but who, of course, inevitably in the end, proved to be totally worthless.

A common enough story, but Charlie's was one of tragic proportions for his wife had drowned herself, together with their little daughter, in the stagnant pond that lay near on the edge of the town. A letter that she had written left no doubt as to why she had done it and who was to blame.

Since then Charlie had lived in a bed-sit, in his own eyes deservedly alone and unloved: sometimes suicidal, sometimes drunk, sometimes engrossed in reading or mindlessly watching television, but at all times desperately unhappy.

The train was approaching the end of the line and Charlie sat observing Cynthia, her eyes closed, ghost-white and twitching. He could see that there was something very wrong with her, physically as well as mentally if the way she'd spoken to him was any indication of her problem. A degenerative disease of some sort he would have said – not that he was any expert.

The passengers in the window-seats would have jumped over Charlie and Cynthia, if it had been at all possible, so eager were they to escape the confines of the train and, therefore, looks of irritation passed across their faces as they waited for the pair slowly to stand, Cynthia because she was incapacitated and Charlie because he was old and arthritic.

"Can I help you?" said Charlie, seeing her discomfort. Surprised that he should want to bother with her, she looked into his eyes and saw genuine kindness and concern there.

"Thank you Mr Burberry, I should be very glad of a hand with my travel bag."

"Have you far to go?"

"I foolishly missed my stop," she lied, "so I've got to retrace my journey. I'm going to stay with my mother for a few days."

Mr Burberry, Cynthia's father, that snide, deceiving, old fox lay lifeless across Cynthia's bed. She had vaguely remembered reading somewhere that strangulation was one of the most painful ways to die and she thought that he deserved such a death. Can you imagine fighting for breath with those inexorable, killing hands around your throat, showing you no mercy, squeezing your life out of your body? She could not, at that precise moment, quite fathom out why she'd killed him or, indeed, how he seemed gradually to have become so much a part of their lives. Well, to be quite honest, everything these days seemed to be a bit of a blur.

Somehow he seemed to have inveigled his nasty little way into their home, so that once a fortnight he came down by train for lunch. When she was in her right mind, however, she was really pleased to see him, for he had apparently accompanied her all the way home when she had been unwell after their first meeting. On this, his final day, she had lain in bed for hours looking at his throat, fascinated by how thin and frail it was. Then, suddenly, it came into her confused mind to wonder yet again why he had decided to return to them now? It was far too late, four decades too late!

"Have you been having a good time these last forty years, Thomas? I bet you have – wine, woman and song – that's been your life, hasn't it? Never mind those who needed you, as long as you were all right!"

The mysterious diatribe continued, leaving him none the wiser. He had never discussed with her mother the previous outbursts that had taken place between the two of them, for they had almost been over before they had begun and were not worth mentioning. Although they had been directed at him, he thought it would be wrong to pry into something of such a personal nature. The formal Mr Burberry!

As for his own tragedy, well, that remained firmly

locked away, a secret from the rest of the world, for he certainly didn't believe in sharing those raw emotions with other people: partly from shame, partly because it was too painful for him to put into words.

He had decided that he would be there at Cynthia's end and try to give her some comfort, in a small way to make reparation for his dreadful sin. He would miss her when she had gone for he had grown fond of her. Her vulnerability and the inevitability of her death had touched him deeply, so he had sat and held her hand as she drifted in and out of consciousness: a daughter, but not his. However, she was not quite as non-compos-mentis as he imagined and that sudden moment of lucidity, mistaken though it was, had so energised her into action that she knew exactly what she must do.

As he bent over her to wipe her forehead he didn't struggle as she grabbed him; perhaps he'd had a premonition all along that this was how it was going to end.

"I hate you, Thomas, you ruined our lives," she gasped. "Why couldn't you love us? Were we so dreadful that you couldn't find anything likeable about us? Forty years of silence is a long time, so why bother to come back?" He heard what she was saying. It was the same old tune, but he still didn't understand any of it. As her fingers tightened around his throat there was no attempt at resistance, for he knew that he was fully deserving of any punishment fate allotted him. Although he died willingly, the end of his suffering finally accomplished, he nevertheless wondered why she was doing it to him and it was the last thought ever to pass through his mind.

For someone in her condition her hands had been surprisingly strong and his old, emaciated body no match for her but, as is so often the case with strangulation, there were no external signs of injury. Therefore, the doctor, seeing this frail old man and already late for his game of golf, was less meticulous than he should have been with his examination. He would never have dreamed that that someone as weak as poor Cynthia after all her suffering, would have been capable, either physically or morally, of such an act.

So it was Cynthia's mother, not Mr Burberry, who sat holding her hand as she died and who was left to wonder for evermore at her last words.

"We got our revenge didn't we, mum? I finally killed Daddy for you and I hope he burns in Hell!"

The Big Question

Where was I last night? Well, my immediate reaction, of course, is to ask what it's got to do with you, because it's none of your damned business. However, of course, that's not strictly true, is it? So I suppose if you really do want to know the answer, then it's my duty as your closest friend to tell you. Especially the state you're in! So don't say I didn't warn you, because you're not going to like the answer one little bit, as you've probably guessed by now!

So, where was I last night? Well, in actual fact, since you're asking, I was lying on my back in the middle of a wood being fucked out of my mind by your husband. How I enjoyed it …and by the moans and groans and all the cavorting and hip movements, so did he!

It's not that I'm particularly attracted to your husband, you understand. By then, anyone with the right bits and pieces in working order would have fitted the bill! It was all just part of the fertility rites of our coven and by the time everyone had quaffed more than their fair share of March ale and brandy, all restraint had flown to the four corners of the earth and a good time was being had by all! Yes, that surprised you, didn't it? I thought I saw you give a little twitch!

You know, you should have tried becoming a witch;

it might have lightened you up a bit, freed you from those inhibitions your husband has not been slow in telling me about. A good dose of fertility worship is just what you needed! I wonder what he tells you he's been doing, when he's been on one of his little magic, spell-making week-ends! An urgent business problem to be attended to in the Outer Hebrides, the sudden demise of a never-before-heard-of old school friend in the fleshpots of Tuscany! I suppose you, in your flannel nighty and falling-to-pieces slippers, believe it all!

I said that I'm not really attracted to your husband and that's quite true. What I am attracted to, however, is his money and I don't think that you, for one moment, deserve all the advantages that it's brought you. Look at this lovely house we're sitting in: swimming pool, tennis court, lawns running down to the Thames, where your very nice boat is moored. Look at your lovely exotic holidays spent in super-duper hotels. Look at the wonderful social events you go to, rubbing shoulders with the movers and shakers of the business world. What a bore it must be for him to have to drag you along!

Just look at yourself! Why don't you go on a diet, stop cutting your own hair, do something about those disgusting spots (and, for goodness sake, stop picking them!) and, believe me, if I were your husband, I wouldn't want those ugly little bitten-to-the-quick nails trying to scratch erotically up and down my spine! Not that you would do that, of course; from what I've heard it's not in your nature, is it?

Perhaps you should treat yourself to a couple of weeks at a health farm. Heaven knows you can afford it! On second thoughts, of course, you don't have to bother, do you? Not now! Because it's too late! Much, much too late, by the look of you! Sorry about that!

I wonder why you're not saying much – because you don't want to or because you can't! Rather the latter I would think: by now! There's probably, however, a whole lot of emotion bubbling away in that little head of yours! I sincerely hope so, because I wouldn't want all this to be falling on deaf ears; I do like an audience, even if it's not an appreciative one!

However, I haven't really answered your question in any great detail though, have I? Apart from the obvious! I think that I'm probably going to wax rather lyrical now, because I do want you to be able to picture want went on last night. After all, that's what has, directly or indirectly, brought you to the rather parlous state you're now in. So here I go!

We witches and warlocks love the fauns and nymphs of the forest glades. We love the Moon Goddess who shines coldly down upon us, watching over what we are doing. (The antics we get up to it's a wonder she doesn't turn from a chaste silver to an embarrassed pink!) We love Venus, the Dark Goddess, who brings us such carnal pleasures. (I won't try to explain those to you: not at this late date!) We love the trees …the birch trees, the willow trees, the oak trees whose bark and leaves we use in our witch's brew and, of course, in our aphrodisiacs. (A good dose of those might have improved your star rating!) We love to gather, as we did last night, in our very special glade, encircling the bubbling cauldron full to the brim with its secret brew of Devil's Weed and other ingredients of which we are never allowed to speak. (Although, I do sometimes suspect that they're nothing more than the out-of-date ingredients of the Great Warlock's kitchen cupboard!) Last night, it was all for you!

So there we were in our black robes and pointed hats, our broomsticks carefully placed in a circle, while we intoned our incantations. To be quite honest with you, of course, and to break the spell somewhat (a bit of a pun there, I think!) half of us don't really know what we're doing, but they do say that the most powerful spells are the homespun ones – more heartfelt, I suppose. I know mine certainly were extremely heart-felt...

What do you think you're doing?

Don't you close your eyes on me!

Pay attention!

You do that again, and you'll get another prod...!

Anyway, as I was saying, there we were chanting away, invoking the Angel of Death and any other spirit who might have been lurking about, trying to summon up the most gruesome of demons: all with the sole purpose of bringing you to an untimely end. While that was happening, of course, we were gradually stripping off for the most important part of the evening: the orgy!

However, because I haven't really got a hundred-percent faith in our magical powers, I thought I'd come along here this morning to work a bit of magic of my own: in other words, my very special, efficacious mixture of ground puffer-fish and Special K (and, no, I don't mean the breakfast cereal!)

Didn't you think that your first G and T tasted a bit strange?

Well, it certainly seems to have done the trick!

Can't move, can't speak, can you?

Though I ask myself, is it actually going to finish you off in the next half-hour?

I have a hair appointment at 12 o'clock that I most definitely don't want to miss...

I don't believe it!

You've done it again!

Look, I've even put on my favourite pointy-hat for you, the one with the gold stars, and you still can't keep your eyes open!

Right, you've asked for it!

Hang on a minute, while I have a quick rummage around in my bag; why can't I ever find anything when I want it?

I know it's here somewhere!

Found it!

Have a look at this then!

Do you recognise yourself?

I hope you appreciate the time and effort (and also artistry, I may say) that went into making this wax doll! Ooh, and here's the pin – can't do without that, can we?

Right, let's have a little jab, shall we...!

Oh come on, you can do better than that – let's have

some reaction!

Sod it, the front door!

Just when I was just starting to enjoy myself!

She's still with us, I'm afraid. In fact, I'm beginning to think your damned wife's indestructible!

For goodness sake, come in here and do something with her. I've got to be at the hairdresser's in twenty minutes!

Can't you take her out in the boat and chuck her over the side? Consign her to a watery grave...!

Ooooh! No, no... I didn't say that! I didn't! In fact, I totally deny saying it.

It's a lie!

It's all a lie!

There's obviously been some sort of terrible misunderstanding!

Anyway, how did you get here?

Did someone call 999...?

The doll? ...

What about it? It's just an ordinary doll; there's nothing special about it!

Yes, I know I'm wearing a witch's hat. So what! Is there any law against it?

We do live in a democracy, you know!

As for her, well, you can see for yourselves that she's not at all well and I have been trying to help her, really I have! ...Would you perhaps like me to call an ambulance?

Might that not be a good idea?

No?

…Oh, you're waiting for the forensic team to arrive… I see!

Well… In that case, I suppose, I'd better put on my coat and come along quietly, hadn't I?

The Cat's Mother

"Remove the pink cushion before you sit down," she commanded. "It's for the cat's use only and he would be most distressed if he were to see you seated upon it!"

The reedy, wheezy, querulous voice belongs to Auntie, she of the mothballs, antimacassars and aspidistras: a relic from some past age. Of course, if you knew the cat in question the last thing you would want to do is to sit on its cushion, but that's not the point, is it? Simply another example of Auntie getting above herself, the old bat!

The command was directed at the Reverend Nigel – Nige – who comes every week to prepare Auntie's immortal soul for the great journey into the hereafter; he'd better get a move-on, however, because it's going to be sooner than either of them imagines! So get your spiritual suitcase packed, Auntie – right now!

The cat, by the way, in spite of the fact that its bits and pieces had been surgically removed by the vet, still sprays everything in sight, although Auntie swears vehemently that the quivering of its tail is merely a sign of affection. Anyhow, the offending cat is, at the moment, absent from the room. Instead, an ancient, tired-looking poodle, with milky eyes that cannot possibly see much, enters, takes a quick sniff at Nige, and plonks itself on Auntie's lap. Curly it's called. Its woolly coat, a faded gingery colour, resembles nothing so much as Auntie's unfortunate, tight perm. Indeed, they could well have both gone to the same hairdresser!

I sometimes wonder if it might not be possible to electrocute Auntie while she is sitting under the dryer, which she does every Friday at about four o'clock when the hairdresser comes to the house, but as my knowledge of all things electrical is virtually non-existent this is to dream in vain. In any case, I need solitude for what I have in mind!

Auntie's eyebrows, those supercilious, heavily-pencilled arches, are raised as she looks at me disapprovingly... I suppose because I've failed to purchase her favourite custard creams, which she likes to dunk into her tea – such a disgusting habit I always think! Nige sits in front of the loaded tea trolley, cup in hand, little finger delicately raised, perching precariously on the edge of the hard, upright cushion-less chair to which he has been relegated.

I do so enjoy looking at him – a late entry into the ecclesiastical life is our Nige – and wondering what's behind that bland exterior. He's certainly not what he seems, that's for sure. At some point in his life he has obviously reinvented himself, for although the doubtful vowels of some lowly Secondary Modern School have now been carefully erased and replaced by the cut-glass tones of a hinted-at Public School, the tell-tale signs of his origins still peep through to those of us who are keen observers of humankind!

He certainly seems to live very well for a man of the cloth… no church-supplied accommodation for our Nige, but a very nice, big house with a live-in housekeeper (the precise nature of her duties we leave to his conscience). He owned a big, flashy, silver Mercedes sports car that certainly didn't come out of his stipend and smart, well-fitted clerical garb, which I would best describe as Savile Row!

Having a good pair of ears and pretty much always merging with the wallpaper, I've been privy to all sorts of gossip – with Nigel very much to the fore! It would appear, that at one stage of his life, he was for some months detained at Her Majesty's pleasure – for bribery and corruption, no less! What do you think of that? If it's true, then nothing that he gets up to here should surprise us. I would like to know if the Bishop has got wind of this! If he hasn't, perhaps it should be someone's Christian duty to tell him!

Yes, I definitely have my suspicions about you, Nige! I wonder if you sometimes sprinkle a little something onto the communion wafer when you minister to the old and housebound, especially those who are alone and well-heeled! I've certainly never quite managed to discover the contents of Auntie's Last Will and Testament, but I strongly suspect that your name is well to the fore; the old bag probably thinks that she's buying her way into Heaven by keeping you happy. Is that what you tell her, Nige? I bet it is …but I'll sort you out at a later date!

In the corner of Auntie's sitting room stands a cage occupied by Barbara Cartland, a rather bilious-looking budgie with a lime-green body. A small piteous lump of feathers is our Barbara, doomed to spend her little life behind bars but, very soon, Barbara Cartland, you will be free for the first time ever, free to spread your wings and to feel the air around you as nature demands!

"Fetch me my knitting from upstairs, Betty, and you can bring my library book at the same time." *No please or thank you, Auntie? Well, why break the habit of a lifetime?* Then Nige adds his pennyworth!

"It's such a blessing that you have Betty to look after you!"

"Look after me! She doesn't look after me! The only person she looks after is herself, but that's young people for you, isn't it!"

Young ...young? I'm fifty-two-years-old and most of my adult life seems to have been spent looking after you and your bloody zoo! Let the cat in, let the cat out, walk the dog, worm the dog, feed the budgie!

Nigel turns his colourless eyes towards me. "How are you these days, Betty? You're looking well, I must say! No more of those funny turns? No more little stays in the Psychiatric Unit?"

You bastard, Nige!

Suddenly, we are all aware of the door being pushed gently ajar. Let the trumpets sound their fanfare, let the drums beat out their welcome, let joy uncontained fill the house! The master is among us. Auntie's face shows such an expression of absolute joy that one would think that the Second Coming had finally arrived! A small, ragged ginger-tom has deigned to grace us with his presence – actually, quite a pleasant cat as cats go, but surely not worth the adoration bestowed on it by this foolish old biddy!

"Come on, Bertie! Onto your cushion, sweetheart!

The cat gazes at us with his bright, green eyes and settles down to watch proceedings. "That will be all, Betty. Why don't you go and prepare the salad for supper. The Vicar and I have a …a rather private matter we want to discuss!"

Auntie is nothing …and very soon will be less than nothing!

I always like being in the kitchen. It's a place of creativity where I can allow my imagination to run free. Despite my dismissal from the sitting room where Auntie and Nige play out their little scene, this is the main arena, here among the pots and pans; this is where the main script is being written – and what a script! A true piece of drama in the making and the star will be Auntie, the cat's mother – before she fades into oblivion!

Therefore, doing as I have been told, I set about preparing the salad. A nice side-salad to a very well-done steak (with, of course, a lovely blood-red bottle of Burgundy). It has always been my favourite meal of all especially as, during my little stays in hospital, I was never allowed to eat meat; they never, never, ever, ever understood my craving! I do so love the mouth-watering smell of roasting flesh, the wonderful flavours of natural juices.

"Bye, Betty!" shouts Nige, from outside the kitchen door. "I have to go now! Evensong calls!"

Give it a few days, Nige and it'll be a funeral that's doing the calling…! Well, that's the salad done! I'll just let the wine breathe for a little… Right, let's go and start the second scene of the drama, shall we?

"Alright Auntie, I'm coming! I won't keep you a moment! Just let me get a box of matches from the drawer…I do so enjoy my meat barbecued – it's just such a pity that Auntie is rather on the scrawny side! On the other hand, this does means that the cooking time can be reduced!"

Yet, the best laid plans of mice and men often go awry, for, all at once, there is an insistent ringing at the front door!

"May I come in, Betty? So sorry to disturb you again, but I've forgotten my Bible. Can't do without that, can I?" The Blessed Nige, Saint Nigel of the Helpless (who by some miracle of faultless timing now saves a member of his ageing flock from an untimely death as well as saving her soul) stands smiling at me from the door-step. Thereupon, in he trots towards the sitting-room and I can hear him, in his unctuous tones, having yet a few more private words with Auntie. Grinding my teeth and with my head pounding painfully within my skull, I know that today is not the day – my plan has been foiled: at least for the moment. Fate and the Church of England have conspired against me! Damn you to Hell, Nigel, for my appetite has now completely gone and my murderous thoughts have evaporated into thin air like smoke from a barbecue.

Nevertheless, the day will not be completely pointless for Barbara Cartland is on the emerald-green lawn enjoying the warmth on her sun-starved feathers while she awaits her imminent release from her long prison sentence. Curly and Bertie lie asleep nearby on a bed of tulips, snoring in tandem.

Right, Barbara Cartland, this is your big moment, the moment I promised you. Off you go! Enjoy your freedom little bird…! Bye, bye, Barbara!

Oh no! No! …God, he moves like streaked lightning that bloody cat does! Let her go, you little sod… I'm going to wring your bloody neck when I get hold of you – and that's a promise…! Poor Barbara, she only managed a few little flutters before he got her… What a rotten, unfair world this is! What a rotten day this has been!

The Dark River

Coralie sat on the damp grass of the river bank with her eyes closed, chewing the skin around her nails until they were bleeding. She had caught her lip on the foil as she pulled the capsule from its strip, causing even more blood to seep out. If only she were able to calm down, control her nerves, for she could feel her throat constricting and her teeth grinding together: a sure sign that she was at the end of her tether.

The cold, night air enclosed her in its darkness, but the fact that she couldn't be seen was of no comfort to her. What if Justin missed her, failed to see her? He was already late.

All their hard work, their careful planning would have been for nothing, for she couldn't do it by herself; he had to be there at her side! Her head throbbed as she contemplated what was to come – if only she had something stronger than these tranquillisers! Really it would be so much easier to forget all about it, simply to slip into the dark river that was flowing past her and end the waiting.

She didn't want to commit murder, but on the other hand she needed them dead.

Justin did arrive; and yes, their plan went like

clockwork and twenty years later an unfortunate gamekeeper discovered, beneath the rich soil of Jensen's Wood, two sets of bones: the fruits of their labour.

"Shut up!" he screamed at the alarm clock as he flung it angrily across the room. The sudden awakening had rattled him, for he liked to lie comfortably in bed for half an hour or so before actually getting up to think over what had to be done during the day ahead. Not that the prospect was ever something to be relished, especially today.

"Did you have to put the alarm on?" he snarled at her. "You're always up at the crack of dawn, anyway, so couldn't you just have woken me?" Picking up the clock wearily, Coralie wondered for the umpteenth time why she bothered with him; he just wasn't worth the effort. However, Justin and she had their little secret, their terrible little secret, so there was really no question at all of leaving him. "I just love your sweet ways, Justin! You're such a lovable guy, aren't you?"

How someone so crass, so unfeeling could possibly have become a therapist she'd no idea. Weren't therapists supposed to be sensitive to the feelings of others but, of course, it was all psychobabble. They were all programmed as to what to say; the response automatically fitted the problem, no actual thinking went on. God help anyone who went to consult Justin today – especially considering the fees he charged!

In precisely two hours he would leave their rather

grand Hampstead house by taxi, still wearing 'The Guardian reader's beard' and the single gold earring of old, but now this image was offset by an immaculate Savile Row suit; the Jesus-sandals and the T-shirts with their socialist slogans were long-forgotten. A strange dichotomy …all the elegance of Harley Street mixed up with the Marxist touch, but that was what Justin had become – a prat, an unhinged weirdo: in fact, just about this side of sane, she sometimes thought.

If they hadn't murdered Peter and Phyllis she most certainly wouldn't have stuck with him, but it had seemed like a good idea at the time. Peter and Phyllis had been very well-heeled, but had not, for a long time, been overly Coralie-disposed, which was why there had been talk of changing their wills in favour of all the abandoned cats and dogs in Little Riding who would, then and forever more, be fed and watered up to the eyeballs. Couldn't have that though could we, so Mummy and Daddy had to die!

Justin, poor as a church mouse, had been a willing accomplice. Instant wealth: well, he'd liked that idea very much indeed and knew that he would never have a better opportunity than the one Coralie was offering him. All he had to do was to marry her and try to ignore her permanently-runny, sore nose and her shakes – the silly little crack-head! Just let him get hold of the money and then he could always make other arrangements sex-wise.

Coralie had been sure that she loved him. Mainly, of course, it was lust, but she wasn't to know that – the advice columns in women's magazines didn't come within her realm of reading material; too busy trying, somewhat dazedly, to get through her English degree course.

She shouldn't have done it, of course (murdered them, that is) but she had no money of her own, no rich girl's allowance, which by rights should have been hers: Daddy had thought her too irresponsible, Mummy considered her too slovenly and a disgrace to the family name, considering all the advantages she'd had. So there was no other way to pay for her addiction – she didn't particularly want to steal – something rather tacky about that and you had to keep doing it. So she decided instead to rob Mummy and Daddy of their lives – a nice, simple, one-off solution to her problem. Anyway, she hadn't liked them very much, so it should theoretically have been no big deal.

However, many are the times when, in her dreams, she saw again the dark river as she had seen it all those years ago on the night of the murders. She knew that Justin too had troubled dreams, for she often heard him muttering and moaning, shouting and screaming, tossing and turning. Down the river in a punt they had all gone: Justin and Coralie both trembling with the fear of discovery: Peter and Phyllis, both with deep, fatal wounds to the side of the head: all went down to Jensen's Wood for the burial.

Justin rolled over onto his back, yawned and smiled, not very pleasantly, as he looked at her from amid the pristine, white pillows. "Would you prostitute yourself for me, Coralie? I think you might rather enjoy it! It would be worth it, I assure you! You do want us to be safe, don't you?" He pulled her onto the bed and whispered into her ear, giggling all the while – he really was very creepy sometimes, she thought.

What was he saying? Jensen's Wood …Mummy and Daddy's bones …found! Oh God – the worst of all nightmares! Where did he find that out – in the evening paper? Why hadn't he said anything earlier? Sometime soon the police would surely pay them a visit enquiring into missing persons. Peter and Phyllis Cadogan, Mummy and Daddy, whose mysterious disappearance twenty-years ago had so intrigued the reading public!

"You want me to open my legs for the Chief Inspector – take his mind off us! What fantasy world are you living in, Justin? This is real life – not Morse, not Lewis, not Midsomer Murders!"

Of course, the bones would easily be identified – but there was absolutely nothing to connect Coralie and Justin to the crime. The punt, stolen and hidden weeks before the murders, had afterwards mysteriously gone up in flames miles away from Jenson's Wood and all the other little details had, Coralie thought, been well and truly covered. No, they were both safe – no doubt about that! Even with her addict's brain she had been meticulous in her arrangement of the scenario, even down to unbreakable alibis. Now, drug-free and with much more experience of life, all she needed were a few gin and tonics to help her think really clearly about the next few days – but not at this precise moment; even she drew a line at drinking her way through breakfast.

Out of sorts, irritable and with an appalling headache, Justin stepped into the taxi, then sat back in his seat and pondered, twisting his earring around with his fingers. He wanted just one more death, one that was long overdue, after which he would be totally free. The dark river was, of course, the natural solution, the fitting end, the completion, you might say, of the circle. Then there must follow another burial, but this one in a deeper, thicker part of the wood where no one could ever find her. He couldn't help smiling at the idea and gurgled out loud, while the taxi driver looked at him curiously in the mirror. Once in his office a nice strong spliff would aid a further ponder.

Later on, as she sipped her ten o'clock gin and tonic in the presence of the police, Coralie tearfully received the news of the discovery and identification of her parents' remains – height, teeth, and pieces of fabric – there was no doubt at all. Looking at the outrageously fat Chief Inspector, his uneven, yellow teeth seeming to take up an excess of space in his mouth, she knew that Justin's little daydream of her sexual romp with a senior member of the police force was not going to happen.

The deep indentations in the skulls ensured that this would be a murder investigation, but it would just have to take its natural course without any blandishments on her part.

Justin sat for a long, long time in his consulting room, doubled up with laughter, the sweet smell of pot surrounding him. Miss Cage, his beautiful, svelte receptionist with whom he was half in love, had been sent home and the 'phone disconnected so that his clients, when they arrived, found everything closed up, the help they so earnestly sought denied them. Their therapist was there, however, firmly locked in his own neuroses, his mind floating in its own dark river.

Coralie, her hands shaking, the ice in her glass clinking uncontrollably, knew that some sort of ending, whether good or bad, was inevitably on its way, that things were about to be resolved, the tale told. She couldn't complain, though, for during the last twenty years they had led a comfortable, though perhaps not a happy, life, because of what had been done on that night by the dark river …and she supposed that ultimately one had to pay for one's sins, either in this life or in the next one, if it exists.

The light of day was beginning to fade and she knew that at any moment the taxi would bring Justin back home. She heard the sound of his key in the door, his footsteps coming along the expensively stained, pale wood floor …and suddenly there he stood in front of her with a stout, wooden mallet in his hand.

He laughed as though this were the greatest joke in the world and raised his arm. "Well, my gin-soaked little rich bitch, this, I'm afraid to say, is the end of the road for you. Peter has gone, Phyllis has gone and I want you gone too. The Cadogan family, in one way or another has condemned me to a living hell, sent me on the road to perdition. I finally want to be shot of the whole lot of you!"

Coralie looked at him unbelievingly and backed away in horror, her glass shattering into pieces as it hit the floor. "Put that mallet down! I'm going to have you committed, Justin, that's what I'm going to do – you're as mad as a hatter or hadn't you realised that? But then, of course, you're not a very good therapist so, no, you probably haven't noticed!"

It was too late to hurl abuse at each other as he brought the mallet down as hard as he possibly could and knocked her head sideways. So into the boot of the car she went, into the punt she went and down along the dark river she went again, until they reached a thick clump of trees and ferns. There he dug and he dug and he dug into the earth so deeply that he knew no one would ever find her.

Miss Cage sat behind her desk, inspecting her beautiful hands, the skin white and soft, the nails expertly shaped and polished; her posture was exquisite and her clothes were immaculate. Justin had failed to appear for the past two days and she had come to the consulting room early, wondering if he would return…

Then the door opened noisily and he staggered into the room, filthy and dishevelled. Miss Cage in her cocoon of pristine tidiness was shocked, for he suddenly sprawled on the other side of her desk, his hands filthy, his nails ingrained with earth and, with his face resting on his arms, he draped himself across her closed laptop, lifting his blood shot eyes and laughing bitterly.

"Go away, Miss Cage, your position here is terminated forthwith, for I'm going on a long, long journey and will no longer require your services. I thought I should let you know face to face."

With a great effort, he then dragged himself to his feet and she watched as he tottered back to the door, slamming it for the last time.

Justin, exhausted and, as usual, drugged up to the eyeballs, was naturally drawn like a magnet back to the dark river where it had all begun and where it would all end. It was to that very same spot that he drove somewhat erratically, half-hoping that he might finish it all by hitting a tree at speed, but that was not really how he wanted the tale to end.

Finally, he sat on the damp grass, beginning to snivel, the contents of his nose dripping onto his already-soiled jumper. He was almost as slimy and evil-smelling as the river. All at once he stood up and said to the empty air, "I think it is time for me to go now for Coralie is calling to me from among the fish – and behind the bulrushes I can see Peter and Phyllis waving."

He raised an arm in greeting. "Hello, Peter! Hello, Phyllis! Did you know that Coralie has risen from her burial place and is here too? Look, Peter, she's down there under the water, just next to you. I can see her quite clearly." At that moment his muddled mind, finally lost control completely and, effortlessly, he slid down the bank like a skater into the river, rotten vegetation gripping him eagerly as he struggled to pass by. His very last thought was to lift his arm towards the world in a gesture of farewell and, as he disappeared from view, he gave a smile – Excalibur to a tee, he thought.

Coralie, of course, was still lying in her deep, wormy grave, maggots and blow-flies feasting on her flesh as Justin became more and more accustomed to watery death. As for the river, itself that abode of horror and murder, it became even darker and more sinister as the years passed.

The Dark Side

The house-lights were dimming, the chatter ceasing, sweet-wrappers finally silent and then, wonder of wonders, the little orchestra burst forth into the opening number as the curtains were magically drawn back to reveal poor Cinderella sitting among the ashes. It wasn't a very good orchestra: slightly out of tune: the players and the conductor not always in total harmony, but Phineas, sitting on his mother's knee, his chubby fingers clasping her arms tightly, wasn't to know that. Young as he was, not for one moment did his concentration waver from the stage – he was totally absorbed, enchanted by what he was seeing.

He didn't even laugh at Buttons or at the two Ugly Sisters, so seriously did he take the whole performance; in fact, tears came into his eyes and his lips quivered when it was time for Cinderella to leave the wood-smoke and the cinders behind her.

Phineas liked her grubby look, her dirty feet, her untamed sooty hair, even her ash-covered dress and was disappointed to see the transformation into Prince Charming's darling, with her sequin-covered ball-gown sparkling under the stage lights like diamonds.

Phineas loved the darkness and the gloominess of the theatre where he felt safe and secure. It gave him the same sort of comfort that he felt at night, sleeping, as he always slept, in absolute blackness, with his head hidden under his duvet. There was never a light left on in his bedroom and whenever the moon shone through the window he made such a fuss that in the end his mother had to sew a lining onto the curtains to stop this intrusion. His teddy bear was black, his train engine was black, his duvet cover was black and grey – everything had to be dark.

At the end of the show, as Phineas was being carried in his father's arms towards the car park, his mother suddenly whispered into his ear. "Look, Phineas, there's Cinderella – there's the actress who was playing the part. Isn't she pretty! And, look somebody's given her a bunch of flowers!" Phineas, however, didn't think she looked pretty at all in her bright, pink coat and her red hair. Why wasn't she wearing black or grey or some smoky colour – she would have looked so much nicer?

All this might make you think that there was something not quite right about a little boy with such an obsession with darkness, but he was really quite normal, nothing peculiar about him at all. No, everyone loved Phineas, so sweet, so cute, just like his little rabbit – but did you know that rabbits, those inoffensive, quiet little creatures, scream when they feel pain?

Phineas had a white rabbit, Snowy, living in a hutch at the bottom of the garden, a long way from the house and there was nothing that the lovable little boy enjoyed more than piercing Snowy's soft skin with a long, sharp needle stolen from his mother's sewing box.

Phineas stood overlooking the Aegean, a glass of ouzo in his hand; on a small, white, decorative, wrought-iron table at his side were plates of sardines and salads, the lunch that he and Suzie had chosen to eat ever since the beginning of their holiday. He adored the view from this rough, stony terrace, admiring the tall, elegantly-shaped Cyprus trees whose outline stood so wondrously against the deep blue sky, and enjoying the blistering heat of the sun on his body.

Suddenly he saw a dark-skinned snake slithering past his feet as though it had no fear of him whatsoever, seeming almost to taunt him, and daring him to react to its presence. It coiled and extended its long shape in a rhythmic movement, ignoring the pots of red and pink geraniums, ignoring the deep purple bougainvillea that nestled against the whitewashed wall, until it reached a hole in the trunk of an olive tree where it quickly slid into its obviously familiar hiding place. Seeing this, something tugged at Phineas' heart, a sense of recognition awoke in him and he suddenly envied the snake its escape into the darkness and coolness of the hollow place.

Phineas appreciated snakes: creatures well able to look after themselves, astute, knowing their own minds. He felt an affinity with them and knew that his own name was related to theirs – for it was a name whose meaning was associated with oracles and serpents' tongues and with Phineas, the Phoenician King of Thrace.

Suzie was a sweet, neat little thing, with her immaculately-cut, short, blonde hair, her discreetly manicured nails with their colourless varnish and her carefully pressed, pale pink dress – in other words, the sort of girl his mother might well have described as wholesome and who until a split second ago, Phineas thought that he might possibly love but, of course, he'd always been on the rather fickle side.

Yet a sudden transformation was taking place. He was becoming what he had once been; he'd always had his peculiar little ways, but a darker, crueller side awakened within him, one that had been buried deep inside his mind, lying dormant for a very long time. He looked at Suzie intently while she sipped her drink as though he were examining every atom of her and knew that this was not the best that life had to offer him. Then, as if in answer to this thought, voices could be heard drifting up from the beach below.

Until this moment they had never had to share their lunchtime with anyone and now, unexpectedly, here were six other people, intruders it seemed to Phineas at first glance. Such smart, sophisticated, bohemian people who didn't have to worry what others thought of them, who were secure and happy with who they were and what they were.

Her name was Leandra and from the first moment he set eyes on her the rest of the world ceased to exist for Phineas. Suzie might as well have been one of the stone statues, which adorned the terrace. As for the other strangers – well, they didn't register with him at all, except for their braying laughter and their strident over-confident voices somewhere on the edge of his awareness.

Tall and slim, Leandra dazzled him with her smooth, olive skin and her abundance of red hair, all shown off to perfection by an obviously expensive long, black sun-dress and by her gold jewellery, but when he looked at down she was shoeless and her feet grubby. His stomach churned at the sight.

"Why, Phineas, how lovely to meet you both. We've all become rather incestuous, I'm afraid, so it'll be like a breath of fresh air to have different company. We've just been spending a few days touring the island by boat and so the prospect of staying in one place and doing nothing for a week or two is positively heavenly."

She clasped his hand and gave him a kiss on both cheeks – how theatrical, how very continental, he thought – and, as her lips touched his skin, he could smell the heavy, spicy fragrance of her perfume and was totally intoxicated by it.

Soon the ouzo was replaced by champagne and, as they stood gazing at each other with the fluted glasses in their hands, he thought her the most exotic creature he'd ever set eyes upon. He guessed she must have been about forty-years-old – too old for him really, but wonderful, truly spectacular as a holiday fling …and after that, who knows? In his imagination he could already picture exciting little rendezvous in discreet London restaurants, secret meetings in exclusive bijoux hotels. It was just such a pity that Suzie was there hovering insipidly in the background, surely now surplus to requirements, cramping his style! However, she was no problem for him; he was used to giving girls their marching orders, for Phineas had a very low boredom-threshold where women were concerned.

More dishes of Greek salad and calamari and pita appeared, boosted by bottles of retsina and more ouzo and more champagne, until the sun set and the calming darkness of night fell upon the terrace. By this time Phineas had adorned himself with a laurel wreath, the supreme victor, mirroring, if the truth were to be told, his own opinion of himself; playing the fool for Leandra's exclusive entertainment. Suzie was in high dudgeon. "You're like some lovelorn loon, Phineas! You really can't imagine how stupid you looked out there," she said to him later that evening.

"For God's sake, shut up, Suzie. If you don't like what I do, why don't you just sod off back to London and let me do my own thing!"

She didn't leave, of course – she just hung around like some presiding spirit casting an atmosphere of ill will and resentment over everything – the proverbial wet blanket!

"Poor Phineas, what a cross you have to bear! Why don't you rid yourself of her; you can surely think of a way. We don't want her here – you, me or the others! She's not our sort at all. So provincial! Where on earth did you find her?"

Where had he found her? Phineas felt slightly embarrassed by such a question, for the answer was that he'd actually found her manning a display of odds and ends of doubtful provenance in an antiques' street market one Saturday morning not very long ago, just at the time when he was looking for someone to replace the woman whom he'd originally been going to bring on this holiday. Suzie was, however, pretty enough, could string two words of English together in the correct order and above all, despite her innocent appearance, was willing to play the little games in which he liked to indulge himself. In fact, until the sudden arrival of the visitors from the sea and the snake's strange effect, he'd been quite smitten with her.

Now he was feeling the old, overwhelming desire to hide himself in some dark place as far away from the light as possible, to find a sharp implement with which he could pierce Suzie's pale skin so that he could hear her screams as he had heard Snowy's. He felt disturbed by these sensations, almost fearful, and knew that he must send her far away before he did her some harm. He was, for that reason, more than happy to agree with Leandra that she must leave – back to London on the next possible plane, to the ends of the Earth if need be.

As darkness fell, he went out again onto the terrace, leaving Suzie to her sulking, and sat on the ground, his back against the olive tree, hoping to catch another glimpse of the snake, for it was still warm enough for the cold-blooded creature to venture into the open – and, sure enough, out it came, its black body covered in dust and dirt – and Phineas began to tremble.

Two days later, Suzie left for the airport, a family

emergency fortuitously precipitating her return. "Lucky Phineas, the gods of Olympus taking a hand in the affairs of men! So I think we should take full advantage of the opportunity they've given us, don't you?"

She stood before him in a grey diaphanous dress, which showed the shape of her legs as the sun shone through it, a large, black, beaded choker-necklace at her throat – always dressed as he would wish her to be without his having to say one word. Always dark, smoky colours, which made her glorious, slightly-dishevelled, red hair stand out even more distinctly, so that all other women paled into insignificance beside her – a Greek goddess truly come to life, only an amphora on her shoulder needed to complete the picture.

Back in London the novelty was beginning to wear thin. Without the background of stone pillars, ancient altars and sacred forest groves, Leandra was somehow less appealing and the monotonous drudgery of working days had superseded the dream-like quality of the glorious nights that they had spent together on the island of myths and legends. Added to which Phineas now suspected that she did not totally enjoy some of the things he did to her.

It was Saturday evening and they were going to Covent Garden. Leandra adored opera, but he just tagged along with her for the ride and hoped that she would give him a nudge if he began to snore. He never bothered to ask what they were going to see and, because she knew he was so bored by it all, she never bothered to tell him.

Tonight, however, there was a change of plan for she had an unforeseen appointment that she couldn't possibly avoid. She would only arrive in time for the second act but this was no problem. She always gave him his ticket in case she was delayed. Deciding against sitting in the bar until her arrival, Phineas took his seat in the stalls. He was feeling tired and work-worn; the prospect of being cocooned in the ever-welcoming darkness of the theatre appealed to him.

The usual rapturous applause greeted the conductor and the overture played through to its end, while Phineas' eyes began to close. He was roused abruptly from his stupor when the woman on his left dropped her handbag onto the floor and, as his gaze focussed disinterestedly upon the stage, his heart felt as though it would explode …for there she sat by the fire amid the cinders, her red hair covered in ash, her feet grubby, her ragged dress torn and threadbare: Cinderella placing logs on the fire whilst the two ugly sisters pranced and preened themselves. He took his ticket out of his breast pocket and in the gloom could just about read what it said – he'd never heard of it before, but what he was watching was "La Cenerentola", Rossini's operatic version of Cinderella, that immortal folktale about cruelty and forgiveness.

Right up to the moment at the end of the first act, when the curtains closed and the lights went up, he sat watching the action with a thousand emotions running through him, his eyes riveted upon the begrimed figure of Cinderella. He was suddenly aware of Leandra's familiar perfume and there she was standing over him, just about to take her seat, but he didn't allow her to sit. How dare she! What was she thinking about, doing this to him? His anger felt boundless and he was completely unable to control it, so he just grabbed her by the wrist and dragged her to end of the row, treading on people's feet, knocking their belongings to the floor in his eagerness to escape into the foyer.

"Was it not to your taste, Phineas? You really didn't like that one, did you? Poor Rossini! And he's so good if you really listen to him!"

"You have no idea how much to my taste it was!"

He was by now gripping her wrist so tightly that it hurt like the devil. He looked her up and down, appalled at her appearance – it was a deliberate insult to him. There she stood in her bright-pink coat, her red hair glowing under the lights, looking like some cheap fairground doll. People sipping their glasses of wine and champagne looked at them curiously, anxiously wondering if they should perhaps call someone in authority to avoid what might turn out to be a very nasty little scene.

Phineas, however, saved them from their dilemma by dragging Leandra into the open air, across the piazza and into Upper St Martin's Lane car park where he'd left his red sports car, for him the symbol of a dashing man-about-town.

By this time, she was in agony and screaming, but

people, in general, are reluctant to become involved in domestic spats – you never know where they might end. Slapping her hard across the face, he flung her into the car and revved up.

Phineas, still ranting and cursing under his breath, had pulled and pushed Leandra to the bottom of the garden, by which time her arm was virtually useless; not that that was going to matter for very much longer. Snowy's hutch, neglected and rotting, still stood in the same place, illuminated by the moon's brilliance. Why, he wondered, couldn't that shining orb do the decent thing and hide itself behind a screen of clouds so that blissful darkness could envelop him. Leandra collapsed on to the damp grass, sobbing and holding her arm, while she watched her aggressor set a match to the empty hutch, soon reducing it to embers and ash. First he grabbed her hair and, pulling her face upward, covered it with the hot residue from the fire and smothered her bright pink coat with wood ash. He then removed her shoes and tights so that he could do the same to her bare legs and feet, now grubby, as he would always have preferred them to be. "What a dirty, slovenly girl you now look, Cinderella – just how I like to see you! That'll teach you to wear the clothes of a slut, won't it?"

A piece of the wire mesh from the front of the hutch was lying amid the remains and Phineas picked it up, shaping it so that it became a pointed weapon, his fingers all the while burning from the heat. With it he started to jab at Leandra's neck, piercing the smooth skin as he had pierced poor Snowy's body.

"Scream, Cinderella, scream, you naughty girl! Louder, louder or I'll set your wicked stepmother onto you and you wouldn't like that one bit, would you?" By now the moon had disappeared and the only light was the glow from the dying embers. "Or perhaps you would like something infinitely worse – Phineas the python to inject you with his venom!" Thus the curtain came down on the final scene of the pantomime with the two protagonists centre stage…a dying Cinderella and a mad villain who thought he was a serpent.

The Flower Garden

The woman's body was misshapen, out of focus, the proportions completely wrong. Why could he never get it quite right? One of the reasons, of course, was that he always removed his glasses when painting – things looked better that way: not authentic, but better. The myopic haze softened reality, helped him to see things that weren't there!

Ralph sat at his easel under the damp sky. At any moment the heavens would open up and his feeble attempts to paint something wondrous would be washed away. It seemed to him as though the white daisies and the red poppies that were around him in this wild part of the garden were thrusting their heads up towards the clouds waiting for the unusually dry spell of spring weather to end.

Meanwhile, the model, her naked form lying before him in the grass, filled him with lust and he moved about uncomfortably on his canvas chair: swollen, throbbing, frustrated. Her scarlet fingernails and scarlet toenails reflected the heat of his rising passion. Rain or no rain, he couldn't concentrate as his imagination wandered into realms that he knew would never become a reality, while the paintbrush within his trembling fingers refused to follow his orders.

He was just about able to see through the dimness that she was asleep and, in his mind's eye, he imagined her mouth provocatively slightly open, saliva wetting her chin. She sighed and stirred as she felt the first drops of rain touching her skin – and then staggered to her feet, grabbing the large-size silk housecoat that lay in a heap under the willow tree. There she stood trying to find some shelter, while Ralph quickly covered his canvas with a plastic sheet, all the while calling to her to follow him towards the house. "Get dressed! Get the dog! Get a move on! You know Bertie doesn't like having his walk in the rain!"

The magic had gone, the dream of unbridled passion dissipated. After all, this was Val – all right when lying down, when seen from a distance, when studied through a fog of short-sightedness, but now he had replaced his glasses and here she was waddling behind him, a behemoth appearing through the rain!

"Why does it always take you so long to do things?"

"It's the pain, Ralphie! It's the pain! Ooh, why doesn't it go away, just for a little while? I try, I really do try to forget it, but it's always there! You don't know what it's like! Aching limbs! Aching muscles!"

"For God's sake, Val, shut up about the pain – we all get rheumatism as we get older. The dog's waiting for his walk – can't you see – the poor little sod's begging with his big, brown eyes?" They both looked down at the black spaniel as it stood softly growling at them both – to be truthful, not a nice dog, but Ralph, for some unaccountable reason, doted on him.

"Why don't you take him out, Ralphie? Please! Just this once!" Ralph hit her hard across the face for her insolence, as he always did when she stepped out of line!

Val, however, had her secrets and Ralph had absolutely no idea just how far out of line she had stepped. A lover – that's what Val had – someone who didn't care that she waddled, someone who didn't mind that she resembled a Sherman tank, someone who didn't have to take his glasses off before he could bear to look at her. The only one privy to this momentous secret was Bertie who had seen it all – the romping in the hay in the big barn at Sykes farm, Val in her black underwear with aches and pains forgotten, Farmer Sykes with his wellingtons, y-fronts and trousers all cast to one side.

Bertie though was a little traitor. Given the power of speech, he would have remained firmly silent over the whole affair because Farmer Sykes was so much more his cup of tea than Ralph – Ralph with his shouting and his pulling on Bertie's choke chain! So unkind! Today, however, Val's lover was at an agricultural show, so that she would be forced, for once, to forego the highlight of her day. Anyway, needs must when the Devil drives and so there was Val, water-proofed and protected from the rain, opening the garden gate, gazing at the poppies and daisies that almost seemed to be smiling at the drenching they were getting.

Ralph meanwhile, sitting in the kitchen, snug and comfortable with a glass of whisky at his side, uncovered his painting, studied it closely and was surprised that it was actually not too bad: in fact, not too bad at all. Val had, of course, been transformed into the nymph-like creature that he had seen without his glasses, but her red hair at least was authentic! He felt a definite stirring in his loins just looking at her! The poppies and the daisies too had turned out quite well. Yes, this painting definitely had possibilities! Could he perhaps put it in for the local painting competition? If Farmer Sykes could enter his daubs of overweight, Rubenesque monstrosities, why couldn't he exhibit this wonderful Titian-haired goddess?

Suddenly, however, the goddess and her red hair seemed to move in front of his eyes, floating away from him, and the daisies and poppies merged together, so that instead of being individually white and red they now looked pink, rather like blood that had been mixed with water. He really didn't feel well, in fact not at all well – so hot, so sweaty, his heart beating uncontrollably. There was a pain in his left arm and another on the left side of his jaw. "I'm going to suffocate!" thought Ralph. "I must get out of here. Get some fresh air, get help! The pain! Oh, why isn't it going away? Where the hell is Val when I need her?"

Well, Val was on her way home, having nothing appealing to detain her, and Bertie was sulking because he'd not been given an opportunity to have a good sniff around the barn. Anyway, suddenly she heard her name being called. What could be so urgent that Ralph would leave the nice, dry kitchen to come out there to find her?

"Ralphie! Where are you Ralphie?" Then she saw him down by the stream that ran parallel to their flower garden… "What are you doing out here in the rain?" All doubled up he was, groaning loudly, not looking his best at all! What on earth was the matter with him?

As she approached he suddenly keeled over and, before she knew what was happening, she found herself standing over him as he cried out in pain at her feet. "Help me, Val, help me! I must have had a heart attack. The pain is awful, excruciating – just take it away! Please, just take it away!"

Val smiled down at him. "Yes, pain is bad isn't it, Ralphie? When you have it, all you want is for someone to comfort you, but I'm afraid you won't find any comfort here, not from me. You're on your own from now on!"

With that she put out her fat, little foot and shoved really hard so that he slid gently down the muddy, grassy bank into the stream, his flailing hands momentarily impeding his progress as they tried to grasp the reeds and rushes. However, once this little holdup had resolved itself, off he went on his way while the rain came down even harder! It passed through Val's mind that if he'd been a Viking she could have put him in a boat and set fire to him, which might have been quite fun, except that it was really too wet for that.

Hateful man! Val smirked and had a bit of a giggle as she heard him cry out for mercy, but he wouldn't last long …not in his condition. Served the little toad right! She then released Bertie from his leash so that he could bound and skip in the muddy puddles to his heart's content – and had the distinct feeling that he was smiling, except, of course, dogs don't smile …or do they? Like a drowned rat, Val walked back to the house, picking daisies and making herself a coronet of flowers, crushing blood-red poppies underfoot as she did so.

Ralph, in his distress, had left the door to the house open and Bertie entered the kitchen, knocking the painting onto the floor in his unconstrained excitement and trampling it under his filthy paws as he frantically clawed at it. It was ruined beyond resurrection.

"Good boy, Bertie, good boy!" said Val and, placing her coronet of daisies on her head, she surveyed the scene of destruction, smiled happily and began to sing a little song of contentment.

The Grown Man

"Don't be such a baby, David! When are you going to grow up, David? Big boys don't cry, David!" Words spoken to him a long time ago by his father, words which, in one form or another, seemed to accompany him throughout his childhood. "It's only a cut, a drop of blood – what's your problem, boy! You're like a dripping tap – for God's sake, turn it off, will you!"

He had, of course, eventually stopped crying, the tears ceasing to fall, but inside his head even now, as a grown man, he was still weeping. He had loved his father, wanting always to do his best for him, but his father had not loved him so his best had never been good enough. Of course, there had been no mother, no siblings to soften the continuous recriminations. He should have hated his father, but couldn't, for his love for him had been unconditional.

Now his father was dead, leaving their relationship forever unresolved, the hurt forever unassuaged. The 'phone call bringing the unexpected news had come only an hour ago, like a bolt out of the blue; his whole life suddenly shifted out of kilter.

Out he went into the night, his stomach churning, not wanting to be alone, wanting to see that life outside his apartment still continued quite normally, despite the fact that his father was no longer among the living.

Hurrying down the street he held back a sob. He had been well indoctrinated not to cry, but surely this was an exception – surely, he would be allowed this small moment of weakness today of all days …wouldn't he?

Nevertheless, the tears didn't come and, if they had, he would have been looked at curiously, for grown men didn't wander the streets of Venice, among tourists and lovers, weeping.

He found himself passing under the tall pillar where the winged lion of Venice looked down upon the darkened city. Passing the cathedral, he saw a group of tourists waiting outside for their guide to lead them into the building. Into St Mark's Square he went; traces of water from that day's high tides sparkled in the lights from the cafés and bars. He was, at this point, only distantly aware of the things going on around him: music drifting towards him from the Café Florian, that most celebrated coffee shop in Venice: lively chatter of tourists with whom he brushed shoulders: the murmuring of lovers holding hands, breathing in the atmosphere of this most romantic of all cities.

All so incongruous when set against his own sense of irretrievable loss. Stopping to look around him, intending to sit outside one of his favourite bars to have a whisky and a cigarette, he noticed the girl. She was leaning against one of the pillars that supported the portico surrounding the square and looking towards him. She suddenly stumbled, one of her high-heeled shoes giving way under her. Down she went onto the damp flagstones, her black-patent handbag flying out of her hand, its contents scattering in all directions.

David stepped quickly forward towards her. He noticed his hands were shaking as he held them out to grasp hers. He helped her up and she dusted herself down, thinking herself lucky not to have sprained an ankle. The two of them picked up her lipstick and wallet and other things that were lying on the ground, then she looked at him in amazement.

"I… I can't imagine how I managed to do that," she said, "silly me! Thank you so much for helping me… I suppose I couldn't repay you by buying you a drink, could I?" Even in the half-light he could see that she was beautiful: dark brown hair, deep blue eyes. As he looked into them his stomach stopped churning and his hands no longer shook. "I'm not in the habit of picking up strange men, you know, but you've been so kind and it would be lovely to have someone to talk to."

He wouldn't, of course, be the best of companions on this particular night, but how could he not accept? It would be the first time in months that he had sat in the company of an attractive woman. So why not? It might perhaps, for a moment or two at least, distance him from his sorrow.

He didn't, couldn't, tell her how he was feeling, but Madeleine, looking at him closely as she sipped her wine, didn't need to be told that this was a troubled, unhappy man. Despite his easy conversation and amusing stories of life in Venice, sparkle and inner glow were absent! So there they sat together! David wearing his cloak of sadness and Madeleine trying to stifle the tears that, these days, seemed always about to fall!

"He's probably as lonely as I am," she thought, "but I'm not going down that route again. You had better keep your distance, my friend, however desirable you might be! He'll ask to see me again, of course, I've seen that look so many times, but I'm afraid it's just not going to be, in spite of losing my head and falling like that! How silly, how irrational that was!"

The square was gradually emptying of people, the lights going out in the bars and restaurants. Abruptly standing up, pulling her coat closer against the chilly air, she extended her hand towards him to say goodnight. It happened so quickly that he had to jump up to take it, almost knocking over his half-empty glass of wine.

Yes, here it came! As she had known it would!

"I don't even know your second name or where you are staying," he said. "I would like to see you again. Please say yes. I've so enjoyed talking to you."

"I'm sorry, David, but I can't. I'm leaving Venice the day after tomorrow and I have a lot to do before then. I just won't have time to see you again."

A lie, of course, but she couldn't allow him any closer. She didn't want to think of him looking for her in vain, searching the faces of people by the canals, on the bridges, in the piazzas. He was sad enough already! In truth, she should never have offered to buy him a drink in the first place, but it was only politeness to have done so, wasn't it? Anyway, she hadn't been able to help herself, had she? With that, she slipped quickly away into the darkness.

Their meeting had truly been, he thought, like two ships passing in the night and, quickly gulping down the rest of his wine, he dropped some notes onto the table in payment and went in the opposite direction.

However, fate or whatever you like to call it, had something else in store, for, looking across the enchanted lagoon at the lights of San Giorgio Maggiore, and seeing again in his imagination the girl's large blue eyes, he suddenly stopped. What if, instead of returning to his apartment, he had followed her? Probably a very foolish thing to do: the impetuous act of a love sick boy rather than that of a grown man! At that moment, he felt as if he were standing at some vast crossroad, rather than there in front of the Doges' Palace with tied-up gondolas bobbing in the water at his feet.

When you have spent the first years of your life believing yourself unlovable and worthless – "a complete waste of space" as his father had so eloquently put it – it's very difficult to enter the adult world thinking differently. Even now, forty-years later, there were odd moments when David had to remind himself that this was just not so. His professional life had been remarkably successful though, on a personal level, things had not gone quite so well. His marriage had ended badly, but there were other relationships that had fared reasonably well, both there and in England.

He always, however, liked to keep a certain distance between himself and his women friends; always careful to shy away from appearing too needy, too vulnerable, too dependent. It would be a great mistake if he were to allow that to happen.

So he felt a distinct sense of embarrassment that he had more or less begged Madeleine to let him see her again. Must be getting soft in the head! Nevertheless, a whole world of possibilities had suddenly been opened up to him by their chance meeting. There had been that indefinable something about her that he knew he would not easily forget.

He began to walk quickly in the direction she had taken, desperately trying to catch sight of her. He must not lose her, or the opportunity to know her better would have gone forever!

Unexpectedly, he heard laughter behind him and, turning his head, saw five or six fantastically masked figures, their costumes shimmering as they moved under the ornate street lights. Today, of course, was the first day of Mardi Gras. In his anguish, he'd completely forgotten about it. However, as the revellers came near, instead of passing by, they formed a circle around him, holding hands to make sure he couldn't escape and then began to jostle and push him.

"What the hell do you think you're doing?" he said, "Get out of my way!"

"Doing? What are we doing? Why, earning our living, of course – robbing the rich to give to the poor. The poor being us, I'm afraid!"

The biggest of them grabbed hold of his arm and began to whirl him around, faster and faster, until he tumbled to the ground, whereupon they fell upon him, punching and kicking. Soon they had relieved him of his expensive gold watch and his wallet, taking even the loose change from his coat pocket.

He bit into the flesh of his lips trying to will himself not to cry out in pain. *"What a racket! You stupid boy! To make such a fuss over nothing!"* No, he wouldn't show them that they were hurting him, that he was afraid, even though six against one was no fair contest. While he drifted in and out of consciousness, knowing that his arm was broken, they gradually grew tired of their sport. Then with a final kick in the kidneys, they skipped away, laughing, as though they had merely been playing a silly practical joke on him.

Rain began to fall and, with a supreme effort he dragged himself away from the water's edge, for he was in serious danger of falling in. However, by then, feeling nauseous and light-headed, all he wanted to do was to crawl into a quiet place and nurse his wounds like a beaten dog. Darkness soon overcame him and he seemed to be teetering at the entrance to a long tunnel, but there was no light at the end of it. When the darkness began to recede he felt fingers as soft as butterflies' wings exploring his face and a coat being placed over him. He could smell Madeleine's perfume and hear her voice 'phoning for help.

"Oh David, what have they done to you? This would never have happened if I had been walking by your side." She sat on the wet ground, his head in her lap, gently talking to him and holding his hand, until the water-ambulance arrived, slurping and slapping against one of the wooden piers that jutted out from the quayside. He then let himself drift into the comforting darkness, no longer afraid, knowing that she was there.

When he came round he saw the morning sun shining through the white, gauzy curtains in his room at the Ospedale dell'Angelo and a nurse taking his temperature. Then turning his head painfully to the side he saw Madeleine sitting with her eyes closed, her face ashen. Her hand was limply resting in his and, when he squeezed it, she stirred and looked at him, smiling wanly. He gazed at her thinking she was the most beautiful sight he had ever seen and he knew in that instant that he loved her.

"How on earth did you find me there last night?"

"Why, I came back looking for you, didn't I, David? I found I couldn't let you go – not what I planned, but that's how it is!

"But, why, Madeleine, why?"

"I know this sounds really silly, and I hope you'll understand. As soon as I set eyes on you in the piazza I had an overwhelming sense of recognition; I can't describe it in any other way. Knowing nothing about you, yet knowing you perfectly! Very melodramatic, I know, but absolutely true. I was so taken aback that I simply lost my balance and fell down. I've been afraid for such a long time, David; afraid of loneliness, afraid of rejection, which is why I came to live here in Venice. My husband had simply discovered that he didn't love me, or anyone else, I suspect! I like to think of myself as the eternal tourist surrounded by people, and beauty, who has no need to become involved in the life here, except on a very superficial level. I suppose I came to Venice to find myself as they say, but, of course, I didn't. I might as well have stayed in London. You take your problems with you wherever you go, don't you? I didn't realise that, of course, until I actually arrived here."

David could feel a lump gathering in his throat, making it impossible for him to speak, so he just looked at her in wonder, loving the sound of her voice and the feel of her small hand in his, recognising her vulnerability.

Madeleine gazed at him, watching the tears starting to trickle down his cheeks, seeing the troubled, unhappy spirit that she'd sensed was there as they'd sipped wine together in the piazza. She gripped his hand harder and laid her head on his chest.

"Whatever it is that troubles you, David, please, please, share it with me. Let it all out, let the tears fall!"

So he wept: a whole life-time of tears.

The Mariner's Tale

Deep in his heart Cramer was lost and grieving. He was also, at that moment, lost at sea, for his boat was spinning helplessly in the middle of a vortex. Within fifteen short minutes the sails had been torn to shreds, the engine had puttered and spluttered into silence and the radio had given up the ghost. It was as though some vengeful weather god had suddenly descended, deciding to punish him.

Thankfully, however – or perhaps for him, not so thankfully – the sea gradually calmed, the rain virtually stopped and the wind eased. He realised, nevertheless, that he would have to drift aimlessly through the darkness until dawn when someone would surely notice his predicament – he wasn't all that far from land – but even if they didn't find him it didn't really matter all that much, did it? He did have emergency warning lights on board, but he simply wasn't interested enough in living to bother using them.

Going below to the cabin, he shut the door firmly to keep out the cold night-air and took off his soaking clothes. Once changed, he lay down on his bunk trying to stop his thoughts straying inevitably to the one thing that consumed him. Concentrating hard, he forced his mind to wander through many different realms until his eyes began to grow heavy and he slipped away mercifully into sleep. For a few hours, he would perhaps escape the demon on his back, escape reliving that fatal second when a monumental, fleeting hesitation changed his life forever.

Reluctantly, however, he soon surfaced, shivering, from a dream where he had been trudging through the tundra of a freezing, icy land – where that had come from he'd no idea – not pleasant, but a damned sight better than the real world. He rose from his bunk intending to fetch a couple of extra blankets that he knew were stored in one of the bulkheads, but first he lit a kerosene lamp so that he could see what he was doing. As he did this, he was startled to hear a skittering, scratching sound on the door. It was a purposeful sound that he had never heard before; one that had no business being on his boat. A rat, a cat, a mouse, some little stowaway? No, the sound was too decisive, one that demanded attention …then footsteps moved away.

Hesitantly opening the door, Cramer, totally astonished, saw by the light of the moon, a woman leaning against the railings of the boat – a big, solid woman with a great swathe of unruly hair.

What the hell was all this about?

As she neared him he felt dwarf-like and, when she spoke, her voice was deep and unfeminine, with a distinct Welsh lilt to it.

"Well, Mr Cramer, what a little pickle you seem to be in! Want to give it all up, do you? Want to die, do you? …What a quitter you are! You should be ashamed of yourself!"

"How, in God's name did you get here? Who are you? What do you want? And who are you to question my feelings? You know nothing about me, nothing about how I feel …nothing about what I did!"

"I know everything about you, Mr Cramer, don't you worry on that score! There's nothing that you can tell me that I don't already know and I object to people who just give up! So I'm afraid I decided that I just had to pay you a little visit in person!"

"What do you mean in person?"

"Because, Mr Cramer, I've been with you from the moment you were born; it's just that we've never actually come face to face."

At this point Cramer felt totally confused – was he perhaps still asleep and this huge woman a mere figment of his dreams? He was so desperately cold that he just wanted to go back into the cabin to wrap himself in the blankets; to stop himself thinking that he had really lost his mind.

The woman, dark-featured and masculine-looking, towered over him and gently pushed him backwards into the cabin.

He looked at her in amazement – this really couldn't be happening – he stared into her liquid-brown eyes topped by heavy, black brows, at her thin lips with just the merest suggestion of a moustache above them and at her eagle-like nose.

"For God's sake just tell me who you are and how

you got here."

"Why, Mr Cramer, I'd have thought you would have guessed by now. Who else could I possibly be but your guardian angel, of course? And as to how I arrived here – well, very easily …it's what guardian angels do, isn't it? Go anywhere, anytime, anyhow, in order to keep a firm eye on our wards!"

Cramer sat down at the table feeling weak at the knees – it was obviously going to be one of those nights – and the woman plonked herself heavily down on a stool opposite him.

They looked into each other's eyes.

Cramer felt the desperate need for a stiff scotch, but for some unaccountable reason he knew it wasn't a good idea; the woman would disapprove of such a totally foolish thought entering his head.

"I'm really surprised at you, Mr Cramer, surprised and disappointed. I would have expected a little more backbone from you …yes, indeed, I would."

This was the most ridiculous thing he'd ever heard in his life – as if he hadn't enough to agonise over without worrying about going mad, imagining he was sitting in his boat, talking to his guardian angel! However, perhaps madness was his allotted punishment for what he'd done and a punishment he certainly deserved. No, that was wrong – not for what he'd done, but for what he'd failed to do! His great sin was of omission.

"If you are my guardian angel why do you always call me Mr Cramer? After such a long and, apparently, close relationship I would have thought that Michael would have been more appropriate!" My God, he thought, I've really lost it now!

"Yes, when you were a boy of course, I would always have called you Michael, but not now – certainly not! Just as I wouldn't expect you to call me Gwyneth. No, you are Mr Cramer and Mr Cramer you will remain, just as I will remain Mrs Jenkins if you don't mind, from Pontypridd!"

Well, well, fancy learning at this late stage that he had actually been sharing the last thirty-years of his life with Mrs Gwyneth Jenkins, a large lady from Pontypridd!

"What you have to do, Mr Cramer, is to give up this self-indulgent grief. You can't change what happened."

"And what you have to do, Mrs Jenkins, is to realise that I loved Laura and I as good as killed her. There's always a way to stop yourself from sneezing if you really want to, but I didn't, did I? So she died! Such a totally ludicrous thing to happen!"

His mind replayed the scene a hundred times a day. Laura and he on the station platform at Rickmansworth, waiting for the train to Fenchurch Street, going up to town to choose her engagement ring: afternoon tea at the Savoy and a west-end show in the evening. In the end, however, they did none of those things because she was dead. He could see her now, so excited, standing in front of him, with her back to the railway line, so near to the edge of the platform, playfully goading him, teasing him and slightly annoying him, were he to tell the truth.

He closed his eyes and again, in his mind, could see her stumble, fall back onto the rails to disappear under the train's deadly wheels. He could still hear the screams of horror and disbelief from those standing near them. He should have foreseen the danger, moved her out of harm's way, taken better care of her; he hadn't, though, had he?

A hundred times a day he relived the moment when her arm, as though in slow motion, came out towards him so that he could put out his hand to save her – but he didn't. What he did, instead, was to give an almighty sneeze that wouldn't be denied. The moment was gone and so was she.

It had been one of life's cruellest jokes, one that made you want to weep – certainly a joke with no humour in it – for his life had ended at that instant. Two lives ended because of a sneeze! In his imagination he could picture a different scenario where he plainly saw his hand going towards her, catching hold of her wrist, saving her life. The image, the snapshot of his hand on her wrist covering her pretty gold watch was isolated from everything else: a close-up shot that the camera didn't take.

"So you see, Mrs Jenkins, why I'm grieving, why I'm tired of living. I just don't want to be here without her! Guilt is a killer, just as loneliness is a killer – can't you understand?"

The large woman's face darkened. "Oh, I understand more than you can possibly imagine. You can't truly believe that you have an exclusive on guilt and loneliness, can you? Grief doesn't wander around carefully picking out its subjects. It's not some exclusive club to which only a few are allowed in."

"So I just have to accept what's happened and get on with things!"

"Exactly, Mr Cramer, exactly! What you need to do is to find a safe haven, both for your life and for your boat and remember, I shall be watching your every move, so please, don't let us need to have any more of these face to face meetings. Now I think you should just lie down on that bunk of yours and get a few hours' sleep until daylight comes."

As tiredness overcame him Cramer could feel a headache coming on, and no wonder! Reluctantly, he allowed her to tuck the two blankets around him so that, as he drifted off to sleep, the last thing he saw was her large, man-like face looming over him. Somewhere in the distance he seemed to hear the comforting sound of the engine as though some phantom had managed to start it up again. As the woman opened the door to step onto the deck, she looked back at him and whispered, "Goodnight, Michael, God bless and sweet dreams!"

It was a glorious sunrise, full of hope and the promise of good things to come; the sun cast a path of brilliance along the surface of the water. Fluffy, new-morning clouds stood out against an orange background; the sort of day on which one was grateful for the miracle of life! Cramer's boat had rounded the whale-shaped headland and now, with its engine again turned off, it was bobbing on the water. The beach of a beautiful cove could be seen from the deck. At one end lay colourful, little boats, turned upside down on the sand, waiting for someone to claim them. The woman sat on the rough, stone wall watching the scene, while behind her could be heard the sound of approaching voices.

"It's Cramer, he's back! About time too! Get the dinghy, Phil, and we'll go and have a few bevies on board with him before breakfast. He'll have plenty in stock, if I know anything about him!"

Pushing the dinghy onto the water, the two men made their way towards their destination. However, neither of them, boarded the boat then, or ever after. There was no need, for they could quite plainly see his body, a noose around his neck, swinging from one of the masts! They were never to understand why he chose such a dramatic death – so much easier just to have slipped into the water, allowing himself to drown. Was there, perhaps, someone he had wanted to impress with the desperation of how he was feeling?

The woman, now standing on the sand, shivered, her frizzy hair billowing wildly in the breeze, tears streaming down her cheeks.

"You poor, silly boy! Why didn't you listen to me, Michael – wasn't I persuasive enough, couldn't you tell how much I've loved you all these years? I obviously didn't guard you well enough, did I? Did I push you too far last night? Should I perhaps have stayed away? Is this my fault…? How do you think it makes me feel,

Mr Cramer?"

Later, when the police arrived they noticed, in the distance, a rather eccentric-looking, large woman gazing out to sea, but what they didn't realise, of course, was that they were also looking at one of the saddest creatures in the whole of God's creation – a guardian angel who had failed in her duty and now had no one to guard.

The Nothing Room

Miss Preston was winding down like a clock that needed a new battery, but in her case it just wouldn't be worth the effort to replace it, for she was slowly but surely dying – not from some fatal illness, but because her reason for living had been summarily taken away from her. She had been stepped upon like some unwanted piece of dirt, thrown out with the rubbish, cast aside as though she'd never been of any consequence to anyone.

She knew it was the autumn of her life, just as it was autumn outside – she was withering away like the dried-up leaves of the trees and very soon she would fall to the ground just as they were doing.

The slowing clock, the dying leaves – one could go on ad infinitum with metaphors describing her condition, but the one that she found most apposite was that of the fading photograph and now here she was, holding in her hands this pristine, perfect photo, newly-revealed to her when she had unwrapped it from its red, shiny gift-paper.

Of course, the photo would have to go. It was very kind of them to have given it to her, but she wouldn't be able to live with it. In fact, she couldn't live with any photo for they always faded, sooner or later. It was like watching someone die, withdrawing from life. Even if you placed a photo in the shadows it still faded, still disappeared, and still died as she was doing. So there were no photos in her house, no albums and, therefore, no memories. Neither were there any books, for she didn't want to remember who had given them to her, what they contained or how she had acquired them. There were no CDs or an iPod, for to play music would be like putting a knife into her – there were far, far too many memories associated with music.

She spent her days in this nothing room – no decorations, no furniture except for her chair with its stuffing gradually falling around her feet. There were no curtains, no light bulbs; she had even scraped the floral patterned paper off the walls. There was only she, with her blank mind that she tried to keep as empty as the room.

Oh yes, Miss Preston was peculiar all right. She knew that as well as everyone else did, but that was what she had become, against her will, of course, because no one chooses to become eccentric or – yes, let's be honest about it – mentally unstable. That was what bitterness had done to her: brought her to the edge of madness!

Really, she should be in a home somewhere; she wasn't so far gone as not to realise that – a place where she would be given medication and looked after. She would not, of course, ever allow that to happen. What she really wanted was to be a nothingness, even more so than she was at this moment. In fact, not to be there at all and, sometimes, she felt so nebulous, so anonymous it was as though she had already disappeared: that her wish had been granted.

Her first thought on waking each day was how much she hated life. Killing herself, of course, was always an option, a very powerful option, but who was to know if the next world might not be even worse than this one? She had always been unsure about the existence of God, despite morning assemblies, but what if he did exist and proved to be a vengeful God? What unbelievably dreadful punishment might he not mete out to someone who had taken her own life? No, far better to stick with what she had. Better the devil you know, as they always say!

She studied the photo they'd just presented to her, a framed memory that they wanted her to keep forever: all the girls and all the staff. There she was, seated primly in the centre of the front row, for where else would the headmistress sit but in the prime position? So many people around her, not just in the photo, but in every facet of her life. Miss Preston had been the centre of the school's universe, the pivot around which everything revolved.

As she looked at the photo the memories came back unbidden, unwanted. Behind the smiling, white-bloused girls seated in rows on the lawn stood the beautiful school building with its long windows. The great, ornate, white veranda extended the whole length of the second floor of what must originally have been a private house. She examined closely the barred windows of the top floor where the servants would have slept, rather like the prison where she now found herself! Just visible at the edge of the serried ranks of girls stood the leaf-laden gingko tree, described by botanists as a living fossil, a descendent of those that had flourished on earth two-hundred-and-seventy-million years ago. Yes, a living fossil – yet another perfect metaphor for her own dried-up bones, for her own useless spinster's body.

Behind the photographer had stood the huge conifer, which had acted as a background for the singing choir, for wonderful performances *of Comus, Twelfth Night* and a myriad of other productions. It was not these memories, however, nor the familiar loved faces that she saw in front of her eyes that caused her stomach to churn. What the photo failed to show, of course, was the man who had been standing at the long window of her study looking out at the scene – Paul, her lover – but no, no more of that; she couldn't let her thoughts go down that path …enough is enough. She'd take the photo out of its frame right now and burn it – there was just too much pain there to be endured.

On went her black, shabby coat, her old slippers now replaced by scuffed, ancient shoes, her untidy, grey hair protected by a brown, woollen hat – but there's no need for me to go on, for you can easily imagine how she looked – after all, you've all seen pictures of bag ladies, haven't you? Into her coat pocket she slipped the now-crumpled photo, a box of matches and, of course, the key – she mustn't forget the key – especially the key!

She made her way along the river bank, the waters swollen by recent rain, while her feet squelched over the sodden, yellow and brown leaves that carpeted the path. The grey, threatening sky watched her as she shuffled onto the wet grass to avoid a deep puddle that had formed in front of her. The half-bare trees, looking down upon her, saw her eyes staring at the ground, for she very, very rarely came this way and certainly didn't want to glimpse her destination before she absolutely had to do so. She thought, nevertheless, that it was the best place to dispose of the photo and of its memories – a fitting ceremony to end finally what had gone before.

Here she was at the back entrance to the school that would lead her directly into what had once been the glorious garden.

She had, of course, no business to have the key, but felt totally entitled to it and who would bother about it anyway, if they knew?

So once more she stood in this deeply-loved spot, the amazing gingko almost bare of its leaves, the grass, once so carefully tended, now encroaching upon the path that had surrounded the lawn, the path around which generations of girls had walked and talked during their break-times.

Standing under the gingko tree, she took the photo from her pocket and set a match to it, holding it up high, ceremoniously, as in some ancient rite, while the charred fragments of memory wafted away into the damp air. Then, finally, through a window carelessly left unlocked, into the building itself for one last, lingering look around! Up the stairs passing her study she went, the smell of damp and decay filled her nostrils! As she peeped into the classrooms she glimpsed one or two desks remaining, albeit on their sides, and forgotten piles of books, maps and charts on the walls to prove that this had indeed once been a living, breathing school.

Miss Preston had been put out to grass, of course. Neither she nor the school was needed. No, what had been wanted was a nice, new comprehensive where everyone could be made to feel equal. There was no place for a small grammar school where academic excellence had been one of the main goals and where girls had been encouraged and happy. That had been three years ago, when at only fifty-nine years old, she'd been deemed fit only for the scrap heap. She had a good pension, of course, but that wasn't the point, was it?

Things could have been so completely different if there had been someone to love, a loving man to soften the blow …and Paul …yes, she would allow her thoughts to focus upon him now, just for a moment or two. Well, he'd grown tired of her eventually, hadn't he? They all had, but he'd been the one; the one that she would never forget and would never ever forgive, however long this living hell of a life might last!

There obviously must have been something very unlovable about her, for after the first flush of lust they all had left her, not just Paul, but all of them!

She went over to one of the tall windows that led

onto the veranda, unbolted it and stepped outside. There she looked down, upon the winding course of the narrow, burbling river that ran along the back of the school, upon the partially-flooded cricket field with its dainty, frilly border of almost leafless willow trees and over the rolling emerald green hills that stretched for miles into the distance.

It was here, on this spot, where she and Paul had kissed and loved in the summer evenings. How surprised the girls and their parents would have been if they had ever learned of such goings-on! Leaning her elbows on the railing she again considered how easy it would be simply to jump over and finish everything once and for all. However, even with her befuddled brain, she knew that it was not the solution.

All at once, she realised that she was not alone, for at her side she heard an insistent, sublime warbling as a rain-bedraggled robin hopped towards her and trustingly landed on her arm. He wants to be my friend she thought …and then she looked into his eyes and recognised him. Without any doubt she knew who it was …in spite of his silly, silly disguise.

"Paul …you naughty boy! Where have you been all this time? Why did you go away like that? It wasn't a very kind thing to do, was it? And why on earth are you dressed in that ridiculous costume?"

The robin continued to stare at her and to talk, but she just didn't understand anything of what he was saying. "I think you should come home with me," she said quietly.

With that she slid her scarf gently from around her neck, carefully dropping it over the startled robin. He wouldn't escape from her a second time.

Past the river, past the muddy, rain-soaked fields, past the ancient vineyards she went, holding triumphantly onto her little trophy – finally she had him firmly within her grasp.

Thus, at long last, Miss Preston brought Paul home. In he went to live in the cardboard box that usually housed her best shoes, whose tenancy now and forevermore would be relinquished!

Into the lid of the box, firmly taped down, she pierced a little hole through which, once a day, if she were very careful, she could just about push a medium size crumb of bread or even, on a good day when he'd behaved himself, a crumb of cake. He had, after all, been verging rather on the plump side and definitely needed to be put on a very strict diet. Nothing to drink, of course…there wouldn't be anything of that sort! Oh no, she certainly wouldn't encourage his drinking habit! She had always thought that he had drunk just a little too much for his own good.

It was strange to see the shoebox sitting there within all the nothingness – it almost made the room look cluttered. She then decided that she would not to speak to him – a dose of sulking on her part would serve him right, a dose of his own medicine. Now she thought about it, he'd always been rather moody and prone to dramatic silences. In fact, the more she thought about it, the more she wondered what she'd seen in him in the first place. Irritably she gave the box a good kick so that it hit the wall.

"I've decided to ignore you completely, Paul – after what you did to me! There will be no talking, no food, no water – nothing, absolutely nothing! Just consider yourself fortunate, in your snug little box, to have a roof over your head. It's more than most people in this world have!" She could hear the fluttering of delicate wings against the inside of the small box and a sweet chirruping that gradually grew fainter, but before long, those annoying little sounds stopped completely and she knew that she had him absolutely in her power.

He would share her nothing-room with her until the men in their white coats came to take her away, or until she eventually passed from this life to whatever lay ahead.

The Owl Woman

The chair stood waiting expectantly in the corner of the room. One of its exquisitely carved and curved legs, suddenly lifted and wound itself around the knob of the bottom drawer of the bureau, gracefully opening it. Thin, filmy threads of every colour, silken gossamer lent to her by spiderlings, filaments of gold and silver: they all tumbled from the interior and began to squirm slowly along the floor towards the Owl Woman.

The artist snapped her long fingers and, immediately, the threads, the gossamer and the filaments curled their way up the spindly legs of the table at which she was sitting. They coiled up comfortably and placed themselves on her palette where they turned to liquid. What joy it was for her to have had this flash of inspiration come so suddenly into her mind – she knew instinctively that she had the talent to do it justice.

There she sat, awaiting the darkness of night so that the alchemy could begin. Two more essential ingredients were needed: the star light that would glow through the round window in the back wall and pour its magic dust on to her palette of colours and the moonlight, which would cast its beams through two small arches high up in the walls of the stone room and would shine directly down upon the paper set before her. Her distillery, her retorts, her glass tubes were all standing by to aid her in the miracle that was to come.

The heart of the Owl Woman vibrated and trembled like the strings of a violin as if her paintbrush were connected in some way to her soul, to her innermost being. She hooted, stroking her tawny, feathery costume, sewn with her own hands, and blinking her dark, sharp eyes through the mask covering her face. Why she had created such a sound and such an appearance for herself she had no idea, but this was how she had to be.

Meanwhile, the Owl Woman's strange cat slunk slowly from his place in the corner and looked at her tentatively. His large, yellow eyes, furrowed brow and thick, red, furry body looked unreal as though from some fable – in other words he fitted the scene perfectly. He gazed at the Owl Woman and, in his feline way, was aware of the excitement and trepidation that she felt as the room darkened. The stars were coming out and, all at once, the cold moon appeared through a veil of cloud. The time had come.

With her hand trembling slightly, the brush started to move; in her imagination she saw exactly what she had to paint, the colours she had to use and the name she had to attach to each creation. With a triangular shaped prism in her other hand, she directed the moon beams on to the paper. It seemed only right that her first masterpiece should be a semblance of herself – thus, tawny feathers, in all their intricate colours, began to appear on the paper.

Then, as her imagination took flight, she added more details: talons, wings, a beak and, by the time the short tail had been painted, the owl was straining to leave the paper and glide out through the arched windows into the moonlight. It was hungry and needed to flit through the trees in search of food.

In this same fashion, the night progressed and the cat was beside himself with excitement, for neither he nor the world had ever seen such things before: hovering Hummingbird, fork-tailed Swallow, a high-soaring Skylark and a taper-winged Nightjar, a sweet-voiced Nightingale and so on.

The Owl Woman's ingenuity was endless. Eventually, her hand beginning to ache, she paused and sat back to enjoy one of her more flamboyant creations who she named Toucan. When she had finally painted in the last of its flight feathers, it pulled away from the paper and started its long journey towards the lush, tropical forests of ferns, palms and waterfalls that would be its home.

One of her favourite paintings had been Robin to whom she had given a red breast and a red tail; she would always think of it as special because unlike the other 'birds' – for that was the word that had come into her mind while bringing these creatures into being – it had not torn the paper in its haste to fly away.

In fact, she had had trouble trying to make it leave, for it insisted on singing to her and trying to capture her attention.

It was at this point that she was most contented with her work, for now she knew that the skies and the forests of the earth would no longer be empty of sweet sounds and graceful movement, everywhere would have an added beauty.

By this time the red cat was feeling somewhat frustrated, his whiskers twitching irritably so the Owl Woman told him to sit quietly or he would be put outside. Nevertheless, the spectacle had such an appeal for him that, finally, he could endure no more of the constant comings and goings of those winged creatures that seemed to taunt him. He would like to catch one, he thought, play with one: perhaps even eat it!

Unfortunately, it was Robin's destiny to be the first-ever victim of an encounter between bird and cat: easy prey. The Owl Woman, by now, was beginning to feel tired, so the cat paid dearly for his mischief and was shooed outside. Cross and upset, she had no other solution but to redo her painting of Robin and hope it turned out as successfully as the first one. For some reason known only to her, she decided, this time, not to paint its tail red.

Thereafter, the Owl Woman seemed to lose some of her artistry and spontaneity for, gradually, everything she painted became less attractive, more threatening and certainly much larger: scavenger Eagle, scavenger Vulture, scavenger Condor… Her imagination had darkened and she was now no longer enjoying the task which, for so many hours, had given her such pleasure.

The Owl Woman would have felt even more

disgruntled if she had known of the little drama being enacted outside, for no sooner had she slammed the door on the red cat, than the flapping of large wings and a menacing, hissing sound could be heard overhead. The red cat was about to breathe his last breath as Condor descended and swept him into the star-studded night air, before disposing of him in a dark, silent place. This modest meal would help Condor through the long hours needed to cross great expanses of sea, desert and jungle, until it reached its destination high in the mountains far, far away.

As dawn approached, the starlight and the moonlight gradually disappeared, bringing the creation of the birds to an end, but there was just one more scene to be played out. Owl Woman was, by this time, fast asleep at her table, her head resting on her arms: so deeply asleep that she failed to hear Owl, whom she had painted with such care, enter the room through the small, round window at the back. He glided silently onto the table, looked at her deeply, considered her existence and thought it unnecessary. There was something not quite right about her: her feathers were wrong, her face far from perfect, her smell out of place and her size out of proportion.

Owl went for her eyes first and, in a split-second, the sockets were empty and useless. As the blood poured down her face, Owl gave a hoot of triumph and tugged mercilessly at her hair. In agony she stood up, knocking her chair over, and blindly careered into her scientific instruments, smashing the glass to smithereens. She fell to the floor with Owl still intent on his attack. Sightless, she fumbled around for a shard of glass with which to protect herself. However, Owl felt he had achieved his aim and, hooting loudly, flew out into the orange sky of daybreak as his creator lay dying.

With the spell now broken, the threads, the gossamer and the gold and silver filaments that still remained had lost their liquid form and were now winding their way in and out of the blood and glass. Finally, they climbed up into the safety of the bottom drawer of the bureau from which they had come. The chair leg, once again, curled around the knob and, this time, closed it.

The Picnic

That was the day that Clarissa's mother threw herself off the roof, breaking her spine and crushing her skull on the hard, unforgiving stone slabs of the terrace: in other words, the day of the picnic.

The fatally momentous tragedy, however, was not destined until the evening, and so, in the meantime, Clarissa sat on the edge of the ornamental fish pond, leaning back, letting her fingers dabble on the surface of the murky water. Poor fish not to have a cleaner home, she thought!

In her coat pocket nestled the beautiful perfume bottle that she had stolen but ten minutes ago from her mother's dressing table. Naughty little thief that she was! Nothing innocent, nothing childlike about what she had done. She had wanted it and, therefore, she had taken it. She was after all her mother's daughter! It was such a pretty, pretty bottle, gold and turquoise – totally irresistible is how she would have described it if she'd known the word.

It was a chilly, autumnal afternoon with the smell of burning bonfires in the air. The only sound to be heard from beyond the garden's high walls was that of carriage wheels and horses' hooves moving at a sedate pace through the tree-lined streets of St John's Wood. It was strange weather for a picnic on the lawn, despite the fact that the sun was trying its hardest to push its way through the clouds, but this is what her mother wanted and so this is what must happen. The large chestnut tree, under which they were all sitting, every so often shed its brown leaves upon them, making untidy the straight lines of cutlery, the precisely placed china and the plates of sandwiches and cakes that all lay in their fixed places upon the snow-white table cloth.

Her mother sat looking at Clarissa, thinking what a plain, sulky-looking little girl she was. There was no joy in her at all; so serious, so fidgety. Here they all were having such fun and still she couldn't raise a smile! Admittedly it wasn't very warm, but they were all well wrapped up, with the ends of their shawls tied round their waists to keep the heat in. Lovely, thick cushions placed on the ground to sit upon! Fur rugs, tartan rugs in which to snuggle! What more could you want? "Smile, Clarissa, smile, for goodness sake! Why don't you come and sit on the cushion here and tell Freddie all about your trip to the zoo! You enjoyed that! I know you did!" Clarissa shook her head silently and sat looking at her mother thinking that she didn't like her one little bit, knowing perfectly well that her mother, in turn, found her unsatisfactory.

Her mother looked at Freddie and thought what an amusing young man he was, as he sprawled on the ground by her side, one arm resting on the edge of the tablecloth, the other holding out his cup and saucer for more tea. In fact, all the young men there were amusing, looking absolutely splendid and awfully handsome in their exclusive cricket-club jackets with their jaunty black, red and gold club caps on their heads.

Her women friends loved these little picnics, loved being able to meet these eligible young men, loved flirting with them. It was all like some pastoral idyll! As she was the only married woman among them, apart from the chaperone, she supposed that she too was in some way responsible for their moral welfare. However, this duty didn't weigh too heavily over her, because, after all, what was wrong with a little harmless fun? Especially in her own case; James was so stuffy, Freddie so available and she so willing!

Clarissa unexpectedly saw the pale, bespectacled face of her father, James, glance down upon them from his study window, a momentary pause from his absorbing obsession with all things Japanese – the history, the language, the art – his desk always covered in manuscripts written in that strange writing! Much older than her mother, she sometimes thought that he looked as withered as the leaves that were falling from the tree, indeed, as ancient as some of his manuscripts. She just hoped that he hadn't witnessed her mother's behaviour, her girlish giggles, the heightened colour of her cheeks – for it was obvious even to a ten-year-old that something unseemly and unacceptable was going on.

The conversation was, at that moment, mostly about Mr Gilbert and Mr Sullivan's comic opera 'Patience', which they had been to see the previous evening. What fun it had been and how amazing the new Savoy Theatre was: totally lit by electricity! Who would ever have imagined such a thing? So much more pleasant, they had all thought, than having to sit there breathing in the fumes from the gas mantles!

Clarissa would love to have seen the opera and the theatre, but neither her mother nor her governess would dream of letting her go!

It had passed through her mind that, perhaps, her mother just didn't want a spy in the camp who might drop a wrong word in front of her father! After all, heaven alone knew what pranks she got up to when she was away from the house, especially in the darkness of the stalls! Her mother needn't have worried, however, because James, wrapped in his cloak of aloofness, was the last person in the world in whom Clarissa would ever have confided anything!

The fact was that he very rarely spoke to her!

Watching her mother purposely arrange her skirts so that a finely-shaped ankle was there for all to see, Clarissa stood up and, hoping that she was unnoticed by anyone, went towards the tree. She desperately needed comforting, so she slowly slid her hand up the rough trunk until she found the hole that she knew was there. Taking off her glove, she was able with her bare fingers to explore her little treasure trove, her hoard of stolen goodies: her grandmother's gold watch (the poor scullery maid had been accused and dismissed for this crime), her governess's silver locket, a pearl necklace that she'd lifted from the jewel box of a weekend visitor and the two glittering rings that were her favourites, one of sapphire and one of emerald, both acquired simply by removing them from a confused octogenarian's hand! For the moment, however, she would keep the perfume bottle reassuringly in her pocket until the novelty of ownership had worn off.

She looked back and saw her mother's eyes staring into Freddie's, a wealth of meaning passing between them – but she wasn't old enough to recognise it for what it was! "What a waste, Barbara, what a waste! James doesn't even love you!"

"I know, Freddie, I know!"

Later on, in the dying light of the day, Clarissa was sitting once more by the fish pond, once more letting her fingers trail backwards and forwards through the water. Her breath was now misty in the cold air and she was glad to be alone, to have the garden to herself again. Even gladder that only the servants were there to hear what she was hearing: voices raised in fury, ugly words spoiling the beauty of the evening. She half-wanted to put her hands over her ears so that she might shut out the sound, but there was a strange fascination about the exchange that compelled her to continue listening.

All of a sudden she heard her mother scream, while windows were flung wide and doors were opened, then slammed shut again. She became aware that two or three of the maids were now standing in the garden looking up towards the noise, shivering, their teeth chattering.

By this time the cold moon had joined them as witness to the scene and was watching the gas lights within the house gleam and glitter. Suddenly there was movement on the crenelated roof terrace where Clarissa always went whenever she wanted to be alone. The furious argument was growing louder and louder until, suddenly, she heard her father call out, "Fly, Barbara, fly! You know you want to!"

Whether of her own volition or not, Clarissa's mother did just that. Holding out her arms like wings, she hurtled downwards towards the cold stone. The maids, as still as statues, were rooted to the spot in horror, their hands covering their mouths.

Clarissa, however, white-faced and dry-eyed, made her way composedly over to the chestnut tree and slowly, carefully retrieved her little magpie collection of gold, silver and jewels from its hiding place. She walked over to her mother and, sliding in the blood, sank down onto her knees, trembling, and began to cry. She then meticulously started to decorate the body with her treasures, gently placing the rings on her mother's fingers, the watch around her wrist, the locket and the pearls on her breast. The perfume bottle she laid upon her open hand. The maids, by this time weeping hysterically, came and put their arms around Clarissa, kneeling with her on the ground.

Abruptly, with a terrifying message, their lamentations were silenced by the report of a single gunshot that came from somewhere inside the house.

So there knelt the unfortunate Clarissa, now a poor little orphan, a poor, sulky, thieving, little orphan, her mother's body displaying her crime for all the world to see! Who would want to look after her? Who could possibly want to care for her? Not her grandparents, that's for sure – too much of a social whirl going on there to bother with such an unlikeable child. Of course, the consolation for anyone taking on the task was that she was now a very rich little girl but, nevertheless, there would be no queue forming!

That damned sea, why didn't it ever stop; why must it always be so busy? In and out, in and out, sloshing, slurping, rushing over the pebbles, making the sand all wet and gooey, always littering up the beach with that ugly, smelly, lumpy seaweed!

Why did it annoy her so much? Because it was imperfection, that's why! It detracted, she thought, from her beauty. Here she was, so perfect in her gorgeous, blue gown, the white veil that hung from her hat wafting in the sea breeze, her blue parasol protecting her lovely face from the sun's harsh rays. Why on earth had Freddie decided to ask the coachman to place the picnic table in this particular spot in full view of everyone? It was such a pretty beach with so many private nooks and crannies.

Nevertheless, she would not complain: she would continue to smile and laugh as though she were enjoying herself – which she wasn't! How could she, not with the hem of her skirts covered in wet sand and her shoes smelling of the sea? However, there were not many things that Clarissa did enjoy. Except, of course, taking things that didn't belong to her, though this had undergone a definite sea-change in the last few years. She had long passed the stage of coveting baubles and trinkets – after all she had as much material wealth as any woman could possibly desire. No, her fun was now of an altogether different kind. So much more entertaining! So much more of a challenge!

Other women's husbands, lovers, admirers; they were her quarry now, they were what she most liked to steal …and what a huntress, what a thief she had proved to be! She hadn't, of course, actually wanted any of them – all the pleasure was in the pursuit, knowing that she had acquired someone who was forbidden to her. Such as Freddie, for example: still possessing the charm that her mother had so enjoyed, but with his hair now flecked with grey, laughter-lines clearly etched on his face.

She had temporarily stolen him for the day from Agnes, that fussy, frilly little wife of his with her carefully cultivated, annoying lisp. Poor Agnes, she had simply no idea that the faithful Freddie was sitting on the edge of a beach somewhere on the south coast whispering sweet nothings into another woman's ears, letting his fingers wander rather too intimately around the top of her lace gown. That, of course, was one of the drawbacks of Clarissa's game; it was so clandestine that no one would ever learn of her triumphs. She had, after all, her reputation to consider! Still, it was all carefully recorded in her diary – every enjoyable, naughty moment!

The champagne had been freely imbibed, the savoury delicacies for the most part consumed, while the coachman sat at a discreet distance always ready to replenish the supply. Gently, Clarissa squeezed Freddie's hand, looking at him wistfully. "What a waste, Freddie, what a waste! Agnes doesn't even love you!"

"I know, Clarissa, I know!"

Her low, husky voice promised him a whole world of delights that would never be completely fulfilled – always leave them wanting more, she thought, that way you always had the advantage. She did just occasionally give in, but Freddie, unfortunately for him, would never be one of the privileged few: too old on one hand, too childish on the other.

Much later that evening, as the sun went down, they walked together hand-in-hand along the cliff top. It was a moonless, starless night and they would have to be careful where they stepped, but there was such a sense of freedom as they looked down upon the sea that, at that moment, the world seemed to promise Clarissa limitless possibilities. She felt there was nothing that she could not achieve.

Sadly, she was not allowed much time to enjoy this unusual feeling of elation. Freddie had stopped to bend down to remove a pebble from his shoe, letting Clarissa go on in front, when she suddenly heard him yell a warning as, behind her, the voice of Agnes lisped through the darkness.

"Once a thief, always a thief – isn't that right, Clarissa?"

So almost before she grasped what was happening, Clarissa was propelled into the abyss, her arms extended like angels' wings, the wind on her face, and the sound of the approaching waves beneath her. A sharp pain went through her as her head struck the side of the cliff and she could picture quite clearly, as in slow motion, her life's blood being blown around in the sea breezes as she descended. Then, for some inexplicable reason, she saw her mother's face appear before her in a mist, but it was too late for regrets …time had revved up a few notches and the boulders below were ready and eager to receive her.

The Potato Peeler

We all have our own particular dreams – love, wealth or fame – the usual things! Few of us, luckily, want what Mabel wanted: to be a first class, top-notch, serial killer seeing her name up there in lights with the greatest of them. Mabel Canute, an ordinary little woman with an extraordinary ambition. She could see it all now in her mind's eye – Mabel Canute, Lizzie Borden, Dennis Nilsen, Peter Sutcliffe and Fred West! How the names tripped off the tongue, but the greatest of them all would undoubtedly be Mabel Canute.

However, she supposed that the fact that no one so far had cottoned on to what she had been doing must prove that she hadn't actually been a total failure. Although, of course, it's only human nature to want some recognition of how clever, how skilful one has been, because that's what it's all about really, isn't it? Approval …which would, of course, have defeated the purpose because she'd be in jail, wouldn't she? So a lot of good that would have done her!

Oh, God! All right, then! I'll be with you in a minute! Shut up, you old crone!

She really should go and feed mother, she thought. What a pain in the whatsit the old biddy was. All those slops she had to spoon into that greedy, ever-open mouth. She always felt like a bird shoving worms down its chick's throat. *You watch it, mother, that you're not the next on my list of victims!*

Murders these days tend, on the whole, to be sophisticated, low-key affairs, excluding, naturally, all the wicked wholesale massacres that seem to be so much in vogue at the moment …and she disapproved of those most strongly. She thought, in her wondrously inventive little mind, that what she really wanted to create was a good old-fashioned blood-bath, swinging the hatchet …rather in the style of Lizzie Borden.

It was not given to everyone to think the way she did, of course, so she supposed that she was very fortunate that she didn't have to lie in bed at night planning the perfect murder, choosing the perfect victim.

With her, all acts were on the spur of the moment, spontaneous – inspired you might even say!

Naturally, she never knew when that moment was going to come, so it added an element of wonder to the whole enterprise.

Also, it was so much more fun that way – the thrill of the unexpected.

There was absolutely no malice in what she did, because she sincerely tried to like everyone and to show Christian charity where it was humanly possible.

If she were not mistaken, it was two months ago that she had murdered her sister – yes, that's right – in fact, almost two months to the day! Her mother, of course, hadn't even realised that one of her daughters was no longer there. As for other people, well, folk in general are pretty gullible and will believe anything you choose tell them, if you're convincing enough.

The house that they all lived in was a pre-war semi and nothing whatsoever had been done to tart it up to whatever former glory it may have had. If Mabel had been in charge of the finances changes would certainly have been made – particularly to the kitchen, which always made Mabel feel like a Victorian scullery maid. Mabel's sister never did any housework, logic dictating that as she was the one going out to work, why should she be bothered to lift a finger? With a couple of male friends hovering in the background she also had more things to think about.

It was not a happy house – there was a strange karma attached to it, but if her sister had known of Mabel's peculiar little ways she would have understood why this was so – for under the floor boards and under the apple trees, were some rather unpleasant souvenirs of Mabel's hobby. Presumably she would have been shocked if she had realised what had been going on, but she too had some rather unsavoury pastimes, mainly shoplifting and, like Mabel, she was very successful in her little peccadilloes. The slippers, for example – criminally expensive – had never been paid for. She'd simply nicked them from the shoe department in Harrods!

On the day of her sister's demise, Mabel had actually been standing in the kitchen peeling the potatoes for supper; she thought a nice cottage pie would go down a treat. So there she was with the peeler in her hand and when she looked down at it she suddenly thought… *You're a nice sturdy little weapon. I wonder what I could do with you!* Her next thought was… *Sweet, sister mine! What couldn't I do with all our mother's money, left just to me?* She then heard the front door open and her sister's footsteps tip-tapping on the hall lino – no expense spared in their house!

Her sister dropped her car keys onto the hall table and opened the door to the room where their mother sat all day, idly surveying the four walls through eyes that no longer made sense of anything. "You don't look very comfortable, mother. Naughty Mabel not plumped up your pillows, then? Not given you anything to eat?"

Mabel Canute heard her sister moving along the passage, now with different footsteps, now shuffling in her smart, fluffy, rubber-soled slippers – got to keep the lino looking nice, hadn't they!

She pushed open the kitchen door roughly and saw Mabel hunched over the old enamel sink; hands plunged in cold water, peeling the potatoes, undressing them down to their bare skins. *Naked potatoes! What a giggle*, Mabel thought.

"You've not fed mother," squawked her sister's nasty, sharp voice. "What have you been doing all day?" she said. "Not gardening, not cleaning by the look of the house, not shopping by the state of the fridge!"

Smelling the stale breath as the ugly little mouth hissed into her ear, Mabel suddenly turned and jabbed the peeler into her sister's heart as hard as she possibly could, noticing a bit of peel still attached to it. Well, her sister always liked her potatoes, so now they were really close to her heart! She finally twisted the peeler, just to be sure, rather as one would if removing potato eyes!

The spontaneity of it all was quite amazing. That was her talent, of course, wasn't it? There was no end to what Mabel could achieve on a good day, and she suddenly thought, why stop there? Have a field day! Make a real occasion of it! So, with her sister's dead eyes gazing at her, she pulled the peeler out and thought... *I wonder what it's like to peel human skin.*

So she did!

Afterwards she wondered how that would have looked on the front pages of the tabloids! Not your normal headlines, that's for sure! 'Watford woman peels off!', 'Hertfordshire householder mistaken for a potato'! At that, she finished preparing the cottage pie and popped it into the oven. *O, sod it, there she was again! Shut up, mother, your voice is well and truly getting on my nerves!*

By the way, Mabel may not have used a hatchet, but she was really pleased by the amount of blood that was produced – and all from a humble potato peeler – and so easy to clean up, thanks to the lino! By the time she finished, the cottage pie was cooked to perfection and, as you can imagine, she felt really hungry after all her efforts!

Only the peelings have since caused any problems;

just today she found a stray piece of desiccated skin when she was sweeping under the vegetable rack! That really wasn't very nice, was it? *You shout out like that again, mother, and I'm really going to get cross. So just watch out that the next skin I've got to clear up isn't yours!* One thing, however, pleased her no end; after a quick application of stain remover, those fluffy slippers came up looking like new; she did so hate waste!

Of course, you're probably wondering what she did with the body. Well, fortunately, her sister had been of only slight build – certainly undeserved after the amount of potatoes consumed – so Mabel, small but strong, was able easily to drag her outside. No guesses where she buried her. Why, in the potato patch, of course!

Needless to say, she hopes that next year there will be an extra bumper crop. You really must go round and have supper with her one evening; believe me, I've tasted her roast potatoes and can tell you that they are to die for.

The Puppet Master

He hit her across the head with a vicious swing of his wooden stick. The pain must have been excruciating! Poor little woman, poor Judy. What cruel beasts children are, for there they sat on the vicar's lawn laughing their nasty, little heads off, completely oblivious to the suffering that this act of domestic violence must have caused.

Billy's eyes were agog at Mr Punch's brutality. He just couldn't understand why the other children were all laughing so much. He wondered if they would still laugh if they could see what his father did to his mother, those large, red fists beating her black and blue as though he were tenderising a piece of steak, bare-handed.

Suddenly Billy stood up and ran towards the booth and put his small hand up so that he could grab Judy, thus saving her from further punishment.

The other mothers had their suspicions about what happened in Billy's house, as did the vicar and the teachers at school, but no one said a word. Even the marks on his legs that looked as though someone had stubbed out a cigarette on them were conveniently ignored, because Billy's father was a big-wig in the village: on the parochial council, on the committee of the PTA and the owner of a factory that produced shoes. Also, more to the point, he gave employment to a fair percentage of Overbury's inhabitants.

Thus Billy was completely alone, totally unprotected in that year of Our Lord 1999 and even He appeared to have forgotten about Billy – halo thereby somewhat tarnished, shepherd's crook awry, His bleeding heart seemingly untouched by any sorrow for one of his youngest lambs.

Billy ran and ran across the lawn holding Judy in his arms like a baby, protecting her from all harm. How he loathed Mr Punch with his eagle nose and hateful, squawking voice. In fact, in Billy's mind, it was almost the same voice and the same face, which at that very moment was sitting behind his father's impressive desk at the shoe factory. The puppeteer, finding his leading lady suddenly missing, darted from the back of the booth and gave chase. The language he used was not what the mothers would have wanted their children to hear, so a watered-down version went something along the lines of: "Billy Jenkins, you little sod, what the hell do you think you're playing at? Bring Judy back this instant!"

While all this was going on, Billy's father sat in his office playing the big man. He was always in charge, always doing what he wanted and Billy's mother was in her bedroom packing her suitcase, for this was the day when Billy's life really fell apart. She had decided that, for the sake of self-preservation, she would sacrifice whatever little happiness he had. She would simply leave and just hope that things would work out for him. He was a lovable little chap – anyone could see that – but her love for him was just not great enough. From then on, if the truth were known, she gave very little thought to him. Billy, however, young as he was, worried himself sick that if he'd done more to protect her, perhaps she wouldn't have left.

Now with his mother gone, Billy was really in for it!

"Well", said his father, "I think it's about time we made a man of you, Billy. You're a wimp, you know that? Saving lost puppies and kittens, communing with nature is okay for girls, but not for my son. No wonder your mother got fed up with you! Six-years-old and boarding school is where you're headed, laddie – and you open that little mouth of yours about things that happen in this house and you'll wish you'd never been born. Understand?"

It was at that moment that Billy finally rebelled. "I'm not going away to school, I don't want to go, I like the village and I want my mother back!"

A quick slap across the head from his father's hand soon shut him up and brought the tears to his eyes. So off he ran, across the fields, until he came to the small church that was the centre of the village's spiritual life, such as it was: only filled at funerals and weddings!

The verger was outside among the gravestones and saw young Billy making his way up the path towards the church door. Bit of a sad figure, especially since his mother had done a runner, but a nice, polite, little lad!

Into the church went Billy, striding up the aisle,

careful to avoid looking into the eyes of Jesus as he hung from the cross behind the altar, blood streaming down his face.

"I'm sorry, Jesus, but if you'd really wanted to, you could have made everything different, couldn't you? It's all your fault!"

With that, he took from beneath his anorak, the cricket bat he'd pinched from the Junior Children's games' cupboard, clambered onto the chair where the verger usually sat and knocked Jesus' head straight off his body.

That evening, black and blue because of what he'd done to Jesus, Billy looked at that hated Mr Punch face, listened to that raucous voice, conscious, all the while, of the close attention he was receiving from the bimbo with long, blonde hair, bright sparkling lipstick and the estuary voice, whose hand was resting high up on his father's thigh. You know the type! No great intellectual, but cute enough to be able to get herself a rich man!

There was no divorce because Billy's mother never came to light again and all his father had to do was prove that he'd done his best to find her. So, once he'd handed over his court fee of £40 – ridiculously cheap at the price – the way was then legally clear for the bimbo to become the new lady of the manor and produce another son.

For protection, as he walked through the depressing

streets where he lived, Billy carried a cricket bat in his left hand. It had been a popular sport at the school where his father had dumped him, where he had sentenced him to a living hell. A sensitive, kind-hearted, timid little boy, useless at sport, and therefore a born victim, he had been bullied mentally and physically through five long years of torture. His father certainly knew what he was doing when he sent him to that particular school.

Then he had run away, was never seen again, and nobody, especially his father, made any great effort to find him. He was just another run-away like the thousands of children who disappear into the blue every year in England.

So how did he cope all on his own, with nobody to love or care for him? Well, Billy was resourceful if nothing else. He had unfortunately learned from his peers and from older boys at his school how he might easily earn a living out in the harsh world and that is just what he did. Young, rather effeminate-looking there was definitely a market for his services, so in this way he survived the next ten years or so.

There was, however, one day that did prove to be different. Billy suddenly decided that there was something he needed desperately to sort out, for his own peace of mind. So for the last time ever, he went back to the village that had once been his home. By now Mrs Bimbo had been replaced by a look-a-like, Mrs Bimbo Mach two.

The house was as impressive as ever and, through a

chink in the velvet curtains, Billy saw his father sitting, surprisingly alone, watching television. Billy was fully confident that his father, within a very short time, would be in hell, suffering with all the other rotten bastards who'd polluted the world. Confident, because Billy was going to be the one to send him there. What would be the weapon of choice? Well, what was good enough for Jesus was certainly good enough for this wife-beating, lecherous, old devil – hence the cricket bat clasped firmly in his hand, but Billy wanted there to be no doubt as to why he was going to mete out this punishment and, of course, who was doing it.

He had changed considerably since his father last set eyes upon him and certainly didn't want him to think that he was simply some unknown yobbo intent on burglary. He rang the doorbell and he was rather surprised that there was no sexy, little maid to answer the door… there instead, standing in front of him, was his father, large as life and twice as ugly,

"Well, dad, this is your surprise of the day, isn't it? Little Billy back to watch you get your comeuppance in a big way!" He held up the cricket bat. "You remember Mr Punch, dad, don't you? What he used to do to poor Judy and what you used to do to mum? Well, this is Mr Punch's stick. Look at it closely, dad, because it's one of the last things you're ever going to see."

His father looked closely at Billy, rather than at the cricket bat.

"Put the bloody bat down, you stupid, little sod and stand under the light so that I can see you better… Now

I get the picture. Surely that's not blusher on your cheeks, is it, Billy? And not Coral Pink on your lips? No guessing how you've been earning your living! You dirty little so-and-so!"

"I'm only doing my job, Dad. I don't hurt people, or destroy them gratuitously for enjoyment like you do. I'm not cruel and unfeeling as you are – whatever the moral failings of what I do may be." Billy held the cricket bat up in front of his father's eyes and then hit him around the head as hard as he possibly could. In this way Billy finally got his revenge; his father's body lay at his feet, as Jesus' head had lain at his feet.

His mother too had destroyed his life, but he would let his vengeful thoughts there go unrequited. After all she also had been a victim. Added to which he had absolutely no idea where she was!

At twenty-two years of age, he really had been alone and lacking in affection all his life – until now, that is – for, as he walked along, he was being closely watched. Grimalkin, feral, unloved and uncared for until Billy found her, looked up at him with her green eyes. The aging, grey cat with her arthritic legs was finding the long walk difficult, but she would never abandon him and every so often he would stop for a while to allow her to rest. Billy now lived in Wandsworth, in a shabby bed-sit, with Grimalkin, the only creature in the world who loved him or whom he loved. He was tired and ill, the result of pursuing such an unhealthy, dangerous profession. There was no one to look after him and any money that he earned was spent on medication for Grimalkin; he couldn't let her suffer.

One morning, however, as they lay on the bed together he knew the time for her to go had arrived. When she looked into his eyes there was no doubt what she was telling him. She didn't want to leave him, but she really didn't want to continue like this and he was the only one who could help her.

So he wrapped her in her pink blanket and took her to the vet's surgery where he sat talking to her, stroking her, thanking her for her love, as she was painlessly put to sleep.

When it was all over, Billy didn't want to part from her so, as the sun was shining outside, he decided that they would take one last journey together to enjoy the warmth that was falling upon them and to watch the buds that were starting to appear on the trees. In his mind he was imagining that Grimalkin too, in her new other-world, could feel and see these things with him. So along the road he walked until they reached home.

He carried her into his small sitting room and sat down with her on his knee, still wrapped in her pink rug. He kissed her on the forehead, then bent forward and switched the tap of the gas fire on as high as it would go. He didn't bother to light it, but merely closed his eyes, laid his head against the back of his chair and started to breathe as deeply as he could.

The Singing Butler

The yacht, which had played such an important part in their lives, had sunk; the beautiful, sleek, white yacht that had brought romance, betrayal and intrigue, had gone to its final resting place beneath the waves.

Meanwhile, Peter, formally dressed for dinner, and Veronica, her dark hair swept up in a chignon, her gorgeous, red dress shimmering in the watery sunlight, had both passed through the veil, through the membrane. Accompanying them were Maud, the maid, in her smart uniform and Jenkins, the butler, who so loved to sing, that he was rarely silent, whistling and warbling like a bird virtually non-stop throughout the live-long day.

Veronica looked back as the mist closed behind them, but no one else was coming through! He can't have drowned, can't have passed into a different place, she thought, that would be too, too cruel, a twist of fate too hard to bear, for she loved Giancarlo to the point of aberration, the only man, she thought, that she had ever truly wanted. He was a roué, of course, an older woman's plaything, Lady Veronica's bit on the side, but, when all you've got in bed with you is Peter, it's not surprising that you would look favourably upon the delights of someone like Giancarlo. He was nothing special, she supposed, as roués go: the usual thing – slim, young, longish hair – terribly attractive, which went without saying, very sexy and with that gorgeous accent whenever he spoke English. As everyone knew, Italian was a language to die for! Nonetheless, he was her roué: on the spot, at her beck and call at any time, available day and night. To watch him mixing cocktails on board the yacht had been poetry in motion: indeed, an erotic experience.

In this strange place where they now found themselves the rain clouds were gathering. Maud and the butler, oddly both wearing hats and holding umbrellas against the inclement weather, could not quite remember how this had come to be and, indeed, the napkin that Jenkins had carried over his left arm as he served dinner was now sticking out of his jacket pocket! What a strange situation this was and what on earth were they doing on a beach? The last thing under their feet, as far as they could remember, had been the fine carpet in the yacht's dining room and, surely, that had been only a few seconds ago! The wind coming from the sea was now so strong that they both, servants and umbrellas, were in danger of being tossed into the air as easily as sycamore wings.

A wireless set then slowly followed behind them through the veil and placed itself on the wet sand; the tango rhythm of 'Jealousy' began to fill the air. Jenkins, of course, could not help but accompany the music in his slightly off-key baritone voice. So the scene was set as Peter took Veronica into his arms and they began to sway in time to the haunting music. Tears were falling down her cheeks to mingle with the raindrops from above, for she longed for another's arms to be clasped around her, longed for another's body to be touching hers. Oh Giancarlo, where are you?

There he was, Giancarlo, with his arms around her, touching her back lovingly with his hand, stroking the soft silk of her long, elegant blue dress. They had passed through the veil together and he was wondering if they were the sole survivors. Was Peter, her reprobate of a husband, at this very moment floating somewhere near the French coast, fish already nibbling at his body?

As the still-warm sun started to sink beneath the horizon, Giancarlo looked into Veronica's eyes. He could see the beginning of crow's-feet and the wrinkles that were starting to appear around the top of her lips. He wasn't sure that he liked her blonde, short, marcel-waved hair, for he preferred long, dark tresses. She'd served a purpose, however, for she had given him the chance to experience a different way of life, enjoy luxuries that had, up until a short time ago, been denied him. Perhaps Peter had gone to the bottom of the sea and would need replacing: an ideal situation, but he would consider that later.

In the meantime, they could see the striped beach parasols still lying unattended on the sand and there was no picnic basket at hand for their romantic dinner. Surely, that was why they were there …or was it? Everything was somehow muddled in his mind.

Moreover, where were Maud and the butler who were supposed to be performing these tasks? Not, Giancarlo hoped, lying full-fathom-five under the water, for he and Jenkins had a little scam going, something that involved a touch of blackmail. Well, all those lightly-clad friends of Lady Veronica had not always kept their hands from wandering as they cavorted on deck and, there had been, during the starlit nights, a great deal of creeping from one cabin to another. However, Jenkins did have that irritating singing habit that Giancarlo would be glad not to have to hear again.

While all this was going on, a veil elsewhere in the cosmos shifted and Lady Veronica was sitting at the bar on board the yacht, her long fingers impatiently tapping, waiting for her drink.

"But, Giancarlo, you silly boy, I ordered a dry martini, not a margarita! And a dry martini is what I expect to get!"

Giancarlo looked perplexed, for that was what he had served her – or had he? How weird, how bizarre! Lately, he noted, this sort of mistake seemed to be happening to him more and more often. Was there something wrong with him...or with world?

He looked at her as her eyes caught his – she was really at her stunning best tonight. How beautiful that green velvet dress looked against her curly red hair! Suddenly and rather cruelly, the moment of magic was shattered by the approaching musical accompaniment that seemed to haunt the yacht as the butler entered to announce that dinner was served.

Meanwhile, as Veronica enjoyed her martini at the bar, Jenkins and Maud sat together, holding hands, while they watched her from their vantage point on the rocks above the beach. She was yelling at Giancarlo who had just made a grave mistake, the sort of mistake that no roué worth his salt would ever have committed. He had just asked her for money! It now looked as though, at any moment, she was going to strike him with one of the parasols, but it was suddenly snatched from her hands and, of its own accord, trundled its way resolutely across the sand, gradually disappearing into nothingness.

On the other side of another veil, Lady Veronica knew that she was growing older – her hair now flecked with grey, her skin less firm, her body less supple. As snowflakes fell from the bleak sky, she still felt the bitter cold in spite of the luxuriant, red-fox furs that enfolded her, in spite of the chic, black cloche-hat that covered her head. She grasped Peter's arm as they made their way towards the courthouse, trying to run the gauntlet of a barrage of reporters and photographers who swarmed around them, cameras flashing, and microphones thrust in their faces. Behind her trotted little Maud weeping into her best pink hankie, the one decorated with a rose in each corner. Poor Maud, trying her best to keep her head down, away from the prying eyes that sought out her every expression!

On the bench sat the judge, magnificent in his robes

and wig, as the prisoners were brought before him: Giancarlo ex-roué and Jenkins ex-butler, now with no song in his heart and certainly with no song on his lips – not in this sombre, sober setting. Two foolish men, small fry, who hadn't realised that they had been trying to chew on the fins of some of the biggest fish in the sea and, for this mistake, they were sent to jail. Not too long a sentence, but long enough for them to see the error of their ways. There would be no more blackmailing from them! As Giancarlo was led away, his eyes fastened on Lady Veronica who just couldn't resist giving the naughty boy a wink; after all, he'd been such fun, so amusing, so satisfying!

Meanwhile, the veiled flickered and there was the yacht moving gracefully through the water: past Nice, past Antibes, past Cannes and, tomorrow, they would moor off St Tropez. Lady Veronica, in her favourite red dress, watched the sun sinking behind the approaching storm clouds as she drew on her Sobranie cigarette, a pink one and, therefore, for once, she was not colour coordinated! She savoured the taste as she watched the smoke rise into the balmy air. She had sent Giancarlo into the bar to mix a highball, though he could just as easily come back with a sidecar.

These days there seemed to be an awful lot of hits and misses with this process, perhaps only a fifty-percent possibility, or thereabouts, that he would get it right! Never mind, though, because it was simply wonderful to have him on board. Everyone she and

Peter had invited along seemed to be having a swell time: the bankers, the parliamentarians, the theatrical crowd – all loving it. If only the butler would stop singing!

In truth, time and space had no meaning for Lady Veronica; she was in a hundred, in a thousand, who knows how many places, all at the same time, the universe continually splitting to accommodate all her different lives, all her different decisions. Sometimes, she herself even sensed that a veil hung in front of her eyes and that, if only she could draw back a corner, she would be able to catch a glimpse of a different self in a different place – a universe made up of her as the central character with all her supporting players accompanying her in her rôle!

The Sorceress

Vaporous swirls of strange matter, dust and other mysterious remnants that had sprung from the singularity at the very beginning of the universe surrounded the wooden tower, which was so tall that it seemed part of the heavens themselves. It sat alone on a high cloud-covered mountain, appearing to float unsupported in space.

At the very top of the tower, enclosed in a tiny, windowless room, smaller than any prison cell, with steps leading out into the dusky night, a solitary figure, dressed in brown, diligently plied her trade: that of making stars and moons so that it would look as though lamps and flickering candles were illuminating the cosmos.

The sorceress was tall and slender, her hands those of an old woman as though they had aged more quickly, worked harder than the rest of her. Her blonde, bushy hair, blue eyes and finely sculpted features belonged to someone much younger.

There was almost no space within the room for anything other than a narrow table and chair. In the roof was a hole through which entered a glass tube that extended down towards a shredder that was attached to the table. Using a handle, the sorceress was able to grind into cosmic dust the wondrous ingredients that constantly descended through the tube and this was collected in a dish.

Nevertheless, there was just about enough space to squeeze in one more vital object, which was an ornate metal cage on a tall stand –the focal point of her work, the pivot around which her life revolved.

"Come on, just one more spoonful, damn you! You know you like it," rasped the sorceress as she jabbed a long, wooden spoon between the bars of the cage. It was the same old struggle: as usual, a pale, infant moon who didn't want to eat the cosmic dust. It just stared at her defiantly – it was at the crescent stage of its development: always a difficult time. Nevertheless, it was growing so quickly that in a week or two it would outgrow the cage, for a hefty diet of this magical dust would make it plump out like a silver ball. Then, it would be set free to roam the universe until it found its allotted place, perhaps in the Milky Way or perhaps not!

The sorceress never discovered where her creations went, for as soon as one had gone, another took its place. Not always totally sympathetic to her young charges, the sorceress roughly forced the spoon into the small moon's mouth, whereupon it spluttered and spat the dust particles out. She was furious.

"Do you know how many hours I spend making dust particles? I know you don't like being in a cage, but I'm a captive too, remember, confined within this tiny room until who knows when. Perhaps forever! Whereas, very soon, you will have the whole of space at your disposal."

Reluctantly, the infant moon saw the logic of this argument, revolved like a treadmill and licked up the precious dust from the floor of its cage.

Some instinct told the sorceress that she couldn't possibly be the sole creator of the stars and moons. There must be others dotted about the immensity of space working on the same project. She suspected, all the same, that she was the sole woman who had been set the task, for in her dreams she could see only men working and talking together in their laboratories, but they were not isolated as she was.

Three weeks later the new, fully-grown moon was led to the door of the high tower and made to descend a few of the cloud-skirted steps. Then the sorceress suddenly gave it a good, hard push sideways so that it bounced, tumbled and then, rather nervously at first, floated away into the ether.

When she re-entered the room she gave the handle of the shredder a turn, looked immediately at the dish and saw that this time the dust was yellow – a sun, a shining star, was about to be born. This cosmic dust was the most amazing material in the universe for everything that existed was made from it: the tower, the table and chair, the glass tube, the cage and, even, she herself. They were all part of one magnificent creation.

As soon as the sorceress tipped the contents of the dish into the cage, ripples and waves of movement showed that the birth of the star had begun – she had long ago lost count of how many times she had watched this miracle. Her eyes began to fill with tears because she knew that she had seen it all too often. Surely, the time to stop was fast approaching. She felt completely hemmed in – within the small room, within her own soul, but she knew of no other way to express herself than in the creation of these objects that had absolutely no feelings whatsoever towards her. There was never anything in the least reciprocal in their relationship, everything was taken from her, nothing ever given in return. So existence was lonely: her only companions nervous, pale moons and red-faced, angry suns. Parasites who gorged themselves on what she provided for them.

As the nascent sun grew, it opened its mouth greedily demanding attention. It glowered and glowed hotly and an ominous churning sound came from its interior. Suddenly, small flames shot up from the sun's surface and the churning became a rumbling.

"What do you think you're doing?" raged the sorceress.

"I want sustenance," demanded the baby sun. "Now! Not later! Not when it suits you!"

"You'll damn well wait until I'm ready."

"We'll see about that, shall we?"

The sorceress was fast losing patience. She'd had so many scenes of a similar nature, with so many potential, celestial bodies, but this little sun was in a class by itself.

What made her feel most upset was all the years and

years that she had dedicated to her task; she suspected to no avail. For the universe was still mostly empty and kept flying away, expanding, leaving even more space to be filled. It was all a nightmare; even if she continued for ever and a day nothing was really going to be achieved.

By this time the sun, incandescent with frustration and anger, was throwing out flames that were really too big for its size.

"Hurry up or you'll be sorry," the little, fiery ball yelled at her.

The sorceress didn't heed its warning and the next thing she knew the table and chair were engulfed in fire, and smoke was filling the room. Fighting for breath and with her eyes stinging, she had no choice but to leave the sun to its destiny. So, she opened the door and descended a few steps. She had long yearned for her lonely, useless existence to end and it now seemed as if fate had given her the excuse. So, with a wry smile on her lips, she held her arms out wide, launched herself off the side of the steps into nothingness and allowed the solar winds to catch her, sweeping her away where they willed.

The Waiting Game

It isn't going to be possible for Frau Schneider to watch while she murders the intermediary. She is a trained killer, has an amazing talent for it: but simply cannot witness death at close quarters, particularly one that she has caused. A strange little foible, don't you think? An assassin who turns her head away and half-shuts her eyes! In her line of work there are always messengers, intermediaries, who know too much and have to be disposed of summarily – the big boys never do their own dirty work. Well, why would they, when they train and pay other people like her to do it for them? At this exact moment in time, she is just such a link between her masters and the victim whose message she will very soon receive.

So she waits patiently, the warmth of the Mexican dawn already making her skin damp and uncomfortable. She really does not appreciate these assignments in hot countries – give her the equable air of her native Austria any time!

I am watching Frau Schneider now as she sits in front of the narrow archway through which she can see nothing but orange light as the sun rises; as though some artist has painted a wash over the entrance, as though this is the only colour in the world. The little courtyard where she waits, however, is filled with a myriad of colours: a small, fold-up red table on which sits a pale-blue carafe of water and an even paler blue cup without its saucer: walls painted a vibrant cobalt blue: next to her, a bright yellow upright chair and, behind her, a tall, dark-green, shiny rubber tree growing out from an earthy space amid the watery-red tiles.

For Frau Schneider her whole world is one of intense colours, a tetra chromatic world – something to do with the way her brain has been wired and connected to her optic nerves. Black and white don't really exist for her literally or metaphorically. Nothing is ever completely bad or completely good; always an amazing variety of shades in between – a unique range of nuances. No one sees a rainbow as she does. No one sees an autumnal scene as she does with so many differing degrees of brownness and yellowness. No one understands the strangeness of the human psyche as well as she does.

Most of us are professional assassins in this organisation, but only she, Frau Schneider, is silly and squeamish about what she has to do; very clever and sly, however, for her training period was long over before we realised her weakness. We watch her like hawks as you can imagine, because we do not want any failures that might bring problems from undesirable quarters: from our American colleagues, for example. Nevertheless, she is so good at what she does that we allow her a phenomenal amount of leeway.

So here we both are: watching and waiting: waiting and watching. Max is the go-between that we are both expecting – he won't recognise Frau Schneider because she's so clever at disguise and now looks as if she has walked straight out of one of Rivera's Aztec paintings. She suddenly stands, walks to the archway, looks out at the sloping, cobbled street with its rich seam of silver running under its surface, and sees the early-risen tourists who are already wandering about, still yawning, preparing themselves for yet another strenuous day of sightseeing.

Ilse, Ilse, you really shouldn't be doing this. What would your mother have thought about this nasty, twisted life you lead? she asks herself. Her eyes expertly scan the unsuspecting tourists – no, there is no Max here, but he will undoubtedly arrive today for the directive must not be disobeyed. *Should you really be spending your time waiting to kill another human being – and not the first by far? Is that how you were brought up? Surely you know better than to be doing this!* There is nothing suspicious, nothing out of the ordinary here as Frau Schneider leans against the archway, fingering her rosary, just another devout Mexican venerating her God.

Get a life, Ilse, a decent life, one where you don't have to walk in the shadows. If only this inner voice would stop talking to her – she has heard it all before, she knows all the arguments – but this is how things are, how things have turned out to be. Perhaps one day she will stop, but not now; they simply wouldn't allow her to make that decision.

You may be wondering who it is who has her so

closely within his sights, watching her every move, doubting, suspecting her. Well, I am Klaus. You might call me her minder, although she does not have the faintest inkling of this fact – someone who will not allow her to step out of line, who will not allow her to enter into any sort of contact with Max beyond that which is stipulated.

Everything must be impersonal: no speaking, no touching, no eye contact.

Those are the orders.

I'll be keeping a close watch on what happens, but they won't see me, of course, neither of them will, for if I think she has the least suspicion that I'm here I can disappear like a puff of smoke, like pure spirit. In fact, I'm almost, but not quite, as good at this game as she is. Then, I shall report back to our masters in that strange building in Vienna and await instructions.

Frau Schneider had, a long time ago, loved Max, but not anymore. He did the dirty on her and she will be glad to be rid of him permanently. Just let him hand over the message and then we can watch what I know she will do to him with her head turned away: with her eyes half closed.

How she will do it I have no idea – something subtle, I would think – no sudden burst of gunfire, no pools of blood, because that would be extremely foolish.

Yes, here he comes, here comes Max. His brilliant, blond hair stands out unmistakably a mile away from all the other colours. She can see him vividly, tossing coins at some kids who see him as an easy touch, but before he reaches the archway, Frau Schneider has slipped into the courtyard as discreetly as some slippery serpent intent on not being noticed: a reptile watching its prey.

She sits down in front of the red table on a large, dark-blue box that serves as a stool and watches and waits. I can almost visualise her long, coiled tongue inside her mouth ready for action; she will stun him with her venom and that will be his end – after, of course, she has collected the message from him. I await his arrival with unbelievable excitement and anticipation!

Suddenly, he is before her and stops short, not expecting her to come so abruptly into his line of vision. He knows she is his contact from the slim, purple tassel that hangs from her hair. She holds out her hand, not saying a word and he, as silently, drops the microchip onto her palm, careful not to touch her as he has been ordered. Who knows what might be on her sleeve, on her shoe, on a skin-coloured latex glove?

As is so often the case though, things are not at all what they appear to be, for Frau Schneider slowly turns around and Max, as he takes a knife from his sleeve, gives one of his cosmetically-enhanced, white smiles. She really should not turn her back on him like that: a very, very silly thing to do…

"Why don't you come out from behind that tree, Klaus?" she quietly says to me. "You are definitely losing your touch. Do you really think that your hair is exactly the same brown as the trunk of the rubber tree and that your dark-green shirt is exactly the same green as the leaves? I'm truly sorry for the deception, Klaus, I really am, but we're just not working for the same masters, are we? And did you really think that Max, my darling Max, would not recognise me, whatever my disguise?"

Max with his over-blond hair, over-tanned skin, over-white teeth, runs his fingers, at some considerable danger to himself, up and down the blade. However, his weapon is, indeed, not aimed at her, but at me – it is a backup in case things don't go quite according to what has been so carefully planned, but things will, naturally, go very well because Ilse never fails.

So there she stands in front of me, in her hand a very small pistol pointed in my direction. "Surely not a pistol, Ilse – how clumsy, how messy! You could have chosen something much more discreet. Think of the blood on the tree, on the tiles: think of poor Señora Luisa having to clean up the mess! You disappoint me – you really do need a minder!"

I know now that the waiting game, the double-game is over as Frau Schneider looks at me; I see behind her, through the archway, a flock of tourists happily passing by, who will never know of the little drama taking place so close to them. I watch her as she fits the silencer onto the gun so that it will give only a gentle whisper that startles no one: then she turns her head away from me and half closes her eyes…

Through the Looking Glass

The little, grey mouse peeped out from its home in the wainscoting, sniffing the air, whiskers on full alert. It looked left, right, then left again with beady eyes that missed nothing and saw Linus, that strangest of strange young men, standing in the shadowy corridor, closely studying his own reflection. Linus, in the looking-glass, saw the mouse but made no acknowledgement of its presence.

So there were the two of them caught at that precise moment in the great circle of time, until Linus, his bland, flabby face as pale as the moon and his grey, deep-set eyes with purple shadows beneath them, suddenly addressed the mouse. "Well, Mousy, who do you think is the fairest of us all …Linus, Snow White or the wicked step-mother? You better give the right answer!" He then quickly swung round to face the mouse who, alarmed by the sudden movement, scuttled off quickly into the safety of its home.

The oval mirror, in its ornate, gilt frame, seemed to Linus to have hung forever in its present place, on the first-floor landing of his mother's impressive country house; four bedroom doors led off from the landing. Linus returned to his intent perusal of his reflection; he always thought it was such a weird experience to do so because he knew perfectly well that what he saw wasn't really him at all – well, how could it be? The mole on the side of his chin, for example, was on the left, not on the right side at all, which is what the mirror showed him.

Everything in reverse, that's what it was! No, not really, however, because he wasn't upside down, was he? There was some sort of magic at work here that he just didn't understand. The most extraordinary thing of all, of course, was that everything behind him: the grandfather clock, the painting of his sister, even, when the bedroom door opposite was open, a view of the garden from the window; all this was squeezed into the mirror, that flat, thin piece of glass that took up no space at all. How was that possible?

The mouse, having taken all its courage into both its little paws, had emerged from its hole, and was again staring at Linus who, without turning round, lifted a hand in greeting. "It's all an illusion, a lie, isn't it, Mousy? Someone, somewhere, is trying to trick me, make a fool of me. I shall investigate further and see what's going on." He put his hand on the glass and rubbed and rubbed all over its surface but, as always, it remained as hard and unyielding as ever. He knew that to solve the mystery he would have to go through the looking glass himself. There must surely be an entrance, a portal that he could use, if only he knew how.

He could never understand how Alice, a frail little girl like her, had been able to pass through it into a different world. Poor Linus, muddled as ever, always got the Alice books confused. He could never remember which characters belonged where, which was why he wondered if perhaps, somewhere through the looking glass, beyond his reflection, awaiting his arrival, was a March hare with a teacup in his hand and a smartly-dressed rabbit with a fob-watch in his waistcoat pocket.

Surely there had to be a spell, magic words that would soften the glass, making entry possible. Anyway, Linus thought, he was probably much too large to go through this particular looking-glass – no, what he needed was a much bigger one. He knew that in his mother's bedroom there stood a cheval mirror that was just the right size – it would be perfect, he thought, even if he had to go in sideways, but she would never allow him into her room; she always kept the door firmly locked... "No, Linus, I don't want you coming in here – you're always touching things and moving them about."

The grandfather clock suddenly chimed half-past-seven – time for dinner – and the mouse, startled by the sound, disappeared.

Linus got down onto his hands and his knees, trying to peep into the mouse hole, and said softly, "I'll leave you for now, Mousy, but just remember that there's no need ever to be frightened of me. I like mice. In fact, I like mice much more than I like people!"

This time it was mirrors and reflections, but his last obsession had been all about gravity and why the stars didn't fall through the night sky and fly down like diamonds onto the Earth. Every day up into the trees he'd climbed, dropping coloured marbles and tennis balls and anything he thought interesting from as high up as possible, like some latter-day Galileo.

Linus's little peculiarities, as his mother called them, were very wearing and embarrassing; every so often, his medication would have to be increased to stop them getting out of hand. After a memorable few weeks he suddenly cottoned onto the fact that time did not always seem to pass at a regular pace. Sometimes it dragged its feet as if loath to arrive at its destination and, at other times, it positively hurtled by in a dreadful hurry, as if it were late for a very important appointment – just like the White Rabbit.

Hours were spent looking at the grandfather clock in the corridor or the grandmother clock in the hall, studying the watch his sister had given him for his birthday. He sat on gravestones for days on end observing the clock on the church tower – all, of course, to no avail. It was little wonder, therefore, that the villagers tended to keep out of his way, hard-pressed to think of anything to say to him. Rather unkindly they always referred to him as Loony-Linus from the Big House – completely harmless of course, but just very odd!

Poor Linus, if only he'd been of a different ilk he'd probably have been spending his life in some university studying mathematics or relativity or quantum mechanics or some rather esoteric branch of science, scribbling frighteningly complicated equations with a piece of chalk on a blackboard – disciplines all completely and utterly beyond the very limited capabilities that destiny had allotted him.

He suddenly saw her as he was walking along the street. He'd known immediately that it was she – who else could it possibly be with her long hair and blue coat? She looked older than when she'd gone to that strange place behind the mirror, for she was now wearing high heels and makeup, but he was sure that underneath her blue coat there would be a blue dress and a white apron, like those she wore in the illustrations in his books.

"Show me the way and then I can follow!"

"Where do you want to go?" Alice asked.

"Why through the looking glass, of course. Where else would I want to go?"

"I'm sorry, but I don't know where you mean. I've never heard of it. Are you sure it's around here? Is it a shop – it's not the new coffee place that's just opened round the corner, is it?"

Linus was beginning to feel cross. Surely she, of all people, wasn't trying to trick him, was she? This couldn't possibly be so, unless for some reason she wanted to keep the other side of the looking-glass just for herself, to keep it a secret, but he wasn't going to allow her to do that. "Of course, you know where I mean!"

He was feeling utterly frustrated, for there he was standing in the pelting rain wearing the wrong shoes, his feet damp and cold, while umbrellas in their hordes came towards him: an advancing army, their sharp spokes like lethal weapons about to gouge his eyes out …and now, to top it all, here was Alice denying any knowledge of the looking-glass.

"Well, if you don't know the answer to that one – what about Wonderland? Surely, Alice, you must know where Wonderland is."

"You've made a mistake, I'm afraid. I'm not Alice …my name is Flavia – a good old Roman name!" she said with a laugh.

Lies, lies, all lies and now here she was laughing at him! How dare she! She was just as bad as the village boys who threw stones at him and called him names.

"I'm sorry," said Flavia, "but I've got to go now – lots of work to do at home! Perhaps someone else can help you. I hope you find what you're looking for!"

She was glad to leave the strange young man behind – she'd found his pale, grey eyes staring so intently into hers and his peculiar questions rather intimidating. She had seen him plenty of times before, in the village, and knew he lived in the Big House, but this was the first time he had ever spoken to her and she hoped the last! However, she was not going to be rid of him so easily.

Linus, keeping well back, followed Alice as she tottered home on her high heels through the puddles. Across the little bridge they went, above the rising waters of the stream and over the Green where even the ducks had sought shelter under hedges and bushes, huddling together for warmth. Finally, he saw her go through the gate and up the gravel path that led to the entrance of a black and white cottage.

He slipped behind a water-logged clump of laurel and watched as Alice, having shaken her umbrella, took out her key and unlocked the front door. Surely the answer to the secret lay somewhere within that little cottage.

Linus gave her a few minutes to take off her wet coat and shoes, then crept up the path and, with his back against the cottage wall, edged his way round to the first window, peeping carefully into the room. Yes, there she was, that naughty Alice!

He hammered on the front door with his fists, almost drawing blood with the force – tomorrow his poor hands would be all red and raw, but his mother would comfort him and soon make them better with sweet-smelling ointment and kisses. "I know you're there, Alice, so you might as well open the door right now!" he shouted, by this time almost beside himself with frustration.

Flavia, wide-eyed and rather shocked to see the young man again so soon, did as she was told, but as soon as he saw her Linus knew that again he'd been sorely deceived, for where was her blue dress and her white apron?

Then, of course, like a bolt of lightning from the blue, it suddenly dawned upon him that this wasn't Alice at all, was it?

How silly not to have recognised the fact much sooner!

However, it didn't matter, because it was only too obvious now who she really was.

Why, with that red dress and those red slippers who could she possibly be but the Red Queen?

He was just rather disappointed that she wasn't wearing her crown and that she should be living in a cottage, when obviously a castle would have been so much more suitable. Anyway, Alice …Red Queen …White Queen …even Alice's cat, Dinah – he didn't care who she was provided she could lead him through the looking glass.

As he pushed past her and into the cottage he was amazed and delighted to see in front of him a very large mirror that made the small room look twice its size – just one more piece of mirror magic for him to solve. So he grabbed her by the scruff of the neck and turned her around, making her face the mirror. "Go on then! Get a move on! You know perfectly well what I want! Show me how you do it!"

He pinched her on the arm, but the Red Queen didn't move. In fact, totally overcome with shock, she didn't even speak. So he grabbed her by her long hair and slammed her head into the mirror, but it still didn't open or melt or do whatever it was supposed to do. So he did it again and, this time, the mirror splintered and he could hear crunching as broken glass crushed under his feet.

He looked at the Red Queen's reflection, now multiplied many times in the cracked glass, and saw blood running down her face. Red blood from a Red

Queen, but surely, thought Linus, it should have been blue! She was, however, still stubbornly this side of the looking glass.

"Say the magic words, then! You must know them!"

She didn't speak, but only moaned softly.

"Say them!" Linus repeated, but there was still no response.

Digging his fingers deep into her neck he shoved her again, even harder, against the glass – surely this would do the trick, but she just slid down to the carpet, leaving a red, bloody trail on the mirror.

Eaten up with fury, Linus kicked the Red Queen in the head. "I have a feeling," he said sternly, "that once I go from here you're suddenly going to rise up and float through the glass leaving me none the wiser." In a fit of the sulks, he kicked her again. For some reason that he didn't understand she didn't move a finger – in fact, she didn't even seem to be breathing.

When he heard a little whimpering sound he looked up and saw, coming down the narrow stairs, a fluffy, white kitten: why, it was Kitty, Dinah's daughter.

"Well, well, Kitty, what a surprise! I didn't expect to see you here. You're a long way from home, aren't you? Don't you think it's time to go back through the looking glass? Look, I'll hold you up in front of it and then we can go through together, can't we?"

Kitty, however, was no-one's fool and didn't at all like the look of this funny man, so she darted towards the front door and out through the cat-flap to safety.

"I won't be bested," thought Linus, though he didn't actually use this word because it wasn't in his vocabulary. This was what he was thinking, however, as he trotted home towards the Big House. The rain, still teeming down, seemed to be doing its damnedest to drown him; his shoes were so squishy that he felt as if they would never dry in a thousand years. "I'm not giving up – I'm going to solve the problem of reflections even if it's the last thing I ever do."

By this time the day was beginning to fade, but through the gloom and the rain he could see lights shining from the Big House.

"Where have you been all day, Linus, in this awful weather?" his mother said, opening the door for him. "You should have been home a long time ago – I was getting really worried." Linus, however, with lips pursed and brows knitted in concentration, slipped by her without saying a word, just giving her a cursory glance of irritation.

He had much more important things to do than stand chatting to her, for he'd had an amazing idea; no longer did he require anyone's help to go into the world of his reflection, no longer did he even need an ordinary, common-or-garden looking-glass. It was such a simple solution, which he should have seen from the very beginning. The great revelation had suddenly come to him as he was crossing over the bridge on his way back from the Red Queen's cottage. A momentary respite in the deluge, had stopped him in his tracks and, looking down into the waters of the stream, he'd seen his own image staring back at him.

The enthusiasm of this moment of enlightenment was still upon Linus as he bounded up the stairs and into the corridor. "Mousy, Mousy," he called out. "I've got it! I've got it! I've found the answer! How would you like to go on a little visit, have a change of air, a change of scenery – you know you would love it?"

Actually, the small, grey mouse was more than content where it was, living from day-to-day with its little family in the hole in the wainscoting – which was the way of mice – until it suddenly smelled the enticing aroma of a nice piece of Cheddar that had been placed at the end of a long, clear, plastic tube closed at one end.

Linus carefully put the open end against the mouse hole and as the peckish, cheese-loving mouse made its way towards the bait, he quickly slid a piece of cardboard over the open end so that there was no escape. A plastic cap then replaced the cardboard so the mouse was totally trapped, only able to view the world from its prison.

The quivering whiskers, the frantically flailing little pink feet, the look of sheer terror, real or imagined, in the mouse's eyes, really upset Linus. "Don't worry, Mousy! You won't be in there for long – I promise! I'll soon set you free but I must go and change my shoes, before doing anything else."

The front door slammed as man and mouse disappeared into the dimness of the evening, but at least the rain had stopped. They weren't going far. The pond that Linus had in mind was in the field next to the Big House and as a precaution, in case the moon failed to appear, he had his torch with him, so nothing would ruin his plan. As he approached he could hear frogs croaking amid the tall grasses and sedges, which formed a frill around the edge of the water.

Holding tightly onto Mousy's prison, he stepped onto the soggy earth and his shoes sank into the mud – he might as well have saved himself the trouble of changing them! Then, miraculously, the moon suddenly appeared from behind dirty-yellow clouds and Linus had no difficulty looking into the water. "Look, Mousy, look, there I am! And there's the moon! And there's you!" he said, as he held out the plastic tube so that the little mouse could see its own reflection.

This was truly a looking-glass of a completely different complexion – not in the least like the gilt-framed mirror in the corridor, not in the least like the mirror in the Red Queen's cottage, for there was nothing solid or fixed about water. It moved and it yielded and he knew that he and Mousy would be able to melt into it, disappearing gently under its surface. Why, the moon could even come with them if it liked! After they had arrived at their destination, he would release Mousy and the three of them, Linus, moon and mouse, could explore the new world and discover all its secrets.

To Sparkle

The verb, to sparkle, means to gleam, to glitter, to scintillate and that's what I have to do right now, get out there and sparkle as I've never sparkled before: give the performance of lifetime. This is my big chance, the only time that the whole country's attention will be focussed solely upon me. This is the opportunity that comes but once in a lifetime. Finally, I'm going to be the star I've always wanted to be!

The publicity given to this event has been absolutely tremendous. I've received an unbelievable amount of support from so many people from so many different walks of life: lords and ladies, beggars and vagrants! Even at this moment I can picture the great crowd that has gathered outside to cheer me on my way!

It's all rather like an audition, I suppose, and to settle my nerves I've just taken a glass of brandy. Though Pernod is actually more my cup of tea, if you see what I mean! If I'm honest, however, I'm actually not too good at auditions ...or at singing for that matter. I've really only sung in rather sleazy nightclubs and those slots only came to me because of other services that I was willing to offer. Nevertheless, my undoubted talents in that direction did lead to much, much more salubrious establishments and, of course, to where I am now!

See this blonde hair of mine, well, it's all out of a bottle: the colour, I mean. I've had it especially done for today. I hope you think it looks attractive and I also hope that you think that I've applied my makeup tastefully. This shade of lipstick has always been one of my favourites; Coral Pink it's called… Well, now that my face is done, I can finally take off my glasses. How I hate having to wear them! It's actually quite comforting, though, to see the world through a haze, as though I've distanced myself from reality and what is going to happen next. This dress has always been one of my favourites! What do you think of it! I think it shows off the colour of my eyes really well – also my figure, of course! It's just such a pity that I've got to wear these thick, padded, calico knickers beneath it! However, that's the rule, isn't, Mr Pierrepoint?

You see, David, this is what you've finally brought me to. The gallows! What a little bastard you were: a real piece of low-life, in spite of the cut-glass accent! Not for one moment have I ever regretted firing those four bullets into your miserable, pampered, over-indulged body. Suddenly finding myself there holding that smoking gun was a moment of pure liberation for me: no more wondering who you were having it off with, no more black eyes and bruised ribs, no more listening to your bluster about your insignificant little career as a racing driver!?

Well, I've always had a distinct talent for choosing the wrong men; during my twenty-nine years I've been rejected, deceived, insulted and humiliated by them. Oh, and by the way, Mr Pierrepoint, if you ever have any problems with your teeth, never, ever make an appointment to see a Mr George Ellis, the dentist from hell! My ex-husband; a drunkard and a wife beater.

It's been a very difficult twenty-four hours for me, you know. I've not exactly relished being able to hear the sound of the scaffold being erected. I think there should be some regulation against that sort of thing! Insensitive, I would have thought, to say the least, but then, I suppose, murderers can't be choosers!

Of course, I've never denied my culpability; I know that people say that with my gammy hand I couldn't possibly have pulled the trigger of a ·38 Smith and Wesson, but that's simply not true. When you want something badly enough, you can do anything and, believe me, David, at that precise moment, I wanted your death very badly indeed. To be quite honest, though, I can't say that I really remember in any great detail what actually happened. I mean, it was me who did it, wasn't it? Well, it must have been, mustn't it? Who else had the opportunity? My friend, Desmond was there, of course, standing behind me, and he's a crack shot; but he's always been so kind to me and to little Andy – poor little motherless boy!

I feel that I've been so used and manipulated in the

last few months by so many different men that sometimes it's rather difficult to separate illusion from reality: so much booze, so many drugs, so many lies, so many secrets, so many double-meanings, so many, many broken promises. I've kept my part of the bargain to the letter, of course, and therefore I really shouldn't be here waiting for you to put a white hood over my head and a noose around my neck, but there's been no reprieve, has there?

I often ask myself what happened to my defence. The truth, though, is that there was no defence to speak of, was there? Couldn't the judge, sitting there in his scarlet robes and white wig, see what a farce it all was? A murder trial that lasted for only one and a half days! A jury that was out for only twenty-three minutes and then, apparently, spent most of the time in the lavatory! What sort of justice was that?

They've let me down, of course: The Establishment, I mean. How could I have realistically expected anything different?

My own fault: too naïve by far!

I just didn't realise what deep water I was getting myself into! Once you're part of the honey trap, you can't escape; you know too much.

Believe me, the world of espionage is a world apart!

You don't know the half of it, Mr Pierrepoint! A prominent Doctor, pimp to the high and mighty groomed me to be what I am. With all his contacts he could have saved me. For he knows everyone – members of the secret service, the aristocracy, government members, even royalty. Of course, they didn't want to save me! I'm safer out of the way! Now I won't be able to spill the beans! Can't have a cheap, little peroxide blonde from Rhyl bringing down Her Majesty's government, can we?

Forget I said all that, Mr Pierrepoint. Please never, never repeat that to anyone! Though obviously it's all much, much too late now anyway. In whatever way it all came about, it was what I ultimately wanted: the little bastard dead! How I hated him, how I loved him!

So this is my final performance; and I dedicate it to you, David. With my love …and with my hate, because there's really very little difference between the two, is there? Right, Mr Pierrepoint, I'm ready, wrists strapped behind me, ankles shackled. I just hope you got all your calculations right and that this is not going to cause me any aggro!

So, sparkle, Ruth, sparkle!

Ishmael

Ishmael leaned heavily against the trunk of an old tree that anyone could see was in its death-throes. It had turned black and, only here and there, could you make out clumps of sickly leaves peeping from the moribund wood. Ishmael was so at one with this poor dying piece of life that he looked as though he were about to disappear into it and share in its death.

His yellow tunic glowed like the sun and was in stark contrast to his pale face that shone as wanly and white as the moon. His long, bony fingers held a flute from which intoxicating sounds made their way into the evening air; so lyrical and melodious that they seemed to form a swirling pattern that you felt you could touch.

The grass at Ishmael's feet was brown and struggling for life on the edge of a pool of brackish water. Pieces of rock lay near him like exhibits from a geological museum, each bearing the enlarged imprint of an ancient fossil: a spiral ammonite, a ribbed trilobite and a variety of others resembling exotic, smooth pagodas that just begged to be touched so tactile were they.

The magic of his flute snatched one rock at a time, the music carrying it effortlessly towards a half-built tower, which he knew it was his task to finish. Within the skeleton of the tower he could see steps that reached up straight and steep almost into the sky itself. These had been built by other hands than his, but the tower would assuredly fulfil the vision of its unknown designer; someone who had shaped the rocks like an intricate and lovely jigsaw, the pieces knowing instinctively where to place themselves.

In the distance, a slumbering volcano rose up into the vivid orange glow of the sky, which was dotted with billions of brightly shining stars. By now Ishmael was weary, only wanting to push his way into the trunk of the dying tree and curl up into a sleeping ball, but he knew he must continue playing, for time was accelerating, carrying him along with it: day and night following one another at a great rate. Soon the tower would be finished and, more than anything, he wanted to ascend the steps to find out where they went; therefore, his tired fingers and his swollen lips must persevere.

Eventually his task was ended, the tower so tall that it was impossible to see its summit. Rather nervously, with his flute tucked into his belt, he approached and began to make his way upward. The soles of his boots echoed sharply with each step taken, so there was no chance that he could hide his presence, but no one was there, so why worry?

As he climbed, Ishmael was aware that the tower was becoming warmer; in fact, touching its walls not only was there heat, but also a pulsing sensation. He imagined that he could actually hear the beating of a huge heart, but this could not possibly be so. By the time he had reached the top of the stairway, however, the tower was throbbing, its walls gently moving in and out as though it were a living, breathing entity.

Suddenly, in front of him, appeared an arched door with a large, black, ornate latch. He paused, fearful at what he might find once he'd lifted it. The breathing lungs, the beating heart, the life force emanating from the tower, made it impossible to hear anything from within even with his ear against the door. Slowly his calloused fingers lifted the latch.

The room was occupied. A young, sad-eyed woman, her head and body completely swathed in blue gauze, sat on a spindly-legged stool gazing at him. Behind her, the shelves of an arched alcove held a variety of wooden caskets and above her the roof was open to the sky: fluffy, dirty clouds, peeped over the edge of it and seemed to hold the threat of rain.

The woman's frail appearance belied her tone of voice, which was angry and resentful. "Why has it taken you so long to finish your work? All you had to do was to play music. What was so difficult about that? Others I have known could have done it in half the time."

"Truly, my lady, I did the best I could. I tried so hard to please the architect of this tower."

"Not hard enough! You are an idle slouch and will pay the same penalty as my other frivolous workmen."

With difficulty, she stood up, hampered by her awkward clothing, which was far too long and flowing, and hobbled over to the alcove to remove one of the caskets. Nearly falling over, she walked towards him and the aroma of woodland flowers assailed his nostrils.

"You will not like what I'm about to show you. However, each casket has the same content, but a different identity; every one of them lazy and underproductive – just like you. I think you will clearly understand the message that you are being given"

She held the casket so that, on lifting the lid, he would immediately see what was inside. Presentiment made his stomach lurch; rightly so, for staring at him was a face and where its neck should have been there was only a bloody scarf. It was a man with skin like yellow parchment, his brilliant, clear-blue eyes opening and closing, his teeth black and rotten, his brown tongue darting in and out. The woman's sweet aroma was drowned by the smell of death.

Ishmael groaned and stepped back in horror propelling himself out of the door that he had not closed. From her voluminous clothing the woman took a knife and stabbed at him, but too late, for by that time Ishmael had turned around and was hurtling down the steps. The walls beginning to close in around him were soft and viscous, pushing him down and out of the tower as if he were being born again.

He leaped towards the sanctuary of the tree and leaned against it in relief, trying to get more air into lungs already over-exercised from the long days spent playing the flute. All at once the ground began to tremble and a great roaring filled the heavens as, in the distance, the volcano started to erupt, spewing out molten rock, which seemed to complement perfectly the orangey-red of the night sky.

"It's like an omen, isn't it, Ishmael?"

He jumped at the sound of her voice. Where had she come from so suddenly, bringing with her the scent of bluebells and oxlips? There must surely be magic at work! Perhaps the eruption was an omen foretelling death and disaster.

"No, you cannot escape from me, for I'm lonely and need company. In spite of your sloth I shall not kill you, but only because you were the only one among them all who loved the tree." She put her arms about him and slowly drew him into the centre of the trunk.

"Just one more of my manifestations," she said as Ishmael felt the same familiar warmth, the same beating heart in the tree as there had been in the tower.

Coming from the old wood surrounding them he could hear breathing that sounded like a death-rattle.

Thus entwined, they snuggled and huddled together and remained there for an eternity of time until they and the tree had mutated and carbonised, joining forces with the earth itself.